In My Father's House

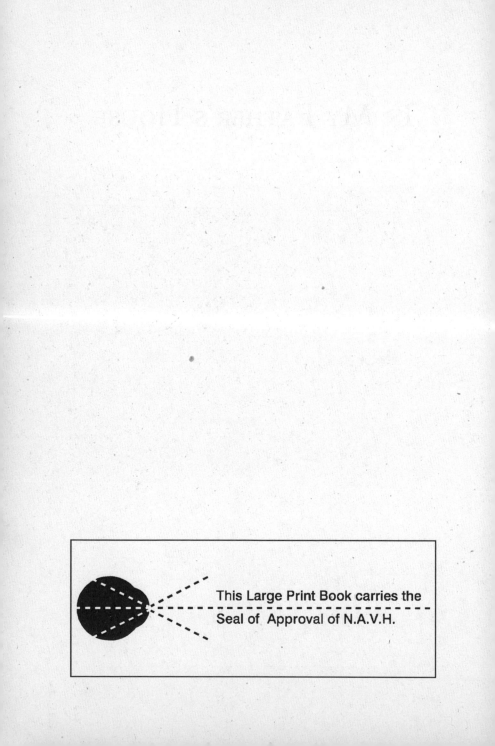

In My Father's House

E. Lynn Harris

THORNDIKE PRESS
A part of Gale, Cengage Learning

GALE
CENGAGE Learning

Detroit • New York • San Francisco • New Haven, Conn • Waterville, Maine • London

GALE
CENGAGE Learning™

LIBRARY OF CONGRESS CATALOGING-IN-PUBLICATION DATA

Harris, E. Lynn.
    In my father's house / by E. Lynn Harris.
      p. cm. — (Thorndike press large print African-American)
    ISBN-13: 978-1-4104-2694-9
    ISBN-10: 1-4104-2694-7
    1. Modeling agencies—Fiction. 2. African Americans—Fiction.
  3. Sexual orientation—Fiction. 4. Miami (Fla.)—Fiction. 5. Large
  type books. I. Title.
  PS3558.A6443I5 2010b
  813'.54—dc22   2010012102

Published in 2010 by arrangement with St. Martin's Press, LLC.

Printed in the United States of America
1 2 3 4 5 6 7 14 13 12 11 10

IN MY FATHER'S HOUSE

PROLOGUE

There are a couple of questions I've been pondering lately. What is the price of true love? Is it honesty, loyalty, or head-banging sex? What is the cost of success? Is it how much money you make or how much respect you earn? For me, Bentley Laroyce Dean, I found the answers at one of the most lavish parties I've ever attended.

I peddle the beautiful life and there is no better place to do that than the city of Miami. So that's where I've been the last three years and that's where I've discovered the answers to my questions. Now before you get the wrong idea, I own a modeling agency that I was trying to make bigger than any of those in New York and Los Angeles. And this party was going to help my agency, but then I met him in that beautiful mansion. That's when he walked into my life and everything changed.

Like most nights in Miami, it was beautiful. A perfect night for a party and even though I had a few reservations about the event, it was simply just too much money to turn down. This was the one engagement that would send my agency, Picture Perfect, soaring into the stars of Miami.

But sometimes it rains in South Florida and it is surrounded by shark-infested oceans. From the moment I stepped out of my car and handed the valet my keys, bad karma covered me tighter than the expensive suit I'd purchased for the party. The sharks, it seems, had come inland that night and ended up on Star Island.

It's when seemingly simple decisions sometimes have a way of snowballing into huge catastrophes. When life becomes like a bad dream, unfolding slowly.

On that night I learned some clues to my questions, but it's not where the daily chronicles of my life begin.

ONE

If I had kept a journal of my love life five years ago it would have read something like this:

Under the soothing pattern of rain I'm in the middle of a crazy, convoluted daydream. Maybe because I could hear the strains of Aretha Franklin crooning "day dreamin' and thinkin' of you" or maybe because I had a big decision to make about my love life.

You see I'm in love with two people.

She. Her kisses are soothing. Sometimes I sank my mouth into the naked warmth of her, a body that was firm and soft at the same time. So warm and velvety that I think heaven couldn't be better.

He. Six feet two of steely muscles, two hundred and ten pounds, with gravy biscuit brown skin who dishes out a dizzying force of manhood, sending pleasure chills throughout my body. Sometimes I crave him more than my next breath.

She. An undeniably sexy woman who has been preparing her entire life to become the perfect wife and mother.

He. Has a sexual swagger who delivers pulse-pounding sex that makes me feel like my ass is on fire.

She loves colorful lingerie, blush-colored wines, and her family and friends.

He loves black sweats, sneakers, and my scent.

She loves me. I love her.

He loves me. I love him.

Love can sometimes be like running from a storm, when all I really need to do is learn how to dance in the rain.

It seemed like a good idea at the time.

Just be honest, Bentley, my inner voice said.

So I told the truth for once in my life — in the place where I'd been perpetrating one of the biggest lies. In bed with my fiancée, Kim. I had just made love to her, and she was curled up around my bare body, purring like a kitten. With her damp cheek pressed to my chest, she cast big brown eyes at me with an expression that would make any man melt and want to stay in bed with her all day. There have been many days when I've done just that and enjoyed every minute of it. Kim, when she's not worrying about her social station in life, is really a fun lady to be around.

But my brain was trying to storm up a scheme to get her out of my high-rise condo as soon as possible. So I could enjoy something and someone even bigger and better.

I glanced at the huge rectangular mirror that sat on the floor, angled longways against the wall. It reflected a picture-perfect couple in a nest of white sheets on my brown leather sleigh bed. With my roasted cashew complexion and black hair, parted on the side and brushed close to my head in tiny waves, I was long and lean.

Kim's black Beyoncé hairstyle fanned over my chest; her skin color blended with mine, as did her slim arms and legs. I could smell the too sweet fragrance coming off her skin. The wall of windows overlooking the bright blue Detroit River and downtown skyline let in sunshine so bright that her four-carat diamond ring glowed as if someone had placed a star on her left hand. Kim was gorgeous, professional, and just bourgeoisie enough to please my parents.

Pleasing me, on the other hand, was the problem. The bottom line was she just didn't have what it took to make me happy or keep me satisfied for a lifetime. I didn't want to be one of those handsome newlywed couples in *Jet* magazine and have former lovers unable to contain their laughter while muttering, "Child, pleeze."

So when she asked a seemingly simple question, the kind that would normally elicit an automatic answer from a man in the afterglow of making love, it had the opposite effect on me. In fact, her question hit me like a truth serum about who I really am. Sadly for her, "husband" is not the answer.

"Will we always be this happy, Bentley L. Dean?" Kim asked with her soft, after-sex voice. As she gazed at me, the black makeup smudged around her eyes intensified her pouty, sexy gaze that demanded an answer. Now.

"Probably not," I replied quickly. The Musiq Soulchild CD had long since ended, so my voice echoed off the cream-colored walls and floor-to-ceiling windows. My words, sounding flat and listless, seemed to hang in the silence. Because I had no more energy to waste on trying to please everyone. It was time to please Bentley L. Dean III. And I refused to live like so many men I'd seen who were married and getting their gay groove on by creepin' on the down low.

12

Damn, I was sick of those two words. My father told us to always be proud of who we are no matter what people think. Maybe he said that because he was convinced that our family were descendants of the talented tenth if ever there were.

No, this is me. And the world needs to accept me as I am. I can't live a lie.

But Kim wasn't ready to hear that. I once heard my father say that sometimes the truth becomes the lie everyone agrees upon.

She raised her head as quickly as if the fire alarm were going off, as if she were trying to determine if yes, the alarm was ringing. And yes, it was time to leave immediately.

My cheek felt cool in the spot where her cheek had been.

"What?" The word shot from her full, heart-shaped lips like a bullet. Her gaze probed my face for signs of a joke. I felt a mixture of heartache and relief. Kim didn't deserve someone like me.

But I stared back, dead serious. And just plain tired of the charade. You see, at the time, I was thinking that I had a few hours to get Kim out of here before Warren, my boo, landed at Detroit Metro Airport and drove the thirty or forty minutes to my twenty-eighth-floor luxury love nest. As soon as she was gone, I would change the sheets, shower, shave, soften my skin with shea butter, and put on the black warm-up pants and tank top that showed off my toned shoulders and chest, my tapered waist, and my muscular ass.

Then I'd be ready for Warren to replace Kim here in my bed. That's when my craving would be quenched. I could hear the message he'd left on my cell phone earlier in the day when in a lazy voice he said, "I'm going to tear that ass down, boi."

That was the truth. And right now, I had just come to the point where I was tired of lying and trying to scheme up new ways to hide my secret from Kim.

"Bentley L. Dean, what in the world did you just say?"

Her eyes grew huge with shock. She looked at me as if I'd lost my mind. Actually, I felt like I'd found it. She and the rest of the world — including my father — would just have to deal with it. Still, I knew dealing with Kim was like petting a kitten where my father would be akin to a tangle with a pit bull. Somebody would come out bloodied.

"Bentley, you're kidding me, right?"

"Kim, I wish I was." My words came out like a sigh of exhaustion. I liked Kim, at

14

times even loved her. But the truth was that I was getting married to please Mother and Father. They are "old black money" rich. As third-generation wealth, they reign from the top tier of Detroit's black bourgeoisie of doctors, lawyers, politicians, and business moguls.

Needless to say, my parents believe very much in tradition. So I was expected to attend Morehouse College and Michigan Law, marry, and have two kids. So the life of Bentley L. Dean III would be a mirror image of the life of Bentley L. Dean II.

That flattery by imitation was my ticket to a seven-figure inheritance. You see, I was born into the black aristocracy. My grandfather, the first Bentley L. Dean, had made his fortune by becoming the first black man to own multiple car dealerships in the state of Michigan. Father expanded the automobile trade, acquired a lucrative soft drink franchise, and purchased several rent houses. The sports lover in him expanded his empire to own an Arena Football League team in Flint. A team I might one day hope to own. Of course, when it was time to marry, he chose a debutante diva with similar status, as my mother's grandfather was one of the first black surgeons in Michigan.

Inheriting the wealth and privilege of their pedigree meant that my sister, Anna, and I would have to become clones of Mother and Father. They expected great things from us, and we both knew better than to disappoint.

So to fulfill my parents' expectations, I chose Kim Boston. She was practically a younger version of Mother, both in looks and in manner. She seemed like a perfect choice. She was beautiful. Educated at Sarah Lawrence and the Wharton School of Business, Kim was working for the governor of Michigan as a policy advisor on new industries.

She could plan a party that would make Martha Stewart take note and had some tricks in bed that made me think I could just stick to women.

But then I met Warren Stubbs and all that changed.

My mouth actually watered the first time I saw him on television. I was sitting in Father's walnut-paneled library, watching the Detroit Lions beat the Dallas Cowboys, when a sports reporter for the local ABC affiliate appeared, larger-than-life, on Father's huge screen.

It was love at first sight. My body and heart reacted immediately, but I had to play it cool in front of Father, who was always quick to condemn a "sissy" or any man who was even rumored to be gay. At that moment, I remembered how one of my childhood friends had exposed Father's hatred for anyone gay. Charlie, who lived across the street from our ten-thousand-square-foot Tudor mansion in Palmer Woods, came out during our senior year at the prestigious Detroit Country Day School.

"You will never be seen with him again," Father had boomed over the dinner table that night. In his business suit and tie, Father was clean-shaven with a Billy Dee Williams mustache. But his usually flawless almond-hued complexion appeared darker. And one of his salt-and-pepper waves, usually combed back in a regal frame around his face, fell to his damp temple. I had never seen such anger flash in his eyes as he said, "We've known him since birth, but Charlie is no longer welcome in our home. And you will never, ever, even think about the disgusting and immoral lifestyle that he has chosen. Not in my house."

So rather than allow Father to see my lust for Warren on the television that day, I took a macho bite of my cheeseburger and chugged a beer.

"Damn, the Cowboys are gettin' an old-school, Motor City beat-down today," I said

17

while secretly devouring Warren with my eyes. He was a dark chocolate god with hazel eyes that wouldn't let me look away and a sexy-as-hell bald head. Warren's deep voice boomed through my chest as he commented about the game in relation to his history as a former quarterback for Purdue University.

From then on, I always watched his reports, and too many times I fantasized about being with him instead of Kim. So imagine my surprise when I went to Chicago with Kim to look at wedding stuff. There in the hotel gym was Warren, in the flesh, even more gorgeous than on television.

With one electrifying glance at Warren Stubbs, and the way his eyes discreetly burned back at me, the life of Bentley L. Dean III as I knew it was over.

Bye-bye, Kim.

Bye-bye, inheritance.

Hello, struggles.

I guess you could say I've always been bisexual. I lost my virginity to a pretty blond cheerleader one week during my sophomore year and lost it again to a football player the next. Something about females excited me and something about dudes left me wanting more. I naturally assumed I was smart enough to make it work.

But now, as Kim asked me why we wouldn't always be happy, the truth serum made me say in a calm and emotionless tone, "I'll always cheat on you. And one day, I'll meet a man that I will leave you for."

She sat up, glaring down at me. She pulled the Egyptian cotton sheet to cover her small but plump breasts.

"Does this mean you're one of those down low brothers?" she demanded.

There were those two words again.

"No, Kim. I'm trying to be an up-and-up brother."

"This *can't* be happening," she muttered.

"Kim, you should be glad you're finding out now, instead of after we've been married for ten years and we've got three kids, a mortgage, and a dog," I said flatly. "Plus, I'm saving you and your parents thousands of dollars. They can keep the small fortune they were about to blow on the wedding—"

"You are *not* calling off the wedding," she snapped. "Don't even think about humiliating me like that!"

"Someday you'll thank me," I said, glancing at the red digital numbers on the clock. It sat on my sleek brown dresser near the expansive view of the river and the blue silver Caesars Casino amid the buildings and lush green treetops of Windsor, Canada.

This conversation felt like a sure bet for me. I had to make her see it was a win-win for both of us.

"If you don't marry me," Kim threatened, "I'll make you the laughing-stock of Detroit. Yeah, I'll take all the money I saved for the wedding and buy a billboard. You know that giant one downtown on Jefferson, as you come off the freeway? Everyone will see it!"

"Go ahead." I shrugged. She would never do that. My family was richer, more powerful, and more prominent than hers by a long stretch. Father was in the Boulé, the oldest black fraternity that was so upper echelon and exclusive that only five thousand people belonged nationwide. Kim's father, a judge and a Kappa, was powerful, but he was no Boulé. My mother was a founding member and now president of her Links chapter. Father sat on multiple prestigious boards; Mother chaired the Bal Africain, Detroit's most important black social event of the year. Her parents didn't come close. And Kim knew better than to make my parents mad. They could cause major problems for her career with the governor, as well as her family's social standing.

"Yeah," Kim said, "I bet your fraternity brothers and your father's business partners would get a real kick out of *that*. I'll take one of your modeling pictures, the one where you wore a pink sweater for Polo. On the bottom, I'll put *Bentley L. Dean III is gay!*"

As she glared down at me, her eyes widened as if a giant spider had just crawled across my face. "Gay! Have you been putting me at risk for HIV?"

"Absolutely not! I'm tested regularly and have the paperwork to prove it." I was wondering why the black community wanted to blame every HIV diagnosis on black gay and bisexual men.

She snatched up a pillow, then whacked me in the chest.

"I trusted you!" she shrieked. "You'd rather have a man than *this?*"

"Kim, calm down." I grabbed the pillow. Her hair stood in crazy clumps around her head. She panted, squinting at me.

"You won't get a billboard and you know it," I said, not caring how mad she was. I couldn't go on like this, no matter what the cost. "Be glad I'm telling you now."

"Bentley, we can get you some help. Let's go and talk to our minister."

"So he can pray the gay away, Kim? What are you going to do about my appetite for swinging dicks and muscular, plump asses?"

Her face twisted with disgust. "Stop talking like that. You love pussy! I know you do, Bentley."

I sat up, covering my lower half with the sheet. "I love yours, Kim. And most of the time, I loved you. But what I feel the majority of the time is not fair to you."

"Did you ever love me, Bentley?"

"Yes, I love you, Kim," I said, but this wasn't enough before Kim had another plea.

"Then marry me, Bentley. Marry me and we'll work through this together. Do you know what my girlfriends thought when I announced I was going to marry Bentley L. Dean? You changed my life. I want the life you promised me."

I shook my head, glancing at the clock. We needed to wrap this up so I could get her out of here and shower for Warren. "Those were promises I can't keep, Kim. One day you'll look back and realize this was the best thing in the world for you. We can still be close. We can still be friends."

"Friends? I don't need friends, Bentley. I need you to be a man."

"I'm a man, Kim. I'm just not the man for you."

TWO

My mother used to always say, "None of us are ever sane enough to not have a good shrink we can call on."

So every other Monday morning I followed Mother's motto, inside the chic, taupe-walled office of Dr. Cindy Fenton in Coral Gables near the University of Miami campus.

I wasn't depressed or anything, but with Dr. Fenton I could talk through things that I normally wrote in my journal. And since running my business left no time for journaling, and I liked the way she challenged me to think beyond my own assumptions, this was just what I needed. It was 2003 when I left Kim, my family, and Detroit behind, yet all that "stuff" still seemed to lurk behind my thoughts every day.

"You look stressed," Dr. Fenton said as she shut the door and sat on a black-and-white-plaid armless chair. She set a red cof-

23

fee mug on the glass coffee table between us as I took my usual position on the black leather sofa. Facing her, I inhaled the amaretto-flavored coffee scent from the steaming cup she had given me in the lobby.

A sudden sense of relief overwhelmed me as I looked at Dr. Fenton. She was a fifty-ish, petite woman with short, mousy brown hair and freckles. She always wore red half-glasses with slim-fitting slacks and sweater sets. But her manner was anything but feminine or mousy. Sometimes I thought she might be a lesbian, but on days when she wore makeup, I'd think not. And her voice was as sharp and edgy as a native New Yorker. "Bentley, talk to me. I see stress with a capital S on your face."

I sunk into the plush leather, grasping the decorative leopard print pillows as if to hold on.

"My business," I sighed. "This economy is making it easy for my models to stay slim. I can barely pay them enough to eat."

She cast a piercing stare over her half-glasses. "What made it worse over the past two weeks?"

"Since I saw you last two of my bread-and-butter clients postponed their shoots until the economy picks up," I said. "I don't know how long I can keep my business

24

open. It's like we're on life support and this month's payroll might pull the plug."

"It's rough out there," she said. "I've had a few clients cancel until things get better. But you're creative, Bentley. Can you collect on any outstanding debts?"

I shook my head, grasping the hot cup against my palms. "The few people who owe the agency money are just as strapped. Once I do payroll this month, my business bank account will be flirting with a zero balance. I don't know if we can make it another month."

"Can Alexandria bring in any new clients?" Dr. Fenton asked. "You said your partner's been aggressively seeking new business."

The rock fountain on Dr. Fenton's nearby desk made a trickling water sound that calmed my panicky thoughts.

"Alex has a few leads," I said, "but nobody wants to commit real money right now."

Dr. Fenton sipped her coffee, then laced her slim fingers around the cup, resting it on her lap. The steam rose as she said, "Bentley, you don't want to hear this. It might sting."

I turned down the corners of my mouth and closed my eyes.

"Either you can let the economy and your

25

stubbornness destroy the business you've worked three years to build," she said, "or you can dial 3-1-3 — D-A-D — H-E-L-P!"

Her words sent something red-hot through my whole body, making me almost shout, "He disowned me!"

I lowered my voice. "And in Father's homophobic eyes, owning a modeling agency full of gorgeous men is about the last thing he wants his namesake to be doing! Especially in South Beach! I might as well be living at the top of the hill in Castro."

She sipped her coffee and shook her head. "He's still your father. I think enough time has passed for you to at least try."

"You didn't see the way he looked at me when I called off the wedding with Kim," I said as the memory of his furious brown eyes flashed in my mind. "He could've spit bullets. He even balled his fists."

Dr. Fenton nodded. "Tell me again what he said."

I deepened my voice to imitate him. " 'Not in my house.' "

It seemed like yesterday that he was standing in the two-story foyer of my childhood home, where the huge double staircase — with its Persian-carpeted steps and polished wood banisters — curved down around a chandelier and a mahogany table holding a giant spray of aromatic tiger lilies. On one side of the foyer was his masculine library; on the other was the two-story ballroom where America's black bourgeoisie attended my parents' soirées that even got featured in *Town & Country.*

"Dr. Fenton, he stood there and pointed to the double front doors. They're wood with stained glass that were custom-made with our family's crest. 'Go!' he said. The sun was shining through the red glass, and it reminded me of blood. Like if you say the word 'gay,' blood doesn't matter."

Her eyes softened as she listened.

"I was so shocked, I just stood there. I'm six-one, but Father is six-four. So he stood there towering over me. It was a Saturday, so he had on a white Detroit Golf Club polo shirt and white khaki slacks. Mother and Anna were standing on the balcony, looking down and crying."

I sighed. I hadn't meant to come in here this morning and get all bogged down in this historic drama. But here I was, and I trusted that Dr. Fenton was doing this for a good reason.

Her pencil-thin eyebrows drew together as if she were hearing this for the first time, not the fifteenth.

"Then my father opened the door and

said, 'Not in my house.' I left. And those were the last words he spoke to me."

I sipped the sweet coffee to wash down the bitter taste in my mouth.

"You're not in his house anymore," Dr. Fenton insisted. "And I'd bet a hundred dollars right now that he misses you like nobody's business. You're still his son."

I stared into the cup and swirled the creamy liquid as if it were a crystal ball. "If he'd take the call, I know exactly what he'd say."

She tilted her head, listening.

"That if I hadn't abandoned his business empire in Detroit to run off and become a model in New York, and if I hadn't come down here to the pastel la-la land of pretty girls and even prettier bois —"

"Stop!" she said. "Don't speculate what he'll say. How would you feel if he died and your sister told you he'd had a change of heart about you?"

Her words slammed me in the throat. I coughed. To never speak to my father again, to never forgive him, or let him accept me as I am —

"Gotcha," Dr. Fenton said with a sassy tilt of her head.

I stared back hard, but she blurred through the tears stinging my eyes. I shivered, hating that she was right.

"Call your sister first," she said. "Test the waters through her. Who knows, maybe she'll loan you the cash to keep your business afloat."

I sipped the hot, sweet coffee. It soothed me from the inside out. But thinking of Father chilled me all over.

I shook my head. "Father would find out. His accountants watch all the accounts like hawks. And since Anna's husband runs one of the companies, their money gets scrutinized, too."

"Do you resent your sister?"

"No!" I snapped, glaring at Dr. Fenton.

She removed her glasses and leaned forward. "Anna has the picture-perfect life. Husband, two kids, European nanny, huge house, financial security, and your parents' approval. That could've been you."

"I can't live a lie!" I slammed the coffee cup on the table. "I'd rather be down here struggling with my business, and being true to myself, than be up there on easy street pretending to be what everybody expected."

She nodded. "Bentley, could you present it to your father in a way that shows he taught you the value of integrity? Now you're living an honest life —"

"No," I said. "I've thought this through

29

frontwards, backwards, and sideways. He told me we couldn't talk about anything until I came to my senses and moved back to Detroit. It's either work in the family business or be an outcast from Father's empire."

Dr. Fenton focused hard on me. "The life expectancy of an African American male is sixty-eight years old. How old is your dad?"

"He was thirty when I was born, so he's sixty-five," I said. "His birthday was —" My gut cramped, either from the sudden surge of caffeine or from the melancholy mood that had struck last week. "His birthday was Friday. Anna said they had a beautiful dinner party for him at Wolfgang Puck's restaurant in the MGM Grand Detroit."

Dr. Fenton raised her eyebrows. "They're celebrating over gourmet food and your models are starving."

I glared at her.

"I won't go crawling back to my father, begging him for money or his love," I said. "I won't let him lecture me again about his disappointment and disgust with my life choices. I don't need money that bad."

"Yes, you do."

"I'll find new clients. I refuse to —"

"Look, Bentley. You're not the first gay man I've counseled through a situation like this. But you may be making it harder on yourself than necessary."

I crossed my arms so hard that I coughed.

"Bentley, yesterday I had a client in a very similar situation as yours. And guess what? His father and his favorite uncle just died in a boating accident. My client hadn't spoken with them for ten years. Now he never will."

Goose bumps raced across my body. How would I handle that? Sometimes I wanted to pick up the phone and call Father so bad. At least it's an option. What if I lost that forever?

Dr. Fenton said, "He and I had had this same conversation for six years. But he responded the same way you are. Then he sat there and cried me a river about wanting one last chance to reconcile with them. But it's too late."

I crossed my arms tighter. "It's not that easy."

"I'm here to help you navigate the now," Dr. Fenton said, "but I want to steer you on the best path for the future as well. So let's review your options one more time. A bank loan?"

I shook my head, remembering that dreadful meeting with my banker just last week. "Most banks won't even give out loans with collateral. They even froze the line of credit

31

I had against my condo. Man, I'm so glad this election is almost over. Our new president has to bring us some relief."

Dr. Fenton made a pretend scoreboard in the air with her fingertip. "Banks? No deal. A loan from your mother or sister?"

I shook my head. "Another thing about my sister is if Father found out, he'd get mad and maybe cut her off for helping me. And since her husband is under Father's complete control, he'd go down, too."

Dr. Fenton marked the pretend scoreboard with her finger.

"Sister, no. Mother?"

I rolled my eyes. "Mother is so caught up with her twenty-four-year-old boyfriend. When she calls, that's all she talks about. She's definitely found her inner Demi Moore."

My biting tone inspired an intrigued look from my therapist, who said, "So she has no time for you. We haven't talked a lot about this. How do you feel about her dating someone younger than you?"

I thought for a minute about Dr. Fenton's question. About a year after I left Michigan, my father and mother divorced after thirty years of marriage. Part of the reason was my father's changed attitude about me, which my mother thought was stupid and childish on his part.

"It's not my business," I said, reaching for the coffee. "I guess as long as she's happy. I haven't met dude yet, but I'm pretty sure he's got a motive. I mean, don't get me wrong, because my mother looks damn good for a fifty-six-year-old woman, but I think this guy has got his eye on her pocketbook." I let out a sly chuckle. "Too bad dude doesn't know Mother like I do."

"Meaning?"

"She's very smart. Nobody is going to pull anything over on her. I don't care how much in love he thinks she is. Lucinda Dean is tight with her money. I guess that's why she still has a lot."

"Then she could help you," Dr. Fenton said as if the matter were resolved.

"I wouldn't feel comfortable," I said. "Mother didn't disown me. But she sort of sent me on my merry way, without any offer to help."

Dr. Fenton marked the pretend scorecard with a question mark. "Mother is still a maybe. So what does this young lover of hers do for a living?"

I savored the coffee, not wanting to waste my energy or my expensive therapy minutes on her boi toy. "He plays football. At least I think he still plays football. The ironic thing is that he plays for the team that Father lost in the divorce settlement. I know that ticks the hell out of him. First he loses his team in the divorce settlement, and then all of his business associates know his former wife is sleeping with someone half her age. And that everybody in their social circles are talking about it."

"So image is everything for your father," Dr. Fenton said.

"Everything! Me, I think it's funny that Mom found a stud muffin that Dad most likely drafted." I laughed.

"Speaking of football," Dr. Fenton said, marking her imaginary scoreboard. "Would your ex help you out?"

I made a disgusted sound. "Yeah, right. Warren is all about Warren. I haven't talked with him for a couple years."

She removed her red glasses and pointed them at me. "Bentley, you sound bitter."

"You'd be bitter if you abandoned your life of luxury for the man of your dreams who turned around and left you for some B-list actress. Ain't that a bitch? Just because I'm not a trust fund baby anymore."

She put her glasses on, squinting over them.

"So much for old-fashioned love," I said. "Besides, I made the choice to be out.

Warren struggles with that."

"Struggles? From what you've told me, 'refuses' is the better word."

"Dr. Fenton," I said playfully, "I can't get anything past you, can I?"

"No, but would Warren consider helping you financially as an old friend?"

I sipped the coffee. It was now as cold as I felt toward Warren. "No, Warren is too busy following the money his damn self. When he gets it, he's keeping it. And every time I open up *Ebony* or *Jet,* there he is with a different woman. I don't know who's stupider, the women or my dumb ass."

My therapist nodded with that perplexed look again. "You haven't used profanity all morning until we've talked about Warren. You don't even feel that angry toward your father. Two men who loved you and basically abandoned you."

My cheeks stung, as if her words had slapped me. I stared down at the heel of my black leather loafer. The inch of ashy ankle exposed by the bottom of my beige linen pant leg let me know just how stressed I must be. I was usually diligent about rubbing shea butter into dry areas to avoid that unsightly dry skin.

"Bentley? Where did you go?"

"I'm right here. But putting Father and

Warren in the same category, that was a sucker punch to the gut."

"The truth hurts," she said. "So I should cross Warren off the list of potential financiers? Even though you said the two of you were once deeply in love."

"Were," I emphasized. "And like my mother, I don't play the fool. Besides, I love *me* more."

"Then you should do everything possible to solve this problem that's draining your vitality," she said, scanning her imaginary scoreboard. "Next source?"

I shrugged. "That's the problem. I don't have one."

"Can you make cold calls? Solicit business from companies you've never worked with? Or tap into a new area of the business?"

I shook my head. "People want to go with what they know in this atmosphere."

"Okay," she said, "let that percolate while we talk about your personal life. Have you met anyone new here in Miami that you'd like to date?"

I glanced at the plump leaves of the jade plant near her desk. "Well, let's just go from bad to worse, okay?"

She half smiled.

"No, I don't have the time to make a new

love connection. I got a few fuck buddies. You know, *friends with benefits*. Besides, I'm not into the Internet dating scene. That's the hot ticket these days. Straight or gay, everybody seems to be hooking up online. That's too scary for me."

Dr. Fenton's eyes lit up as if she were having a lightbulb moment. I sat up straighter. Maybe she'd just figured out how I could bankroll my business for the next couple of months.

"Bentley, tell me something. What if Warren *did* come back into your life, on your terms?"

My excitement deflated. "It's not going to happen."

"Why?"

"Because men like Warren will never be able to admit who they are." I set down the coffee cup; it clanked against the glass like an exclamation point after what I said.

"Bentley, you were that way once."

"I was, but I'm smart. With that, anyway. But not smart enough to solve my problems at the moment. Personally or professionally."

"Hopefully we've opened your eyes to some new possibilities today."

My session was almost over. But instead of feeling like I'd found some solutions, I felt like Dr. Fenton had helped me pry open a big can of worms. And instead of the relief that I'd felt as I walked in forty-five minutes ago, I felt more confused than ever.

THREE

The hot sun was shooting down from the skylight in the office of my modeling agency, making me feel like I was literally in the hot seat. Financially, anyway. Because as I sat at my desk, every bill I reviewed only filled me with more panic. We just didn't have enough money to cover the basic expenses of rent, utilities, phone, and Internet, and the few subcontractors we were still using.

White envelopes and bills stamped OVER-DUE! in red ink blanketed my work space. It was only paper, but it seemed like the weight of our modeling agency's financial burden was threatening to crack the glass-topped desk and bend its shiny chrome legs. The papers surged up in a mess around my desktop computer, like waves trying to engulf it.

In my gray leather chair, I spun around to the credenza behind me. I flipped through my Rolodex, then scrolled through the contacts on my phone.

Somehow, some way, I just had to score some cash to keep my dream business alive. And it wasn't all about Bentley L. Dean III. It was about the struggling models that depended on me for jobs to pay their rent and eat.

"Bentley?" my assistant called as she knocked softly on the open door.

"Yeah," I said, my voice sounding more irritated than I intended. I sliced open yet another envelope with my sleek chrome letter opener that resembled a silver dagger. Damn, I sure hoped Laura wasn't coming in with an armful of today's mail. That would only mean more bills.

"Bentley? Excuse me? But there's a man in the lobby? Sterling Sneed?"

I slammed the letter opener on the credenza and spun around. "Girl, I told you to stop making everything sound like a question. Declare it. Say it like you own it."

Laura's twenty-something, cappuccino-hued face turned milk white. Wearing skinny white leggings, ballerina slippers, and a loose turquoise top, she froze. The shock in her eyes made me realize I must have sounded like a bear.

"I'm so sorry, Laura," I said, shaking my head. "These bills —"

"It's okay," she said, fingering her shoulder-length braids, "everybody I know is like totally freaking out about money, too. Oh, and I'm working on the way I talk." She laughed nervously. "Just habit, I guess."

"You can handle the office like nobody's business, Laura, but you need to sound more businesslike. Like Alex. Listen to her," I said, referring to my business partner of five years.

"Okay," she said, "I will."

"Now, who is this, somebody I don't know, who's out in the lobby without an appointment but wants to see me?"

"Sterling Sneed," Laura said. "He said it's really important that you talk with him now." She glanced at the mess of bills. "Maybe he can help?"

"That would be the answer to my prayers," I said. "Did he say what he wants?"

"I tried to find out," Laura said, "but he insisted that he could only talk to you."

"Does he look crazy?"

"More like he just stepped off the pages of *GQ* and into like, a corporate board-room," Laura said. "I think his suit could pay my rent for the rest of the year."

"Laura, you know I only see people if they have an appointment," I said. The time in the upper-right corner of my desktop com-

41

puter said 11:40 A.M. "Besides, I have a lunch date at noon. How much time does he say he needs?"

Laura shook her head and raised her arms out slightly, sending a gust of patchouli oil scent my way. "He didn't say. You want me to ask him? I'm sorry for sort of breaking with protocol, but he looks like someone you'd want to see. Either rich or important or both."

I had nothing to lose, and about fifteen minutes to spare. It was either take another torturous dive back into that tidal wave of bills, or talk with this man.

"Send him in," I said, buttoning the top of my baby blue dress shirt that I wore with pleated navy trousers and loafers. As Laura left, I gathered the bills into a neat pile and tucked them into the top drawer of the credenza. A messy desk, Father used to say, was the sign of a cluttered mind, and a cluttered mind was too clogged to let success take hold. Suddenly I remembered how, when he'd take me to his grand office overlooking downtown Detroit, he would always clear his desk before seeing a visitor. And his secretary had strict orders to declutter the entire office, every evening.

Now, my back was to the door when I heard a deep voice say, "Mr. Dean, I presume?"

I turned around, looking into the face of a tall, slim African American man who was extending his hand toward me.

I shook his firm grip. "And you are?"

"Sterling Sneed," he said with cocky confidence. With mocha skin and a close-cropped black beard and hair, he had dark eyes that were slightly slanted. Before I could offer him a seat, he gracefully sat in one of the white leather armchairs facing my desk, then crossed his leg so that his expensive pant leg draped elegantly over his dress sock and shiny oxford leather wing tips that matched his belt.

My inner voice sounded an alarm: *He's dressed like a banker!* My heart raced. Was he here to evict us? Tell me we'd defaulted on our line of credit? Or was he offering some special new financing to bail out small business owners?

I took a deep, calming breath as I walked around the desk and assumed the dominant position in my office. I felt in control behind my gleaming desk that, with the rest of the furniture in our office suite, had consumed far too big a chunk of our budget back when I thought business would always be booming.

"Thanks for seeing me," Mr. Sneed said,

crossing his hands on his lap. The bright sunshine accentuated the shininess of his manicured fingernails and the diamonds on the face of his gold watch. That was too flashy for a banker.

"What company are you with, Mr. Sneed?"

He tilted his head as if he were in charge. "That's not important, Mr. Dean. This is a private matter."

I was the epitome of cool and controlled when I said, with an almost blasé tone, "First of all, Mr. Sneed, I don't usually see people without an appointment. Secondly, I don't meet with people until I know who they are, where they're from, and what they want."

"Then why are you seeing me now?"

"I'm starting to wonder that myself," I said. "I have a business to run. I don't have time to play guessing games. And I don't think I have any private matters to discuss with you."

Mr. Sneed leaned forward as if he were about to give me a winning lottery ticket. His face lit up as he said, "I have a possible engagement for your agency."

Did he have any clue that my agency was on financial life support? With the Internet these days, was he from some unscrupulous

44

company that could tap into records and see the bank had closed my line of credit? Or that I was behind on some of our bills? I studied his face for hints.

"A very *lucrative* engagement," he said with a sly smile. "And if you do the first event, well, there is a chance for substantially more business."

Fairy godfather or deal with the devil? I still wasn't sure. But if he was talking money, I was listening. A sleazy proposition, however, would earn him an immediate eviction from my office.

"Mr. Sneed, I'm listening." My somewhat impatient tone let him know that I wasn't easily impressed. And surely not one to get suckered. "We're in business for big engagements. Tell me, how did you hear about our firm?"

"I did some checking," he said, looking hard into my eyes, "and my client and I have decided that you're the best firm for this job." The way he said "my client" with emphasis made it sound like he was talking about the president.

"And what, may I ask, is the job?"

The corners of his mouth rose, but he wasn't smiling. It was more like a Cheshire grin, or the cat that was about to swallow the canary and try to play it cool. And that always spiked my internal distrust meter into the red zone.

Mr. Sneed's voice deepened as he declared, "I need fifteen of your best-looking men. They must be gay, bi, or very open-minded."

I said flatly, "I don't have any bigots working for me."

"There is more," he said, delighted with himself.

"About the assignment?"

"Yes." His tone was so upbeat, as if he were offering me the most irresistible deal of the century. "My client requires that each of the models selected will have to sign a nondisclosure agreement. It states they will not discuss any of the guests or anything that goes on at the event. Ever."

I leaned back in my chair, squaring my shoulders. What was this man asking me to do?

"What's the event?"

Mr. Sneed really smiled this time. His teeth were small and his thin lips glistened as if he'd just put on lip balm. "It's a very high-profile party with guests who are very discreet. Your models will have the once-in-a-lifetime opportunity to interact with some of the most powerful men in the country."

"Interact with," I repeated flatly. I had been in the modeling business and in Miami long enough to know exactly what was up. But the promise of money to fix our financial mess kept me listening and hoping that I was wrong. If business had been booming, I would have straight up asked him if my models were expected to have sex with these guys. But today, I only vaguely admitted to myself, my monetary neediness softened my approach. I needed to listen intently to what he wanted before I made a judgment.

"Mr. Sneed, what will be expected of my models?"

He extended his folded hands to his knee. "Our expectations are simply that your models enjoy the evening as grown men. It's a private gathering where discretion is the utmost priority. Your models will act accordingly, with full understanding that they are, to put it bluntly, 'eye candy.'"

"Eye candy," I repeated. "Anything else?"

"Indeed," Mr. Sneed said. "We want them to dress to a tee. We'll provide money for clothes, which they will get to keep. They need to look good and like they belong. We don't want any youngsters and bois with their pants dragging to the point that we can see if they wear boxers or briefs. Do you understand?"

"I think I do." My inner voice was repeating my mother's mantra, *If it sounds too good to be true, it is.* I had heard about parties like this where high-powered men who played straight to the world invited in a bevy of boi toys for their private pleasures. Still, I had to find out more. "What is the age limit? Are you looking for a particular type of guy?"

Mr. Sneed nodded. "I would say at least twenty-one and with very nice bodies. That's why we came to you. I did my homework and found that you are one of the best in town when it comes to our type." Then he spoke as if he were ordering off a man menu: "We would prefer black, Hispanic, or even Cuban, guys, as long as they speak English. And we'd like a few light-skinned brothers and some dark-skinned ones, too."

I loved that my agency's reputation on the Miami modeling scene had brought him here. But this was reminding me of that proposition I'd gotten when I'd first gone into business. A hip-hop mogul sent his representative to me to "order" two dozen hunks of every race to attend his yacht party. The catch? He said, point-blank, that the men would be generously paid for any "additional services" that they would be

48

"expected" to provide during the moonlight cruise.

That was one deal — despite the bricks of Benjamins that he was offering me — that I said without hesitation, "No, thank you."

But right now, Mr. Sneed was making his offer sound legitimate.

I cast a hard stare at Mr. Sneed. "Are you asking me to supply guys for sex? Because if you are, Mr. Sneed, I think you've found the wrong agency. We're not in that type of business," I said firmly. "This is a modeling agency. Not a gigolo service."

He shifted on his chair and chuckled. "No, that's not what I'm asking. Did I mention that each guy will receive a $2,500 clothing allowance in addition to a flat fee for the night? It's absolutely imperative that they have the proper attire."

I studied his eyes; he never looked away. "Will I be able to see the guest list?"

He shook his head. "Our client list is very discreet. So the answer is no. Besides many of our guests will be using aliases. They are quite reserved and guarded when it comes to meeting new people."

I asked more firmly, "Will your client expect sex from my models?"

"No, Mr. Dean. But like I said, we need adults who can make adult decisions."

"So there's an age requirement?"

Mr. Sneed ran his fingers over his diamond-faced watch. "We don't want anyone under twenty-one. And we will pick the models that you invite."

"I don't know if I have fifteen guys who fit your description," I said, typing into my keyboard to call up our online catalogue.

"Can't you do what they call a casting?"

"Yes, I can do that," I said, staring at the handsome faces on the screen. "I have several who meet your criteria but a casting is a good idea."

Mr. Sneed smiled. "So do we have a deal?"

I focused on the screen, loving those buff bodies and stylish clothes that earned my agency its excellent reputation. "I need to get more details and talk this over with my partner. When do you need a decision?"

"The party is in two weeks."

I met Mr. Sneed's probing stare and asked, "Where is the party?"

"On Star Island. If you take this engagement, then I will give you the address."

"Will I be able to do a site visit?"

"A site visit? What is that?"

"I would actually visit the place where my models are scheduled to appear," I said. "It's a standard practice in the industry. So I know what to expect."

"Sure," Mr. Sneed said, "that's fair."

"And will we be able to put a time limit on how long my models are expected to stay?"

"Absolutely," he said. "But they will have to be on time."

"Alcohol," I said, going down my mental checklist as I did for every assignment. "I prefer that my models not drink alcohol on the job. Are they expected to drink?"

"Sure."

"What if I don't want them to do that?"

"What's a cocktail or two for a grown man?" Mr. Sneed flashed that cat-eating-the-canary smile again. "Alcohol is not a deal breaker, but I think we should just let the guys be who they are. We're talking about adults. Right?"

Normally I would demand a no-alcohol clause in the deal. But a sudden surge of excitement shot through me as I realized this could be the answer to our financial crisis. "I guess you've got a point," I said. "Now tell me more specifically how you found out about my agency?"

Mr. Sneed looked around at my office walls, which were covered with silver-framed eight-by-tens of my models' head shots. Above my credenza were three silver-framed posters of huge campaigns we'd done for a jeans company, a designer perfume, and a local gym.

"Your work speaks for itself," Mr. Sneed said. "And we let our fingers do the walking through the phone book of who's who in Miami modeling. Every time we asked which agency would most likely have the kind of men we're looking for, the answer was Picture Perfect. Every time."

"Well, that's good to know," I said, wondering if I should believe this is as the truth or dispel it as a flattery-will-get-you-everywhere tactic.

My tone remained strictly business. "And will I be able to get information on your client?"

"Mr. Bentley," he said with a tone like I had no clue who I was talking to, "let me assure you that my client is one of the most important men in the world. He is first-class."

So was the hip-hop mogul who wanted my guys to work as sex toys at his yacht party. I didn't care how much money they were offering. Today, however, I did. I hated that it was my major motivator for even considering a deal that had too much gray area between the black-and-white facts of the business deal.

"How will we be paid?" I asked.

52

"We will pay fifty percent once the contract is signed," he said proudly. "The balance would be paid the day of the event."

So maybe this was a legit affair. I mean, except for my music mogul experience, when was the last time I'd heard of anyone having a legitimate business contract for call bois? That kind of thing was never documented with paperwork.

I wanted to smile, but I didn't. My best poker face masked my excitement. Maybe the goose that laid the golden egg had just landed on South Beach. At Picture Perfect. In my office.

"I'll need to discuss this with my partner," I said coolly. "And I'll have to do a casting."

"How long will that take?" Mr. Sneed snapped. "We're working with a short time line. We need to make sure that you'll be able to deliver."

"Trust me, Mr. Sneed. If we take this engagement, then we'll deliver." I stood. So did he, extending his hand to shake across my desk.

"I don't doubt that one bit, Mr. Dean. Here is my card with both of my cell numbers. I'd like to hear from you within twenty-four hours. Is that possible?"

I walked around my desk and took the card. "I'll give it my best shot."

We stood a few feet apart as I continued to assess his believability. Father used to always say, "When in doubt, don't." But the doubt that I felt hinged on one thing: whether my models would be propositioned for sex, and whether that was Mr. Sneed's secret intention. Then again, how many times had I sent models off on shoots where perhaps they were propositioned for sex — in exchange for money, favors, or gifts — but they never told me about it?

"Your best shot," Mr. Sneed echoed. "I guess that's all I can ask for." He tipped his head toward me.

Excitement pumped through me. Finally, some relief from worrying about money.

"Have a delightful day," he said. "And let's hope your casting finds the hottest young models in Miami for our party."

The way he said "hottest" singed my excitement. And the look in his eyes spiked my internal distrust meter even farther into the red zone.

FOUR

A vague sense of wrong burned in my gut as I walked into my partner's office. A yellow beam of sun was shooting down from the skylight, glowing brightly on the sleek glass-and-chrome furniture. And shining like a spotlight on Alexandria Wells. If I were straight, she'd be the kind of woman who'd make it hard to concentrate on anything but her beauty. That's exactly what I'd thought when I'd met her four years ago in New York on a modeling job. Now she was thirty-six and as stunning as ever, as if she'd ripened into womanhood and just *knew* it.

She was standing beside her desk, looking like a pillar of glamour. I loved the femme fatale visual. But it didn't make me think about sex. It made me think, *Badass bitch businesswoman.*

The sharp points of her black stiletto pumps let me know she could kick ass even in the toughest business situations. The sleekness of her trademark black pencil skirt, which hugged her slim but curvy hips and behind and tapered into a small waist, let me know she was in control of her diet and exercise. In the office that translated into the discipline to get deals done, no matter how much work or time they took. The crisp white blouse, starched so tough that her collar stood up around a glimpse of cleavage, was the perfect mix of professional and stylish. And the half-carat diamond solitaires sparkling in her ears looked classy and expensive, but not flashy.

Her hair, tinted dark auburn, was blown out and slightly curled back in sassy little tendrils that might look like a swirly helmet on anyone else. But on Alex, it worked.

Her face, however, was looking pretty stressed right now. It was usually a smooth chocolate brown oval, with a little mushroom of a nose and full lips that looked like a figure eight set sideways and glossed in bronze. Anger radiated from her dark gray eyes, which she'd inherited from her white mother and accentuated with black liner and mascara.

Now, her neck jerked just enough to show her sista was about to come out on whoever was on the phone. The air of anger around her only intensified my worry about whether

Sterling was trying to lure me and our models into something sleazy.

"You can't do this to us at the last minute!" Alex's deep voice boomed up to the slanted white ceiling. If I hadn't seen the ceiling fan, I would've thought her tone had made the wispy plants sway. "We'll sue the lenses off your damn cameras!"

I stood in the doorway, listening for clues about who was trying to jack her day. As if our firm needed more problems.

Alex ran the film and television side of our agency and the women's division, while I ran the men's print and runway division.

Why Alex hadn't applied this toughness to claw her way to the top of the modeling industry — to become a supermodel — I don't know. We'd clicked right away. Her female companionship so soon after my breakup with Kim had been comforting. We'd check out those gorgeous Roman god statues at the Met, take in a Broadway show, and blow our diets together on pasta in Little Italy.

But one thing Alex loved was the fast lane. A little too fast for me. So I let her take her walk on the wild side with her model girlfriends, while I focused on my work.

Then once she'd gotten her fill, she left the runway for the classroom, heading down to NYU to earn an MBA.

That makes her a bad sista unto itself. How many beautiful women do you know who can strut their stuff on the catwalk, and then go get a Master's in Business Administration from one of the best schools in the world?

I was so impressed, she was the first person who came to mind when I decided to open the modeling agency here in Miami. It was only natural for us to team up in business once we both retreated from the concrete coldness of New York for the pastel sunshine of South Beach.

But beachside bliss was hardly what we were feeling right now.

Especially when she slammed down the phone.

"I can't believe these assholes!" Alex crossed her arms and perched on the edge of the desk.

"Who's trying to play bad guy?" I asked, stepping into the office. The soft vanilla-musk scent of Hanae Mori perfume radiated from her.

"They can't just cancel a movie that's supposed to start shooting tomorrow," she snapped. "I booked ten people for this bastard. He can't just call and cancel!"

She reached for the phone. "He needs to

honor this commitment. I am *not* going to call our people and say they don't have work tomorrow." She started dialing.

"Alex, what's his reason for canceling?"

She shook her head. "He said something about losing their financing at the last minute. But it didn't sound like they had looked elsewhere. Damn, this economy sucks!"

"Maybe they'll get new financing and the job will be rescheduled. Think of it as just postponed for now."

She almost smiled as she looked at me. Her tone softened as she said, "You're so optimistic. Bentley, I was counting on this job to get us out of this hole."

"Let's find out more before we go making demands," I said.

"Can we sue them?" Alex asked, her hand poised over the number pad.

"We can't afford an attorney. We owe our lawyers, too."

Alex gripped the phone and held it in midair. "Ugh! Something has got to give!"

"Other jobs will come our way," I said with far more confidence than I felt. Sterling's proposition sat on the tip of my tongue. But my inner voice said, *Wait.* Alex was so squeaky-clean when it came to business, I was afraid she'd hop up on her high horse and tell me I was crazy to even consider anything that looked the least bit questionable. Even if she was strapped for cash.

"You look like you know something I don't know," she said. "Like Congress is about to send us the Bentley bailout."

I smiled, thinking that my new client might actually be about to do that. "I wish."

Alex slammed down the phone. "This day has got to get better. Tell me you were coming in here with some good news."

"Mine can wait," I said. "I think you need to decompress. Go for a run or something."

All that wrong in my gut burned even hotter as I left her office. As I walked down the hall, I hated that my father came to mind. I'd left the stability and luxury of his world up in Detroit. A world of financial security and prestige that was my birthright, except for the fact that the real me just couldn't conform to their expectations.

So I'd set off on my own, doing what I love.

And now it felt like my business was a house of cards that could come tumbling down any day.

FIVE

I woke up this morning just before five, hating that my entire being ached to hear my father's voice. I pressed my head deeper into a fluffy pillow and pulled the soft beige sheets up to my chin. The white ceiling of my bedroom reflected the blankness, the emptiness, which made me feel hollow right now. Hollow, except for all the question marks slicing through me.

Was Mr. Sneed trying to bamboozle me and my models?

Would I look away and play naïve so we can all get paid?

Would that mean I was selling out?

Should I call Father? Should I reach out for help from my sister or Mother? And would I ever see Warren again? Would I ever feel the comfort of being in his arms or enjoy that happy vibe that lovers create together, even when they're sitting quietly on the couch?

I stared at the sleek gray phone on my nightstand. The blue numbers cast an eerie glow over the dark room. The price of the sleek black furniture I'd bought for this master suite — after leaving everything behind in Detroit and New York — could have paid the bills at the agency for a few months. I had to stop thinking like that. What was done, was done. I wasn't going to sell my furniture.

I reached for the phone. Father always followed Benjamin Franklin's advice about "Early to bed and early to rise makes a man healthy, wealthy, and wise." Right now he'd be down in the kitchen, drinking coffee and reading *The Wall Street Journal*, *The New York Times*, and the *Detroit Free Press*.

While he was far more Internet savvy than most of his colleagues who relied on secretaries, Father was old school when it came to the newspapers. He had to read them in his kitchen every morning. Though he had stainless steel appliances and every modern convenience, he said a successful man stuck to certain habits to anchor his day.

I needed to anchor my heart and soul by speaking with my dad. But a wave of resentment washed through me, along with a cold splash of fear. What if he heard my voice and hung up?

I bolted out of bed. Fifteen minutes later, I was at the gym. South Beach had several gyms. This morning I chose the one where I could run on the treadmill and pound away all this anxiety. This was the serious gym, where I could have a workout without guys ogling me or hitting on me by asking things like, "How often do you work out?" or "How'd you get those rock-hard abs?"

My runner's high soothed me a little bit, but the ache to hear Father's voice still made me feel sad. After showering and dressing at the gym, I walked down Washington Avenue to my favorite bagel shop. I had a cup of coffee and a bagel with smoked salmon. I resisted the cream cheese, hating the restrictiveness of my low-fat diet that kept my body sculpted and strong, but loving the results. It felt like everything in my life was restricted now. No romance. No new business except for a questionable proposition. No money. No Father.

The caffeine rush from my coffee gave me a sudden surge of courage. I snatched up my phone. As I dialed his cell, my fingers trembled and I wondered what I would say. I thought about these options:

"I'm sorry, Father, that I disappointed you, but I'm still your son and I need you." Would that sound weak?

What about, *"All right, old man! You're only getting older. One day you'll need me to run your businesses or make sure you don't marry some young chick who'll take advantage of your old ass."* I could never speak to Father like that.

Or, *"I love you and miss you."* What man didn't want to hear such precious words from his only son?

I didn't use my speed dial, but punched the numbers in one at a time to make sure that I remembered my father's number. It was now just after seven. Father would be up and in his office, handling his business. After three rings, I thought maybe I was wrong. But before ring number four, I heard his voice.

"This is B. L. Dean, Jr." The deep bass of his voice boomed through my phone. Into my ear. My heart raced.

I froze. The words "Hello, Father" and "Daddy" were like little ice cubes on my tongue, which refused to warm up and spit them out.

He changed his name!

Shock paralyzed me. The people in the bagel place around me blurred into grayish streaks; I stared at the potted palm tree just outside the window.

He was using his initials instead of his

name! I remembered when I would call him from prep school and from college; he always answered the phone, "This is Bentley L. Dean, Jr."

Does he hate me that much?

Had I — the third in the line of Bentley Deans — embarrassed him so that he had forsaken our name?

SIX

As Alex and I walked into one of Miami's lunchtime hot spots overlooking the ocean, I felt calmer than I had in days. The bright blue expanse of the ocean, the palm trees, and all the beautiful people packing the outdoor tables jolted me with the excitement that I used to feel. Not that we could really afford this world-famous restaurant. One of Alex's clients had given her a two-hundred-dollar gift card last year, for a job well done, and she was just now taking time to use it with me.

"I need your opinion about something personal," she'd said when I'd arrived at the office this morning looking more somber than I'd intended. Little did she know, she was providing the perfect opportunity for me to talk with her about the party assignment. Why I was acting like it was a choice seemed a little ridiculous when I really thought about it. We needed the money. Period.

"How's this?" the maître d' asked, seating us in a prime people-watching spot over-looking the outdoor terrace.

"Picture-perfect," Alex said. "Bentley, this is a good place to scout. All the waiters are gorgeous."

The delicious scent of garlic, tomatoes, and basil wafted around us as a hunky blond passed with a plate of bruschetta. The supermodel types at a nearby table stared him down, giggling and pretending to eat their salads. The fast-paced New Age music almost cheered me up.

As did all the people wearing buttons in support of my presidential candidate. That filled me with optimism that he could take office and make the economy boom once again.

"If I scout, I need some jobs to lure them in," I said. "Speaking of —"

The waiter, who looked like a living, breathing Ken doll, took our orders. Despite all the fresh seafood on the menu, I couldn't stop myself from ordering a cheeseburger, for nostalgia's sake. That's what Father and I used to always enjoy during football games or outings to collect rent from his income properties around Detroit. Back then, it was White Castle, a secret indulgence that health-conscious Mother still didn't know about. But this upscale place, full of men dressed like Mr. Sneed and wealthy matrons and the young, hip crowd, was hardly White Castle. Still, I needed the comfort of a big, juicy cheeseburger and fries.

"Anything to drink?" he asked after Alex ordered her favorite, red snapper.

"I want a margarita like nobody's business," I said, "but it's lunchtime. I'll be good and take lemonade, please."

"Make that two," Alex said. "But make mine half iced tea, please."

When the waiter left, she said, "Bentley, these people are like, '*What* recession?' All those luxury cars in valet, they don't look like they're missin' a beat." She pointed to a thirty-something woman in a designer dress. "Her designer bag alone could ease our worries for a whole month. I want to go table to table and ask if these people need any models."

The waiter brought the lemonades.

"You might not have to," I said. "Yesterday I got an offer to supply fifteen models for a party. And they want to *pay*. A lot."

Alex smiled and toasted me with her lemonade glass.

"Cheers to you, Bentley L. Dean. Workin' it!" She tilted her head. "Why didn't you

68

tell me this during my meltdown yesterday?"

"I had to think about it," I said. "My mother always says, 'All that glitters isn't gold.' "

"Uh-oh," Alex said, almost slamming the glass on the pink linen tablecloth. "What's the catch? Wait, you don't even have to tell me."

She crossed her arms over her crisp beige blouse. "He's looking for call bois."

I shook my head. "Of course that was my first thought. But he didn't say anything blatant to imply that."

"Everybody has a price, even if a job seems totally legit," Alex said.

"Well, I don't have a price for that," I said more confidently than I felt. "I've checked him out and made it very clear that we are a modeling agency and casting agency. Nothing more. I promise you, Alex, I wouldn't do anything to damage our relationship and the reputation we've managed to build."

She nodded. "I know that, Bentley. I trust your judgment."

The waiter brought our salads of mixed greens with gorgonzola crumbles.

"The sleaze factor is out there, big-time," Alex said. "I can't tell you how many calls I get a week. People ask for female models but they really want call girls. I'll be getting all excited about a potential booking, until the alleged client says something stupid like, 'We only want girls with big knockers and small waists like strippers.' "

I stabbed my fork into the salad and took a crunchy bite. That gorgonzola was so delicious. The flavor reminded me of the steak house Warren and I used to frequent in New York; for some reason everything there tasted extra flavorful. Or maybe everything tasted extra flavorful because I was madly in love with the man across the candlelit table that he hoped looked like a business dinner to everyone around us. The way he was looking at me like I was the big, juicy steak, Warren Stubbs wasn't fooling anybody except himself.

Back to the present, I focused on being glad I had skipped the cream cheese this morning.

"When I tell these sleazy moods that we don't employ strippers," Alex said, "they come back at me like, 'I know, but we want classy girls who can *pass* as strippers.' But, Bentley, in this case, you're right. The money we'd make on the job would be good for the firm. We could finally go after Hollywood in a big way."

"We sure could," I exclaimed, even hap-

70

pier as the waiter approached with my mile-high burger. "It seems like it'll be a onetime thing."

I closed my eyes and inhaled the scent of the food.

"I'm gonna eat the butter and the sour cream on my potato!" Alex said like a giddy child ordering ice cream. "I worked my ass off at the gym this morning —"

"No, you didn't," I teased.

She playfully swatted me, and then took my hand across the table. We bowed as she said, "Dear God, we have faith that you are always working in our best interest. Please bless us with new opportunities, both personally and professionally, that help us live our best lives."

"Amen to that!" I declared, raising my cheeseburger to my mouth.

Alex took a few bites. We ate silently for a few minutes, loving the luxurious taste of this delicious food and our fancy surroundings.

"We took this for granted in New York," she said. "I think we ate out almost every night. Spending money like water. Now I have to pinch pennies just like I count calories. And I'm not even gettin' any."

"TMI," I said playfully.

"Sorry," she said, taking a big forkful of

71

sour cream–covered potato.

"So you're cool about us doing the private party?" I asked.

"You're going to do it," she said. "It's a boi thing, so that's your side of the business. But I don't have any problem if you feel good about it."

"I do," I said, dipping a long fry in ketchup. "We won't regret it."

"Good," Alex said, clearing her throat. That meant she was about to change the subject. She cast a piercing stare across the table. "Bentley, do you think I'd be a good mother?"

"What?" I stared to make sure I was hearing her right. "I need to check your ID. Back in New York the Alex I knew used to look down her nose at baby carriages. She said she'd never ruin her figure by having some man's baby. And she'd have a certified fit if she had to sit next to a crying baby on an airplane."

She laughed.

"Are you pregnant?" I asked with a shocked tone. "I didn't even know you were seeing anyone seriously."

"No, silly! I'm not pregnant! And no, I'm not dating anyone special."

I scanned her face for clues.

"I've been feeling the mommy gene," she

said seriously. "So I'm thinking about having a baby on my own."

"What?" A thousand emotions pumped through me. I was happy for her, but being a single mom was no walk in the park. And kids were expensive. With the agency on life support, and no man to foot her baby bills, it didn't sound like a good idea. "Why now?"

Disapproval must have flashed across my face because she crossed her arms again and looked down at the shell of her potato. Her voice was as melancholy as I had felt this morning when she said, "I'm not getting any younger, Bentley. And neither are you."

Father's face appeared in my mind. And Dr. Fenton's warning about him getting old and dying before we could reconcile echoed through my thoughts.

"I understand," I said. "Age has a way of making you think about things."

She exhaled. "I'll be thirty-seven next month. And I left that long line of suitors back in my twenties."

I shook my head. "Alexandria, you are still so beautiful. I'm sure if you put your mind to it" — I glanced out at the bustling restaurant — "you could find a suitable husband and father. A brotha with a good

73

J-O-B and wholesome values. You could even do a white boi."

She shook her head. "I've already made my decision. Now that I see I don't have your support —"

"I support anything you do," I said. "I just want you to be happy. And that's a huge commitment."

"I don't have time to scour the streets for Mr. Right," she snapped. "So I've talked to my doctor about being artificially insemi-nated. It's all so very modern now."

"What? A test tube instead of making love?"

She smiled. "No, silly. I mean you get DVDs that show you profiles of the sperm donors. A lot of them actually will meet the children if I decide I want them to."

I thought about my friend from Country Day who was there on scholarship because his dad had abandoned the family and his mom was never home because she worked two jobs. "But it's hard being a single par-ent, Alex."

She sighed. "I know, but I want to be a mother so badly. There are health concerns as well."

I reached for her hand and squeezed it. "What do you mean? You're okay, aren't you?"

74

Alex looked longingly toward the beach. I knew she was thinking about her mother, whom she lost to breast cancer about three years ago. They had been extremely close, even after her mother dropped two bombs on Alex along with the cancerous death sentence. First, her father was not her biological dad. Second, her real father was a rapist frat boi who'd taken her mother out on a date during her freshman year and impregnated her with the baby who'd forced her to drop out of college. Alexandria.

All this had been too much for Alex to bear. But after a few days of furiously giving her dying mother the silent treatment, she had forgiven her and nurtured her until death.

Now, Alex's eyes glistened with tears. "Everything is fine and I want to keep it that way. But I read somewhere that I can reduce my risk for breast cancer if I have a child."

I put on my best poker face, the one I learned from watching Father and his golfing buddies as they played cards on our back patio while I pretended to swim in the pool. Not that I was frowning; I just didn't want my thoughts to show up on my face and make her think I disapproved of her decision.

"Now, Bentley, I know that might sound selfish, but I think I'd really be a great parent. Single or otherwise."

I squeezed her hand again. "I have no doubt you'll be a great parent, Alexandria. If you decide to do this, I'll be there for you. I'll do whatever you need. Including helping you pick the sperm donor. Or, I mean, the father of your child."

Alex smiled. "Really? Because if I do this, I know I'll need your help. I want you to be the godfather!"

Hearing the word "father" made me want to cry. Why was fate suddenly putting this in my face? How could I serve in a fatherly role to Alex's child without constantly being reminded of how much I missed my own father?

"I'm there if you need me," I said, "but don't give up on finding Mr. Right. You're too good of a catch for the right man not to come around. Just be patient."

The waiter brought the bill and Alex pulled out the gift card.

"What about you, Bentley? Is your daddy gene talking to you?"

Alex would have been very comforting if I shared the whole saga and longing for my father. But I didn't feel like getting into it right here or right now.

"So you don't want kids?" Alexandria asked.

"I do," I said. "I'm thinking about adopting an older kid from the foster care system. A lot of those kids come out of that system really damaged."

"You're a good person, Bentley. Your parents raised you right."

I leaned back, not wanting this leisurely lunch to end. "My mom might think that, but you might get some disagreement from my father. He still thinks he failed me since I'm gay."

"Hmmm," Alex said, "I just don't *get* that. You're his flesh and blood! So I guess this means you still haven't talked to your dad."

"You'd be correct on that assumption."

"Do you miss him?"

"I guess if I was talking to my doctor or maybe somebody who couldn't read me, I'd say no. But I do miss him. Terribly."

My throat burned with sadness. That meant tears would be trying to blow my cool any minute now.

"Bentley!" Alexandria grasped my hand. "Why don't you make a move on reconciling?"

I looked at Alexandria for a moment in silence and blinked back a single tear. "I don't think I can stand to see that disappointment in his face again."

SEVEN

It was a tight deadline for the engagement. I needed to hold a casting *and* get pictures to the client before the week's end. But I sure would rather have this kind of anxiety — about getting a job done well — than to sit here as I had just twenty-four hours ago, worrying about how to stay in business.

You can do it, Bentley L. Dean, my inner voice said.

So I logged on to www.modelmania.com, where I'd had success in the past finding mostly black men looking for representation. Sometimes you found some real winners, but most of them weren't signed with an agency for a reason, like being too short or just flat-out busted.

My announcement for the casting call read: "MALE MODELS WANTED. Are you a good-looking guy who's considered 'eye candy'? Are you willing to do artistic nudes and underwear modeling? Then you

79

may get the modeling job opportunity of a lifetime." That wasn't what I was looking for for this assignment, but I figured this would bring out the open-minded freaks.

I had also arranged a few interviews with models on my current roster that might fit the bill as well. First up was Tristan Foxxe, a former Marine and a really good-looking sports model from San Diego. I didn't know his sexual orientation, but he was friendly and clients always rebooked him.

He walked into my office wearing head-to-toe white: drawstring linen pants, a V-neck T-shirt, and boat shoes. The outfit looked good against his skin, which was the color of a glazed donut. Tristan was six foot five, two hundred and thirty healthy pounds of man. I remember sitting in on a photo shoot he did for an underwear line. Damn, I couldn't get his plump, muscular ass out of my mind for days.

"What's up, Bentley?" Tristan said as he took a seat in front of my desk. "Did I hear your message correctly? You got a job for me? Brotha sure could use some spending money."

One thing I loved about owning a modeling agency was the power to help young men like this earn a living by doing something they enjoyed. Maybe it was Mother's constant indoctrination of "God loves a cheerful giver," and sermons in church about how you always get back a million times more than what you give.

Or maybe I just liked looking at all these fine-ass men.

"Good to see you, Tristan. I sure hope I have a job for you. How's the personal-training business going?"

"It's all right." He shrugged. "But I think everybody in South Beach is a personal trainer. It's tough getting and keeping good clients. Then when the season is over, the good-paying snowbirds go back to Europe. I see modeling ain't doing all that good as well."

"We're still standing," I said. "And things might be picking up."

"So what's the job? An underwear or swimwear gig?" He had light eyes with a rim of darkness around them, straight teeth, and full lips. I knew the client would like him, but I was not so sure he would do it.

"Tristan, this job isn't like your other ones. It's actually just attending a party and smiling and being nice to the guests."

"Are you serious?" Tristan asked.

"Yeah, that's it. It pays five thousand dollars. *And* you get a clothing allowance."

Skepticism swept across his face. "What

kind of party is it?"

I wanted to be honest, and I wanted him to take the job. But how should I answer this? "Well, I know it's on Star Island."

"Is it a celebrity party?"

"It could be."

"It's not any faggot shit, is it?"

I hid my surprise by smiling awkwardly at Tristan.

Cross him off the list, my inner voice said.

"I don't know, Tristan. I'm sure that there will be gay men there. Is that a problem?"

"I *know* it will be gay men there," he said in a tone like he wanted to announce he wasn't born yesterday. "But if it's a gay thing, then I got to be able to bring my girl and they gonna have to pay her as well. She's a real good-looking lady and models for Elite."

I made an expression like I was considering that idea when I knew Mr. Sneed would never agree to that. "I don't know if you can bring guests. Let me check with the client. Now look, Tristan, you know if you turn this down, I'll still send you on other assignments. Don't take this job if you'll feel uncomfortable. Besides, I can't assure you that they'll hire your girl. They asked me to supply them with men only."

"Pffft," he said, slumping back in defeat.

82

"Yeah, it must be a gay thing. I've heard about these parties. If it's one of those circuit type of events, then I have to pass. I don't care how much money they offering."

I shook my head. "Tristan, I can assure you, it's not a circuit party. But let me see what information I can get from the client. So do you not want me to submit your comp card? I mean, the client has the final say about whether you're even invited."

He looked annoyed as he stared at the floor. "I don't care how rich your client is or how broke I am. I ain't tryin' to be gay for pay."

Tristan looked up at all the photographs on my walls, especially the sexy jeans ad that had generated a lot of hype in Miami — and cash for my models.

"Yeah," Tristan said, looking wishfully at the pictures, "you can go ahead and submit my head shot, but no nudes or underwear shots." He glared at me and said, "I don't want some freak whacking his shit off to my pictures. You feel me?"

I'd really heard enough of him, but I was relieved that he agreed. "I hear you. Thanks. I'll submit your picture and see what happens."

"You da man, Bentley Dean," he said, standing. "Is that it?"

"Yes, sir. I take it you have the same cell phone number."

"Yeah. When will you find out?"

I stood and came around the desk. "I'll submit your pictures today. The client is moving fast, so I think real soon. I'll try and find out the guest list. But I don't hold out too many hopes of that, since they want you to sign a nondisclosure agreement stating you won't talk about the party or guests. Will that be a problem?"

Tristan turned down the corners of his mouth. "Yeah. Sounds like some gay shit. And that won't be a problem if I get picked and decide to do it. That is some long paper and could last me between clients. Just as long as no one expects any sexual favors from me, it might be cool."

"Now, Tristan, you know me better than that. I'm running a modeling agency here. Not an escort service."

The truth was, I wasn't certain that I was going to submit his comp card. I didn't know if I was dealing with a closet case or if somebody had approached him before. The client had been specific about being gay friendly.

"I hear you," Tristan said, giving me a quick embrace. "Just let me know what's up."

84

I couldn't wait for him to get his foul mouth out of my office. "Will do, Tristan. Good seeing you. Hopefully things will pick up for the both of us."

"I hope you're right, Bentley," he said as he walked through the door. I admired his beautiful physique. "Hit me up when you find out something."

Damn, I hated it when something I thought was a sure thing turned out to be a question mark. Maybe this casting wouldn't be as easy as I thought.

EIGHT

As soon as Jah appeared in the doorway of my office, I switched into my fun-loving but protective big-brother mode. Jahron Anthony Borden was the little brother I'd always longed for as a child. Today I was taking time out from work on the party to have lunch with Jah and catch up on his life as a college student.

"What do you feel like eating, Jah?" I asked, walking around my desk.

"It doesn't matter, B," he said, smiling and standing there in his too-tight blue jeans, light blue boxers visible, tan Timberlands, red mock-neck T-shirt, and a brass belt buckle that said JAB in block letters. He was so handsome, and his natural charisma glowed like a spotlight around him. "I'm just glad I'm getting to spend some time with you." He gave me a big hug.

I had this overwhelming urge to shield him from all the bad stuff in the world. I

86

wanted to guide him every step of the way through his life so he never felt any more of the terrible things that he'd already experienced.

I had taken him on as a mentor some three years ago when I met him at a foster care home in North Miami. We'd hit it off right away when he jokingly said my name sounded so fancy. That was when he'd started calling me "B." Back then when I met him, he was only fifteen, but he said he was interested in modeling. I told him this was a tough business, but that I would let him give it a try once he turned eighteen.

But I'd also insisted that he go to college, so I helped him get a full scholarship at Florida International University. Now that he was eighteen, I was so proud that he was earning good grades, studying hard, and making school his top priority. Jahron wanted to be a lawyer and become an advocate for children's rights. I'd promised to do whatever I could to help.

Six months ago, I helped Jah move into his own apartment. I will never forget the image of Jah, his eyes filled with pools of tears, the first time he sat on his bed, slowly taking his hands over the bedspread we found at T.J. Maxx. He did the same with the shiny pots and pans I bought him because he loved to cook.

The model scout in me had recognized Jah's potential immediately. A shade over six feet, he weighed about a hundred and eighty-five pounds. He had dark curly hair with sun-glazed skin and beautiful green eyes the color of peas. He was a boi with a man's body. Jah had accepted the fact that he was gay at the age of fifteen and had already had several boyfriends. Still, he had not yet engaged in full-out sex. He had spent the majority of his young life in the foster care system of Florida, having never met either his father — who he knew was African American — or his mother, who was Hispanic.

When he was twelve, he was almost adopted, but his foster parents brought him back for what they called his "sissy tendencies." I hoped that the time I spent with him would show him the love and acceptance that he'd never felt from an older person.

"Jah, let's go get some subs at that sandwich place you like off of Washington Street."

"That's cool, B. You know they deliver. We could just eat here in your office."

"Are you sure? I thought you wanted to go out."

"I know, but you're busy." Jah glanced

toward my desk, which was covered with eight-by-ten glossies and copies of the nondisclosure agreement that I'd been reviewing for the casting. "I just wanted to catch up with you. To let you know how school is going." He looked up at the posters on the walls. "Hey, B, you got any modeling jobs that have come up that might be good for me?"

I stood between my desk and Jah so he couldn't see my work for the event. "I'm working on this big party, but I don't think it's right for you. It's more grown folks stuff. But let me look around on some of the other requests that have come in. I'll see if any of them are good fits for you, Jah."

Excitement sparkled in his green eyes. He tried to look around me at my desk. "Why do you think I wouldn't be right for the party? It sounds hot! You know I like older men, anyway. I may be just eighteen, but look at how I've had to grow up. B, you know better than anybody, I'm more mature than most teenagers."

I shook my head. There was no way I was going to send this gorgeous young boi into that swarm of sharks.

"You did have to grow up fast," I said, "but some things can wait. I don't think this crowd is right for you. Let me see if I have a menu to the sub shop."

"Aw, B, you're trying to change the subject. Tell me about the party."

His boyish face reminded me of when Anna and I would demand to know what our parents had gotten us for Christmas. All we wanted was a little hint. And the more they said no, the more curious we felt.

"I don't know that much, Jah. Now I've told you, it's not right for you. End of story." I found the menu on my credenza. "What kind of sandwich do you want?"

He shot me a playfully annoyed look. "Just maybe tuna and cheese with tomatoes and lettuce."

"You want any chips?" I scanned the list.

"Sure," Jah said, sitting in one of the white leather chairs facing my desk. "I met a new guy on campus the other day. He's really cute and I think he plays on one of the sports teams, but I haven't found out yet."

I glanced up from dialing the restaurant. "How do you know if he's gay?"

Jah smiled. "I don't know, but I saw the way he looks at me in my English comp class. Trust me, I'll find out soon enough."

That protective feeling shot through me again; I hung up the phone. Young people just didn't understand how dangerous it was out there. Everything from gay bashers in

90

public, to diseases in the bedroom, were just waiting to destroy a young man trying to find his way in the world. "Well, make sure you remember what I always tell you. Be safe, Jah."

"I'm always safe, B. So you don't have to worry."

I phoned in the order for our lunch. Jah walked over to the window and stared down below. His white pants might as well have been tights, the way they showed off one of his best assets, his ass. It was as hard, round, and muscular as the Alvin Ailey male dancers. And that filled me with panic, because my modeling career had taught me just how many predators were out there, waiting to devour fresh meat like Jah. I couldn't help but worry about this boi who'd been forced to become a man way too soon. I wondered if I could have managed to move from home to home, never feeling like I belonged, and come out of it without being mad at the world.

But Jah didn't walk around with a chip on his shoulder. He had a people-pleasing personality. And he talked about moving to California after college to pursue modeling and acting, even though he was a great writer and artist.

The restaurant said the order would be

delivered in fifteen minutes. I stepped beside Jah at the window, watching cars and people on the sidewalk below. "So how do you like living in your apartment?"

"B, I love it," he said, smiling at me. "Every day I say, 'Thank God for Bentley.' I never could have gotten such a nice apartment or gone to college without your help." I loved feeling like I was making a positive difference in his life.

"I feel like I have everything but a man," Jah said, staring longingly out the window. "I mean, I have the whole package. And I can cook. I gotta have you over for these southwest-style omelets I made the other day. They'd put Emeril to shame."

"A man?" I asked, alarmed at the determination in his voice. "Jah, you're in school. You don't need a man to distract you."

"I just want someone to love me. To hold me while I sleep. And talk to me like he cares about me."

I shook my head. "You've got the rest of your life to enjoy that. Right now, Jah's focus should be on Jah. Period."

He crossed his arms and tilted his head in annoyance. "You're too old to understand."

"Excuse me?" I asked with mock anger.

"You don't remember what it's like."

"The hell I don't. But when I was your

age, I was still dating girls. You have an advantage because you're comfortable with who you are. You don't have to hide." The second those words came out of my mouth, I wished I hadn't said them, because Jah would take them as a license to find the so-called man he wanted. Deep down, though, I admired — maybe even envied — the freedom that Jah had by knowing who he was and celebrating that, no matter what the world thought.

"Don't be in such a hurry to grow up, Jah. You should enjoy this time of your life, young man."

"I do enjoy my life. It just seems I've discovered my inner freak at a young age." Jah laughed.

My voice was stern: "Like I said, be careful, Jah."

"I want to take acting classes."

"Will you have time for that, with classes and all?"

"I'll make time. I don't have time for the gym, but I make time."

The thought of him in workout clothes in the middle of that meat market known as the gym made me shake my head. "Are you still going to the David Barton gym?" It's just as much of a pickup place as it is a fitness club for all the beautiful people, straight and gay.

"Whenever I can get a monthly membership," Jah said, "because you know it's very expensive. But one day real soon I won't have to worry about money."

"How are you going to avoid worrying about money?"

He looked at me with a face full of confidence, optimism, and dreaminess. "Because I'm going to be rich."

I felt like I was bursting his bubble, but he looked naïve with a capital N. "It's good to have a big dream, but you've got to be realistic. Remember, I left my family's wealth so I could be myself. Money isn't everything, Jah."

"But it takes care of a lot of things," he said with a look that let me know he wasn't even trying to hear me.

"And it can bring a lot of problems if you're not careful," I said.

My assistant, Laura, knocked on the door and walked in with two yellow bags. She set our lunch on the small glass table between the two leather chairs. Laura, in a flowy orange dress with sparkly earrings, said, "Bentley, can I talk with you for a second?"

I followed her into the hallway. Laura whispered, "I tried to use the company credit card to pay, but it was rejected. So I took a twenty out of petty cash."

"Did you tip the guy?" I asked coolly, not wanting to deal with another minute of financial stress.

"Yeah, I gave him fifteen percent."

"Cool," I said confidently. "I'm sorry I didn't ask you if you wanted anything. And don't worry, the credit card situation will be resolved today." I was so glad I had said yes to Mr. Sneed. I spoke low so that Jah couldn't hear me. I could see out of the corner of my eye, he was craning his neck to eavesdrop. But I hated to admit just how desperate my financial situation had become.

"My mom had the same problem at the airport," Laura said. "The credit card companies are like going bonkers on everybody." She smiled. "I'm brown-baggin' it today so I can afford a manicure during my lunch break."

Laura was about to step away when I said, "Please just take messages for the next hour for me, unless it's Alex."

Laura's earrings sparkled as she nodded. "Okay. Alex is in a meeting in Fort Lauderdale, so I think you'll be free to enjoy your lunch."

I turned back to Jah, who still had that dreamy look in his eyes. Hopefully, after the agency got paid for this mysterious job, I'd be feeling that optimistic about money, too.

NINE

Sometimes on the weeks when I didn't see Dr. Fenton, I would have a session with a mentor and friend, Mitch Proctor. He owned one of the hottest male modeling agencies in the country called Mitchell Men of Miami International. He had the most gorgeous white and Italian male models in America.

I had met Mitch at a modeling seminar when I first started my agency, and he immediately took me under his wing. I liked him because he seemed sincere and honest. During one of our first meetings, he said he admired me for having an agency that used only African American male models. His agency never got calls for any, so Mitch never hired any. And on those rare occasions when he did get calls, he would refer his clients to me.

This Wednesday morning, we met for breakfast at the Setai resort in the heart of

South Beach. When I arrived at the upscale, Asian-style restaurant, Mitch was already on his second cup of coffee.

What he lacked in the looks department, he made up for with his money. Mitch was short and a little pudgy, but everything about him said "rich." His year-round tan could give George Hamilton a run for his money. He was about five foot eight and could have passed for a Miami businessman if he were not so fond of pinks and light blues. Today he was wearing a dark pink oxford shirt with a blue sweater hanging on his back, white slacks, and alligator loafers without socks.

"Sorry I'm late," I said as I leaned over and kissed Mitch on the cheeks. It wasn't my normal way of greeting business associates, but this was Mitch's style.

"No problem, Bentley." Mitch's blue eyes glowed with happiness to see me. He had a clean-shaven baby face that would have looked more mature if he lost weight and had some cheekbone definition. His sharp nose was always slightly pink with sunburn, as if he'd just gotten in from a leisurely day on a sailboat. His straight brown hair always looked freshly trimmed and brushed back. "Did we have a hot date last night?"

"I wish," I said as the waiter poured me

some coffee. "How are you doing?"

Mitch pushed a small black square plate holding sugar cubes and a tiny pitcher of cream toward me. "Doing great, considering the tough times we're all facing in this business. If things don't pick up, I'm going to have to dip into the trust fund," Mitch said with a laugh.

I only used a little cream and sugar. Then I looked over the menu and decided on an egg white omelet and some fruit.

"I know you can't be watching your weight, Bentley. I'd kill to have a body like yours," he said, sipping his heavily creamed coffee. "And don't forget what I told you about if you ever decided to go back into modeling. I would get you some bookings, buddy."

I smiled. "So I'd be your first African American model. Wow. Do you think we'll ever live in a country where there are no more 'first this' and 'first that'?"

"Now, Bentley, I think our country has come a long way," Mitch said. "And if Mr. Obama comes through, I think that day will come real soon. And you can celebrate at my party. Election night. We'll have flat screens all over the place. Fabulous food. An endless bar. And a waitstaff to make sure you don't have to do a thing but cheer for

President Obama."

I smiled. "I'd love to come to your party, Mitch," I said, remembering his phenomenal high-rise condo with 360-degree views of Biscayne Bay, the Miami skyline, and the Atlantic Ocean. His place was on Fisher Island, one of the ritziest pieces of real estate in the world.

Mitch raised his coffee cup as if it were a champagne flute. "Cheers! To our new president, and to you gracing us with your presence at the party."

I felt happy about watching the election results and hopefully celebrating in a gay-friendly scene.

Mitch said, "I can't believe he's leading in Florida, because I believe if he wins this state, it's a runaway."

"I know, but I doubt if he wins here. I still think it's Bush country."

"Mr. Dean, please don't ruin my breakfast. How is business coming?"

I smiled. "Looking up. I might be booking a big party, but I don't want to talk about it until it's in the book."

"I understand," Mitch said. "I'm sending about five guys to Milan for the runway shows and it's helping me to pay some bills. I really would like to go, but that's a frivolous expense my firm can't handle this month. So I'll just stay here and enjoy what Miami sun I can find."

As I enjoyed my omelet and he devoured pancakes with bacon, Mitch told me about some of the areas on Lincoln Road where he'd seen a lot of good-looking black guys. He recommended that I might want to spend some time down there scouting.

That was an example of why I liked Mitch so much. He was always giving me pointers. We also had a lot in common. Mitch was from old-money Texas, having been raised in Highland Park, a tony Dallas neighborhood. He had been educated at Rice University in Houston and was in his second year of law school at Southern Methodist University when he decided he wanted no part of the family business and outed himself.

Just like me, he faced resistance from his father, but support from his mother and sister. Mitchell moved to Miami and never saw his father again. When he died suddenly of a heart attack, Mitch fell into a depressed mode for almost a year. He, too, had a female co-owner, Trudy, who saved his ass while he nearly drank and almost drugged himself to death.

There was also one other difference between us besides the color of our skin. In the middle of his year of despair, Mitch contracted HIV while having unprotected sex during a drug binge. But thanks to remarkable meds, Mitch's HIV was currently undetectable and he lived an active and seemingly happy life.

"So have you met anybody lately?" I asked. "Or are you still happily single?"

"The latter, for sure," Mitch said, wiping his mouth with a linen napkin. "And I can't tell you how wonderful safe sex is when you're simply under the influence of the moon."

"I know that's right."

Mitch always looked at me like he really cared about how I was doing, both as a friend and as a business associate. I didn't get the feeling that he wanted anything from me except for that. And in the modeling business, and in Miami, that was a rare feeling.

"What about yourself?" he asked. "Are you still against meeting someone on the Internet?"

"Yes, most definitely," I said. "Mr. Right will have to meet me without the help of modern technology."

Mitch's face lit up. "Oh, Bentley, I got a call the other day from the office of tourism for the island of St. Lucia. They're using some of my guys, but I'm going to suggest we use some men of color. Do you have any guys that might fit the bill?"

Cha-ching! I played it cool as I secretly wanted to pump my fist with excitement. A job like that would bring in some nice bricks of Benjamins for the agency and my models.

"I'm sure I do have the models you're looking for," I said. "I guess you'll need Island guys, or mixed."

"Or all black. I will let you know."

"How many do you think you might need?" I asked as the waiter refilled our coffee cups.

"Can I get you gentlemen anything else?" the waiter asked. He was an attractive white guy with brunet hair and I watched Mitch give him the once-over. When the waiter left, Mitch said he was going to give him one of his cards but thought he'd seen him on the Boss Models of Miami roster. Boss Models was Mitch's only competition.

"How is that young guy you mentor?"

"Jah? Oh, he's doing fine."

" 'Fine' would be the right word to describe that fine young specimen," Mitch said. "Now I really think I could manage him and when people hear his story, I think it makes him even more marketable. Let me know if you think you're too close to market his look right. If you can't be my first, then maybe Jah can."

Now here was one subject where I didn't need Mitch's advice.

"I'm bringing him into the business slowly," I said. "I want him to concentrate on school. I don't know how long the state will pay for his education, so I want Jah to get his degree as quickly as possible."

"He's lucky to have you in his life," Mitch said.

"And I'm lucky to have you in my life," I said while lifting my coffee cup and gently tapping it against Mitch's.

Around 5:30 P.M. on Wednesday, a dream walked into my office in the form of Daniel Baxter. He was a referral from Boss Models in New York and had sent me some pictures by messenger the day before. He looked better than his pictures.

Daniel was a mixture of African American and Puerto Rican, with golden bronze skin, dark curly hair, and a body, from what I could see, that was awesome. This guy was so handsome that I could hardly look him straight in his hazel-green eyes. I found myself stuttering as I told him about my agency. The conversation took a different turn when I mentioned the upcoming party and asked if he might be interested in making some good money.

Daniel's deep voice was just as intoxicating as his appearance. "So basically what your client is looking for is eye candy."

"I guess you could say that," I said, sitting behind my desk.

"That doesn't sound right to me," he said, taking one of the white leather seats. Daniel said with authority in his voice, "I think they're looking for more."

I looked him straight in the eye and asked, "Why would you say that, Daniel?"

He looked at me like he wasn't born yesterday. "I think I did one of those parties when I was living in Los Angeles. They're looking for more than eye candy, Mr. Dean."

I put on an air like I didn't need to stoop to that level of thought or conversation. "Please call me Bentley. Let me assure you, I'm running a respectful modeling agency here. I have made it clear that my models are models. Not escorts."

"I'm sure you are." He shrugged as if he understood that I wasn't going to acknowledge the unspoken, just as Mr. Sneed hadn't. Daniel radiated authority as he said, "But I think I'll have to pass on this."

I showed no reaction, hoping he would change his mind. He would be perfect for the party.

"I love sex as much as the next guy," Daniel said, "but I'm not selling my body to a bunch of old men who think they can buy people with their money. Daniel Baxter does not have a 'for sale' sign across his forehead or his ass."

Daniel stood up to show off what he said wasn't for sale. He was just over six feet tall, about one hundred and eighty-five pounds. A muscular body with a tiny waist. Daniel's ass pushed out of his tight jeans so firm and plump that you could have placed a tea service on it. It looked so yummy, I was getting aroused. Good thing my desk was protecting me.

"You don't have to do the party, Daniel," I said with a cool tone, "but I would like to bring you into the agency. We do a lot of sports modeling. It looks like you would fit the build on what most of our clients are looking for. In fact, a friend of mine is looking for models with your look to do a high-paying job in the Caribbean."

Excitement flashed across his face for a split second.

"Of course," I said, "that means we do a lot of swimwear and underwear modeling assignments. Do you have a problem with that?"

He squared his broad shoulders and said, "Of course not. Just 'cause I don't want to sell myself to these sick men doesn't mean I don't want to show my body." His voice got lower and softer. "Matter of fact, why don't I give you a look at what you'd be sending out."

"Excuse me?" I asked as he stared hard into my eyes. "That's not necessary —"

Daniel popped open his shirt and dropped his jeans without a hint of shyness. His muscles rippled under smooth bronze skin. I didn't know where to look first: the bulging biceps that tapered down from his buff shoulders, his round, hairless pecs, his washboard stomach, or those muscular thighs. Standing right in front of my desk, he was a living, breathing underwear ad in a pair of black boxer briefs as tight as his own skin. He either had a huge dick or his average-size one was fully erect.

I forced myself to stop my jaw from dropping. And my body was on fire, hard as a rock there behind my desk.

"You think your clients will like this?" Daniel asked. I was trying not to stare, so I picked up his comp card and acted like I was studying it.

"Mr. Dean, you're avoiding me," he said with a teasing tone. "Do you think I'll get a

107

lot of work with your agency?"

"I'm sure you could, Daniel. You have a very nice body."

"Would you like to see more? I think you would," Daniel said as he dropped the boxer briefs. Now I was really in trouble. His hairless body was flawless, the kind gay men dreamed of, with its soft, smooth skin over hard muscles.

"Daniel, you don't have —"

He walked behind my desk and stood in front of me totally nude. "Would you like to touch my abs?" They were so cut, and in my face, it looked like I could run my fingertip through the ridges and trace little squares.

"I don't think I can do that," I said, trying to maintain a professional and firm tone of voice. I couldn't help inhaling the mix of his cologne and that clean, musky man scent that made me feel weak. Still, my voice was strong. "You might say I sexually harassed you, Daniel."

He let out a low, sexy laugh. His huge dick swung like a pendulum in my face as he said, "No, it's perfectly clear that I'm sexually harassing you, Bentley. I think you're quite handsome yourself and this has nothing to do with me signing with your agency or not. This has everything to do with me wanting to see how it feels to have you inside me."

As Daniel talked, my dick was getting so brick hard that I was sure it would tear through my underwear and pants. I'd heard of things like this happening in auditions, but it had never happened to me. Should I tell this handsome man to put his clothes back on?

Or should I just clear my desk?

The cool, controlled businessman in me took over as I said, "You don't even know me, Daniel. I thought you came in for work."

"We can talk about work later," Daniel said as he got on his knees and reached for my zipper. When his warm hands covered the head of my dick, I felt defenseless. He licked the pre-cum off my dick. It stiffened even more.

"Damn, Bentley, you taste good," Daniel said, pulling on my pant leg. "Take these off."

"That feels good," I groaned. "Can you take it all?" I whispered as I let my pants drop to the floor.

"Let me see." Then he *showed* me the answer: yes. Because he took me in so deep, I could feel his lips brushing against my nuts.

It felt so good to focus on the pure plea-sure of the moment. Nothing else. After about five minutes, Daniel stood in front of me. He smelled so good. My eyes met his penetrating gaze.

His voice was deep and dominating as he said, "I want you to take this splendid piece of meat and fuck me, Bentley."

"Do you have condoms?"

He looked surprised. "Don't you?"

"Not at the office," I said as my dick began throbbing.

"Damn, don't you want some of this?" Daniel asked as he turned his ass toward me and tooted it up in the air.

"You know I do," I said, running the palm of my hand over the perfectly round curve of his ass.

He looked me in the eyes and ordered, "Sit your ass on your desk and let me ride it."

"But we don't have condoms," I said with a tone to let him know this conversation was over.

"I'm not going to let you put it in," he said, "but I want you to see how good it's gonna feel. When you get some free time, we can do it right."

I moved some folders from my desk. It felt cold as I sat my bare ass on it. Then

Daniel sat on my lap, facing me. He placed his arms around my neck and laced his fingers to lock his grip. He kissed me gently and choreographed every move until his plump, naked ass brushed against my dick. Then he started grinding and teasing me.

Damn, I thought, *I ought to just take a chance and get some of this ass.*

He had the sexiest look in his eyes as he whispered, "You want it, don't you?"

"Yeah, I do," I groaned, running my fingers over his baby-soft but rock-hard pecs.

"What you gonna do with it, Bentley?"

"I'm gonna fuck the shit outta you."

"Sure you are," Daniel said as he bounced his ass up and down on my dick and his own hard dick against my stomach.

"Don't play with me, boi," I said. Daniel continued to grind his ass against my dick. It felt almost as good as I knew that it would once I got inside. Before I knew what was happening, the pre-cum turned to a nice little load of cum, but not as much as normally jutted from my dick.

"Shit, dude," I said deeply. "You got skills. I haven't come that way since I was a teenager."

Daniel smiled as he dismounted off my lap. "Just wait 'til you put it in. Be prepared the next time."

"When will that be?"

"Soon. Give me your number."

I got off the desk and pulled my pants up. I scanned my desk for a notepad so that I could give Daniel my number. "Where do you live?"

"Fort Lauderdale. And yourself?"

"On South Beach."

"Must be nice," he said, pulling on his boxers.

"Not on the nice side."

"Every side of South Beach is nice." Daniel stood there in that underwear model pose that I could imagine on the side of every bus in Manhattan. Or workin' it for Mitch's agency down in the Caribbean.

"So do you still want to work for me?"

"If it's a good opportunity," he said, pulling on his jeans, "I'd be interested. But none of those parties where people gawk at me and think flashing cash will get them a piece of ass."

"So this isn't going to cost me," I said playfully.

His tone was hard as he said, "Don't step to me that way, Bentley. You know better."

"I'm sorry, just trying to make a joke." My office was silent and felt a little awkward as I finished writing my number and address on the notepad.

"I know," Daniel said as he pulled his shirt down his arms. "You seem like a cool dude. I've been looking for a new FWB."

"FWB?"

He poked his head out of the shirt and said, "Friends with benefits, silly."

"Oh," I said, handing him the paper. I didn't ask him for his because I figured if he really wanted to see me, now he had the information.

"Thanks, Bentley. I'll give you a call. Or maybe I'll drop by when you least expect."

"Do that," I said, challenging Daniel, even though I didn't like surprise guests. I just wanted to see if he was bluffing.

"Okay, but don't say you haven't been warned."

"Warned about what?"

"This ass. It's addictive."

TEN

Two days before the big party, my client threw me a curveball. Mr. Sneed rang my cell phone, instructing me to replace one of my masculine "top type" guys with a slender, feminine guy. His casual and comfortable use of that term raised my suspicions once again that sex was secretly on the agenda for this event.

Because what Mr. Sneed meant by "top type" was that some gay men prefer to be on top during sex, as the one who does the penetrating. Whereas a more feminine guy would be a "bottom" as the one who gets penetrated. Guys who did both were called "versatile."

Still, Mr. Sneed played it off in the visual sense, focusing on how the guys would look as "eye candy," not on how they would perform in bed.

Why hadn't he told me this at our first meeting? I could have chosen from several feminine guys at the casting. Most of the several dozen models who showed up — forming a line that snaked out the door and down the street — were masculine. They made it easy to satisfy Mr. Sneed's initial request.

Now I was starting over. Since I didn't have any feminine types on my roster, I had to go back to Model Mania's Web site. I placed my ad and received a couple of responses. I invited two into the office for interviews, but only one showed up.

When he walked into my office with such command, I didn't know who was interviewing whom. He was obviously gay, and slim-hipped with an auburn and black Mohawk hairstyle. Wearing tight, skinny jeans and a sheer black shirt with a white T-shirt under it, he had a scarf tied around his neck. He carried a brown leather man purse.

"I'm Bentley Dean," I said, extending my hand.

Instead of giving me a handshake, he rubbed his delicate hand across the top of mine and said, "Charmed, I'm sure, Mr. Dean."

"And you're Gabriel." His face was oblong and hairless, with flawless mocha skin that looked more than familiar with facials. His nose was somewhat pointed, which blended nicely with his high cheekbones. His eye-brows were waxed into perfect black arches. And his dark eyes appeared seductive and smoky, because he was either wearing black eyeliner or had permanent makeup tattooed into the bases of his eyelashes that were curled but natural-looking. Whether the dark pink hue on his full lips was natural or not, that was a big question mark.

"Yes, Gabriel Teal, like in Halle Berry's baby daddy, Gabriel." His gold hoop ear-rings shook a little.

"Have a seat, Gabriel."

"I think I will," he said. Gabriel removed the neck scarf and dusted my chair before sitting down. What was that about? There was no dust on my furniture.

"So how long have you been modeling, Gabriel?" I asked as I sat behind my desk and scanned the comp card that he handed me.

"Since I was sweet sixteen." A choking cloud of his floral-scented perfume came at me across the desk.

"All in Miami?"

"No, I did a little in New York and some in Los Angeles. Mostly runway shows, but some print. I got a fierce walk. You want to see?"

"Not right now." I took another look at

his comp card.

"So tell me about this job," he ordered.

"Excuse me?"

His brown eyes flashed impatience as he looked at me. "You said I could make some nice money. What's the gig?"

"I have a client who's having a private party and he wants some nice-looking young men," I said. I saw no need to mention the "gay friendly" part.

"All men?"

"Yes. Is that a problem?"

"Not for me. No, no, not at all."

"Great."

"Now, whose dick am I expected to suck?" Gabriel's bluntness startled me.

I set down his comp card and looked at him to make sure I'd heard him right. "Excuse me?"

"Now come on, Mr. Bentley. Gabriel has been around the block a time or two. Is this some kind of sex party?"

"Mr. Teal, I'm not a pimp," I said with an irritated tone. "I'm running a legitimate modeling business."

"Sure you do. But you still didn't answer my question. Whose dick do I get to suck? And are these white men, black men, or a little of both?"

I shook my head, not bothering to hide

117

my annoyed expression. "You will not be expected to perform any sexual acts, Gabriel."

"But there will be dick there, right?" Gabriel spoke as if he were asking if Roscoe's House of Chicken and Waffles had fried chicken on the menu.

"I'll ignore that."

"But you shouldn't. Am I going to be your token fem guy? I've been to the parties before where everybody walks around the room like they're the king of the butch queens, but when the lube comes out, they all have their asses tooted up for the big dicks." Gabriel laughed and said, "My mom always told me, 'Today's trade is tomorrow's competition.' "

I showed no reaction and said with a flat tone, "Are you interested in doing the assignment, Gabriel?"

"Is there going to be dick there?"

Tired of that question, I responded, "It's going to be all men."

His face lit up. "Then dick will be served. I think I'll do it. Where do I need to be? And would you like me to wear something tight?"

"You can wear whatever you like."

"Panties or not?"

"Panties?"

"Yeah, I have this married executive type who likes me to wear purple or red panties. I'm sure you'll have one like that there. I like to please my clients."

I could not wait to end this conversation and my bored tone of voice let that be known. "I don't care what you wear under your clothes, Gabriel." This guy — and I use the term loosely — was tripping me out, but I had to satisfy my client's needs. He was just what Mr. Sneed had ordered.

"Am I making you uncomfortable, Mr. Bentley?"

"It's Mr. Dean, and of course not."

"Are you sure?"

I flipped through a pile of mail, giving him a hint that it was time to wrap up. "Why would you ask me that, Gabriel? I'm simply trying to fill a job order."

He smiled as if to say "you can't fool me." "Oh, I've met your type before. I don't think you qualify as closet, running a modeling agency and all. I'm sure you'd like to fill this order with one of your Ralph Lauren or football-type models. But I'm telling you, the brothers who act straight in public with their wives and important careers, they still like us fems in private. You know, we make them feel more like men."

I logged on to my computer. I thought

about going straight back to Model Mania to find another guy who was not as offensive as Gabriel, but something stopped me.

"If I pick you," I said, looking at him over my desk, "then you'll have to sign a nondisclosure form."

"But of course."

"There is a clothing allowance."

Gabriel clapped. "Oh, goodie, new panties!"

"I haven't said you got the job for sure."

"Oh, you'll hire me," he sassed.

Gabriel had sent me into a "Calgon, take me away" moment. I needed to be reminded why I was interested in *men*. Warren. I focused on my computer and logged on to Facebook. I typed in Warren Stubbs. It said he had 2,393 friends. And every face I saw was a beautiful woman of every hue and hair color. A couple of dudes were in the mix. But it was clear what kind of face Warren was trying to show to the world: a ladies' man who loved ladies only.

Gabriel's voice made me realize he was still talking.

"Who else is as cute as I am? And you know I'm exactly what your customer ordered. I'm telling you, Gabriel will be the hit of this party. And who knows? Your client might give us both big tips. Don't miss out on a good thing, Mr. Dean, because I make you a little uncomfortable." He chomped his cosmetically whitened teeth into the air between us and seductively said, "I don't bite — unless I'm *asked*."

"I can reach you at this number?" I asked, trying to hide my face behind the comp card.

"I can be reached there 24/7. But I don't know why you just don't stop playin' and tell me where I need to be and when."

"I will call you either way."

"Sure you will," Gabriel said as he stood up. For the first time, I realized he was tall. He peered down at me, making me feel as small as my attitude.

"Thanks for coming in," I said, standing up in front of my desk. Again I extended my hand and again Gabriel brushed across the top like a paintbrush. He didn't say a word as he swished out of my office, leaving his floral scent behind.

Eleven

The night of the big party finally arrived. I was standing in front of my dressing mirror, trying to decide if I should wear a tie with my navy blue suit and crisp white shirt. I placed a yellow and pink tie against the shirt, then a red one, and finally an all-white one. None of them looked right, so I decided to go with the open collar look.

I liked to take my time when getting ready for an event, so I could arrive feeling fresh and relaxed. Nothing made me more irritated than rushing and dealing with last-minute drama. So far, everything was going smoothly.

I brushed my teeth and swirled some mouthwash before squirting a little Tom Ford cologne behind by neck. I was ready to go and wanted to get there at least forty-five minutes before the first of my models arrived.

As I was looking for my keys, my cell

phone rang. The display glowed with blue letters: TRISTAN.

"Hello, Tristan. You ready for the party?"

"What's up, Bentley?" He sounded nervous.

"I'm good," I said impatiently. "What's the matter? You lost the address to the party?"

"Naw, but I got some bad news for you."

I scanned the kitchen counter for my keys. "What bad news?"

He paused; the suspense only made me feel more irritated. Then he said, "I'm having second thoughts about this party. I don't think I can do it."

"Why not?" I snapped, dashing into the front entryway. Maybe I left the keys on the small glass table by the door.

"I was talking to my girl about it and she's giving me some flack," Tristan said. "I guess I let it slip out that you said I need to be 'gay friendly' to do the party. Now she's freaking out, asking me if I was one of those down low brothers. So I think I'm going to have to say I can't do it."

"What?" My pulse was racing. I felt like I was about to break a nervous sweat from rushing around and feeling so irritated. My thoughts raced over my roster of models, and guys who'd come to the casting but didn't get chosen. Would any of them be available and willing to attend the party on a moment's notice? Damn!

"But why wait until the last minute, Tristan? I promised them fifteen guys. Why didn't you call me this morning or something?" I looked at my watch. I only had thirty minutes to get to the party, and I still couldn't find my keys. They were not on the front table.

"I feel like a punk," Tristan said. He must have heard me thinking those exact words. "I'm sorry, Bentley. I've been thinking about it all day. Man, I really need the money, too. But I don't think it would be worth all the grief my girl's givin' me. She'll be checking up on me like she's a detective on *CSI: Miami* and shit. I'm sorry, Bentley, but I just can't."

I was not about to let Tristan jack my event. So, to convince him, I forced a nicer tone out of my mouth. "What about you coming and just staying for thirty minutes? What kind of clothes did you buy with the clothing allowance?"

He sounded excited. "I bought some real fly shit." But then he was depressed again as he said, "I haven't worn it and I can take it back. I'll bring the money by the office later in the week."

"Are you sure about this?" I hurried back into my bedroom.

"I'm sure," Tristan said. "I hope this won't hurt me for legit assignments down the road."

"This *is* a legit assignment, Tristan." There, my keys were on the dresser. I snatched them up and said, "Nothing is expected of you but to look good and be nice. And by that I mean with sparkling conversation. But I'm not going to try and talk you into something you don't want to do. Now I've got to run and try and replace you."

I clicked off the phone and sighed, wondering where the hell I was going to find another guy at the last minute. I was heading to my home office when my cell rang: JAH flashed across the screen.

"What's up, big bro?" His playful voice eased my tension a little.

"What's up, Jah?" I didn't let him hear my annoyance. It wasn't his fault that Tristan had punked out on me, the party, and all that money.

"What are you doing, B?"

I sat down at my computer, not even sure where to start looking for a last-minute model. "Heading to a function I got tonight. What about yourself?"

"Chilllaxin'. I was going to drop by. I forgot this was the night of your big party."

"Yeah," I said as I thought about asking Jah to take Tristan's place. But was that the right thing to do? Jah was basically a kid and this would be a party for a bunch of grown-ass men. But I told myself if I kept him close by, everything might be okay.

"You still there, B?"

"Yeah, Jah. Hey, you got anything nice to wear besides jeans?"

"Yeah. I got some real nice off-white gabardine slacks that hug my ass in all the right places and that black silk shirt you gave me. Why?" He sounded excited.

Liking the image of him in that outfit, I didn't even bother to log on to my computer. "I don't know if I should do this, but one of my guys just canceled on me and I need another guy for the function."

He reacted like he was a kid and I'd just asked him if he wanted to go to Disney World. "Please, please let me go. I promise to do whatever you ask, B. I could use that money! And who knows? I might meet someone."

I stood up. "Jah, I think you might be too young."

"But you need me, B! Let me do it."

I thought about it for a few minutes.

"Okay, Jah. Get dressed in something nice. I'll meet you at the Ritz-Carlton on South Beach. Park your car there and meet me outside. You need to hurry."

"Don't worry, B. I'll be there in a minute. And thanks a lot. You won't be sorry for this."

"I hope not." A sinking feeling suddenly hit me and I knew in my gut that I'd just made a big mistake.

Just as we arrived at the sign directing us to valet parking, I went over my rules with Jah one final time. As I followed a line of luxury cars through a gated drive lined with palm trees, I turned down my 50 Cent CD that Jah would have blasted if I let him.

"Now remember," I said, turning to him, "no drinking alcohol."

"Okay, I promise, B." He was so excited, he could hardly sit still. As I looked into his eyes, I could practically see his imaginary visions of glamour and gorgeous men that he thought he'd see at the party.

"And stick close to me," I ordered. "Always within my eyesight."

"I will."

I inched my car closer behind the black BMW sedan ahead of us. "And if anybody asks you how old you are, what are you going to say?"

"Twenty-one."

"What do you do?"

"I go to the University of Miami."

"What year?"

"Freshman."

"What?" I shouted.

"Oh, I'm sorry. I forgot. Senior."

I looked at him with a serious expression that was just short of threatening. "Don't exchange numbers with any of these guys. And if they ask you if you want to go for a swim, say you're afraid of water."

"But I love to swim. Come on, B! Let me have a little fun."

I shook my head. As we proceeded forward, the mansion came into view. It was an enormous, Tuscan-style palace with a white tent where rich-looking men were getting out of their Mercedes, Lamborghinis, Porsches, limousines, and dark-windowed Escalades.

Jah's jaw dropped open as he stared at the cars and the house. "Remember I told you I'd be rich, B? This is proof. You have to speak it to get it."

"This isn't your house, Jah."

"It could be someday," he said dreamily, craning his neck to look up at the second floor.

"Listen," I snapped. "If anybody comes on to you, tell them you have a lover."

He crossed his arms. "I wish! But if that's what you want me to say, B, I will. But what if it's somebody around my age who comes on to me? Can I get his number or give him mine?"

I drove forward. We were next. "Jah, he won't be your age. Oh, if they ask you if you signed the nondisclosure, tell them yes."

"Okay. Can I eat the food?"

"Of course you can eat. Just make sure you don't drink, smoke, or let anyone give you something you haven't seen them pour."

I didn't like Jah's rebellious tone as he said, "Man, you need to stop trippin'. Everything's gonna be fine."

We reached the young man at valet. As I opened the door, I looked over at Jah and said, "It better be."

When Jah and I walked up the steps to the beautiful Colonial-style mansion, a million butterflies suddenly filled my stomach. Would tonight be perfect and go off without a hitch?

"This shit is off the chain," Jah said as he looked up toward the Miami sky like only a young person could.

"It's nice, isn't it?"

"How big is this mug?"

"I haven't seen it all, but when I did my site visit," I said, as we followed two well-dressed, gray-haired men up the stairs, "I was told that there are fourteen bedrooms."

Jah gasped. "That's sick!"

"Now remember, Jah, act like you've been somewhere. These are important people and I don't want anyone to consider how young you are."

He smiled. "I'll be cool, B."

"Don't forget, you need to show the security guard your identification. Pull it out now."

"Okay." Jah took his wallet out of his back pocket.

I pulled my cell phone from inside my suit pocket as we approached the security station, which included a metal detector.

"Can I have your name, sir?" The security guard asked me before looking down at the guest list.

"Bentley Dean and guest."

"Do you have identification?"

"Here you go." I handed him my driver's license.

"What about your guest?"

"Jah, show the man your identification."

"Cool." Jah laid his ID on the black marble table.

The security guard looked at our IDs and checked them against the list. "Have a good time, gentlemen."

As we walked toward the two huge doors with gold fixtures, Jah leaned over and whispered, "He called us gentlemen. That's big-time."

"And don't you forget it," I whispered back.

We walked through the doors into a brightly lit marble foyer. Handsome waiters with flutes of champagne greeted us. More waiters followed close behind with trays of boiled shrimp, sushi, and other fancy appetizers.

"Would you like some champagne, gentlemen?" asked a very handsome Cuban-looking waiter. I made a mental note to give him a card and see if he was interested in modeling. Damn, he was hot.

"I'll have a glass," Jah said as he eyed another equally gorgeous waiter.

I quickly grabbed Jah's hand and said, "No, thank you." I gave Jah the evil eye. Had he already forgotten my instructions?

We walked into the main area where several nicely dressed men drank and listened to a jazz ensemble. I scanned the room for Sterling. But to my surprise, I didn't see him or any of my models. I had warned them all to be on time, but then again, I was early.

The huge, high-ceilinged room had tall fireplaces, French doors leading to a terrace and pool, and clusters of fancy furniture with a lot of gold accessories. I looked toward the left side of the room where, finally, I saw Sterling walking toward me. Maybe I would finally meet my real client.

"Bentley, so good to see you." Sterling was dressed to the nines in pleated black slacks and a crisp white shirt with an open collar and a black suit jacket. He looked formal and casual all at once.

"Same here, Sterling. This is one of my models, Jah."

Sterling looked at Jah like he was a platter of fried chicken. He put his hand on Jah's shoulder and said, "I don't remember seeing this handsome young man's picture. Is this a new addition?"

I fought the urge to remove his hand from Jah's shoulder as I said, "Yes, one of my guys got sick at the last minute. Fortunately, Jah was available to fill in."

"Well, well, aren't we lucky," Sterling said in a way that I didn't like at all.

"Nice meeting you," Jah said. "This is a beautiful house."

Sterling all but licked his chops as he

faced Jah. "It's not mine, young man, but please allow me to give you the tour before the night is over."

"Cool."

"Did you bring your swimsuit?" Sterling asked Jah, not me.

"Swimsuit?" Jah cast questioning eyes my way.

"No, I forgot to tell him, with it being last minute and all."

Sterling looked Jah up and down. "How tall are you and how much do you weigh, Jah?"

"A little over six feet and one hundred and eighty-five pounds," Jah said.

"Then I'm sure we have something that will fit you perfectly," Sterling said.

"Cool," Jah said, looking around as more men filled the room, forcing us to talk a little louder amid all the deep voices. "See if you got something in black. I look good in black."

"I bet you look good in anything, Jah."

Jah cast a flirtatious look at Sterling and he said, "I try my best, S."

"S. I like that," Sterling said, nodding his head and admiring Jah's beautiful body.

Just as Sterling was getting ready to take us to another section of the mansion, we heard a shrill, high-pitched voice say, "The party can start now! Gabriel has *arrived*. Gabby is here!"

I turned around. There was Gabriel, standing in the foyer with his hands high in the air like Diana Ross in a *Mahogany* pose. He wore a nice black suit that looked like it could fit a male or a female, and a white hat with a black band.

As I looked at Sterling, he raised his eyebrows and said, "Who dipped him in sissy sauce? I guess that's the fem I asked for. Great casting, Mr. Dean."

"Thanks, and exactly." I pressed my lips tight to hold in my laughter.

"I need a drink," Sterling said. "Come with me, Bentley."

Sterling led me into the media room, where two men immediately pulled him aside for a private conversation. I figured I was on my own for a while. The giant screen showed a porn flick of gay men having group sex.

I looked around the room. And he was the first person I saw. Our eyes met immediately.

Warren.

I smiled nervously at the man I once thought was the love of my life. What the hell was Warren doing here? He always told me that he didn't do gay events. He smiled

134

back at me and began walking in my direction. And excitement filled his hazel eyes that were so striking against his dark chocolate skin. Damn, he was more gorgeous than any man had a right to be. His tan linen pants and loose-fitting jacket did nothing to hide his football physique; his tan leather belt with a gold buckle cinched his tiny waist where a form-fitting white V-neck left nothing to the imagination about his rock-hard, sculpted pecs and abs.

Suddenly I felt like I was overheating with the thought of his nude body, the way his broad shoulders tapered down and his hamstrings curved from his ass to the backs of his knees. And his ass . . .

This was not how I had told myself I would react if I ever saw that man again. But my heart felt like it was beating twice as fast as normal. All those butterflies fluttered back into my stomach.

As he wove past people and the red velvet chairs, he was smiling like he was glad to see me. And when he was standing right in front of me, Warren laced his fingers with mine. It seemed like both our hands were shaking slightly.

But aside from that, I wasn't about to let my face or my voice snitch on how I was feeling. No, my expression was cool and my

135

tone was even cooler as I said, "Warren, how are you?"

"I'm good. I'm surprised to see you." His deep voice could have made me melt inside, if I weren't trying to put the deep freeze on my reactions.

His eyes sparkled at me. "I guess I could say the same thing. I would have never expected to see you here. How long have you been in Miami?"

Warren's fingers squeezed mine. "I came down for a job interview and one of my bois from Cali invited me to the party. I guess I forgot that you lived here."

I didn't like the nonchalant way he said that. As if I were so easy to just forget. But I shrugged, with an expression like I just didn't care, and said, "That's understandable."

"B —" Warren was about to say my name when a gentleman in his early forties came over and stood next to Warren.

"Here's your Henny, baby," the guy said, handing him a drink. Warren released my hand and took the glass.

"Thank you," Warren said. "Bentley, I want to introduce you to Radford Johnson. He's an actor and director."

"Nice meeting you," I said politely, but I was not impressed. The guy was well-groomed, but average in the looks department. Medium brown, my height, slim, wearing gray pants, expensive loafers, and a white dress shirt. The only thing about him that stood out was the slightly exotic slant of his brown eyes.

"Nice meeting you as well," Radford said. "Isn't this a fabulous party?"

"Yeah, it's pretty nice," I said, noticing that Warren was watching our exchange as if he'd forgotten about our history. I also didn't appreciate that he'd been so secretive about our relationship, but here he was at a who's who event with this dude. I played it cool and said, "I still haven't met our official host."

Radford said, "I don't think he's made his grand entrance, but he will soon, I'm sure. Fasten your seat belt, because it will be a shocker. Is Bentley the name?"

"Yeah, Bentley Dean." I looked around at all the rich-looking men. Many wore wedding rings. I recognized the CEO of a major Fortune 100 company. I only knew his name because he was featured in *GQ,* thanks to his reputation for dressing well.

"Bentley Dean," Warren's boyfriend said, making me remember that he was there, trying to engage me in conversation. "That sounds like an actor name. Are you in the business?"

"I own a modeling agency," I said flatly.

"Oh, so you must have supplied the eye candy. I can't wait to see what little morsels we have tonight."

I looked back at him with an almost snobby tilt of my chin. I wanted to say, "Your ordinary ass wouldn't have made the cut for my agency or this party." Instead, I bragged, "I have some great guys who work for me."

"I bet you do."

I turned to Warren and asked, "How long are you here, Warren?"

"It depends on how my interviews go."

Radford pawed on Warren like he was a prized teddy bear. "Oh, he'll get the job if he wants it," he said. "Look how handsome he is."

Warren said modestly, "They're looking at a lot of people."

Radford's face lit up as he took Warren's hand. "Do you think Warren ought to be in the movies, Bentley?"

Without looking at Radford's love-swept expression, I said, "I'm sure Warren can do whatever he sets his mind to."

"See, boo, your friend agrees with me," Radford said.

Boo. Warren and I used to call each other

that. He also called me Bent, in private. And he was my boo boo.

Radford leaned too close to me, as if he were sharing a secret, and said, "I'm trying to get him to audition for this independent movie I'm doing. He'll be perfect for it. He would play a black James Bond character."

"I've never acted before," Warren said.

"Just be yourself — the dick daddy that you are." Radford looked at me like he was announcing breaking news. "Warren is bigger than being a sportscaster, even if it is a national station."

"So it's network, Warren?" I asked. "That's been your dream for a while."

Warren said modestly, "Well, it's a cable network."

"Still sounds like a wonderful opportunity."

"I think he can do better," Radford said, "and I'm going to stay on him until he relents and gives it a try."

I looked at Warren, thinking, *I bet Radford will stay on you long after that.*

The awkward silence that ensued was my cue to exit stage left.

I needed to find Jah. I scanned the room for him and Sterling. I had to make sure everything was okay.

"Nice meeting you, Radford," I said,

139

hardly looking at him. "And, Warren, it's always great seeing you." I glanced into his eyes, wondering if I would ever see him again, and if I even cared.

"Nice seeing you, Bentley." He smiled. "I'll give you a call before I leave."

"Maybe we can take you to brunch or dinner," Radford offered.

"That would be cool," I said.

Like hell it would. I was about to step away when Warren said, "Take care, Bent."

A chill shot through me. I was shocked to hear him call me that private pet name in public. That was a first. It never happened when we were together.

I needed to leave now, before I got into a catfight with Radford over Warren.

"I will," I said coolly, stepping away. "You guys enjoy the rest of your evening."

"Oh, we will, Bent," Radford said.

My pet name on his voice hit me like fingernails across a blackboard. Yeah, I had to get the hell away from both of them. Now.

I looked around the media room, but Jah was nowhere amid the red velvet theater-style seats, the popcorn stand, or the huge white screen where men were mingling. As I hurried toward the door, I almost bumped into Sterling.

"I was looking for you," Sterling said. "I have someone I want you to meet."

"Who?" I asked impatiently. "Have you seen Jah?"

"Yeah," Sterling said casually, "Jah is changing into some swim trunks. He's doing fine. Really nice young man."

"Yeah, *young* man."

"Follow me." Sterling led me down a long hallway. I couldn't help but notice how nice everything was in this beautiful house. Expensive crown molding, Brazilian wood floors, and very rich, bright colors. I followed him into a modern, metallic kitchen that was bigger than most restaurant kitchens. Men and women in white chef uniforms were preparing fancy foods over open flames. It smelled like I had walked into culinary heaven.

"This is our chef for the evening, LaBron Wolfe," Sterling said.

I bowed slightly toward the thick-waisted man with a cappuccino complexion and tiny beads of sweat at his temples. "Nice to meet you, Chef LaBron. What's on the menu tonight?"

Sterling teased, "Yeah, Chef LaBron, what's on the menu?"

The food sizzled in a pan as he shook it over the flames. It smelled so good, I just kept inhaling.

"Well, right now, I'm working on a creamy seafood risotto and a fennel and sausage risotto. We're going to have yogurt marinated lamb kebabs, and of course the Emperor's favorite, stuffed flounder with frizzled mint and ginger."

"Sounds great, LaBron," I said. "I'd ask what's for dessert, but I'll let you surprise me."

"It will be the grand finale," LaBron said proudly.

As we walked away, I whispered to Sterling, "Who is the Emperor?"

"He's the one paying your tab. He's my boss and that's where I'm taking you now."

Sterling and I got on an elevator with gold doors that were so polished, they were like full-length mirrors. When it opened, we walked out into a huge master bedroom that had a sitting area bigger than most living rooms. A male butler was putting a bow tie on a tall man whose back was facing us.

"Emperor," Sterling said, "I have Bentley Dean here to meet you."

The Emperor turned around.

And I could have fallen over. I was speechless. Unless he had a twin, I was looking at Seth Sinclair, one of Hollywood's biggest — and probably richest — actors and directors. His movies made millions. And he was not only popular in the African American community, but in the entire world. As in Tom Cruise, Tom Hanks, and Will Smith would kill for his box office receipts. I had just seen him and his wife, and their young children, on the cover of *Ebony,* under the headline THE FIRST FAMILY OF HOLLY-WOOD. Alex was always following the celebrity gossip about his wife, because they had modeled together in New York.

Time had just featured Seth Sinclair on its list of the top fifty most important people in America.

And I was standing in his bedroom, supplying "gay friendly" models to his all-male party. He was wearing a Ralph Lauren Black Label tuxedo and I couldn't help but notice his black Italian loafers. Seth looked even more handsome than he did on screen. Several inches taller than me, he had cinnamon-colored skin and large brown eyes that made you feel like he was seeing more than what normal people saw. His wide jaw, nose, and cheekbones had the sculpted look of a model, and his black hair lay in tiny waves close to his head. And when he smiled, it was like you'd just walked into a snow blazer.

"Bentley," he said, "so nice to meet you.

Sterling tells me you're providing us with some of our honored guests. I'm looking forward to meeting some of them." His voice was so smooth and deep. It was strange hearing it in person, after I'd watched him star in so many movies and present at the Academy Awards last year.

"N-nice m-meeting you," I stuttered and shook his hand. What other surprises awaited me?

"I hope you'll have a good time at your first PGC event," the Emperor aka Seth Sinclair said.

"PGC?" I asked.

"That's the name of the organization the Emperor heads," Sterling said. "It stands for the Prosperity Gentlemen's Club. You have to be invited to join, and membership dues start at one million dollars."

"Are you serious?" I tried to make a joke. "I guess you wouldn't have a lot of people on the waiting list for membership."

"You'd be surprised," Sterling said.

The Emperor smiled. "Well, I need to finish getting dressed. I shall see you downstairs." He turned his back so the butler could finish securing his tie.

"Everything is ready," Sterling said. "The members and the guests are waiting for your arrival, sir."

"I will be there momentarily, Sterling and Bentley."

When Sterling and I got back on the elevator, I asked, "So what's really going on here, Sterling?"

"What are you talking about?" Sterling focused on the gold elevator buttons and pushed one.

"Is that who I think it is?"

"What do you mean?" He looked at me as if I had just spoken another language.

I cast a look that told him he could not play me for a fool. "That's the famous actor and director Seth Sinclair. I've seen all of his movies, but I've never seen him in person."

Sterling chuckled. "Well, I guess that's not true anymore, but you must refer to him as the Emperor and not any other name." But nothing was funny about the threatening way he looked at me and said, "I need to remind you of your nondisclosure and you need to remind your guys. If a word of this gets out, then we'll sue your firm with every lawyer in our employ. Do I make myself clear?"

"Understood," I said, "but I didn't have a clue that was who you worked for. I thought he lived in San Francisco with his wife and twins."

Sterling glanced at his diamond-faced watch. "Don't believe everything you read. And since it looks like we'll be doing more business together, it's very important that we trust each other, okay?"

I was getting that same slippery, half-truth vibe as when he'd first visited my office.

"Bentley, if there are guys we like from tonight, can you fly them to our next event?"

Was he just dangling a golden carrot to make sure I followed his rules? Or was this really a chance to make more money? I said with my usual calm, cool business tone, "I'm sure if the guys want to come, we can work something out. How often do you have these events?"

"Every month. Each time in a different city. Members are not notified until the week of the event about where the party will be. I think next month will be in Hawaii. In the summer, we tend to travel abroad because the Emperor has business outside the country."

"You mean making movies," I said, thinking of the St. John detective series Seth had made so popular. They had even eclipsed the James Bond series.

Still, this didn't make any sense. I'd never heard any rumors about Seth Sinclair being gay or even bisexual. And I usually heard all the rumors. All you ever heard about him was praise that he was such a big family man and how his beautiful and socialite wife was building private charter schools in poor communities. The Sinclair name was so popular that many people actually thought he could have been the first African American president if he wanted.

"No," Sterling said, "I mean conducting *his* business. Now, enough with the questions, because it's important that I continue to trust you."

The elevator made a *ding* sound and the button for the first floor lit up. The golden doors started to open, but Sterling pushed a button to keep them closed. He gave me that warning look. "Bentley, there will be some more surprises as the night plays out, if all our current members show up tonight. And we do expect them because we had such a nice time the last time we had a party in Miami. You'll see several other people you might recognize. Don't gawk. Just act like you see them every day."

I didn't appreciate Sterling's subtle attempts to intimidate me, but I had to keep reminding myself that he was the well-paying client who was actually a godsend for my agency.

"Honestly, Sterling, that might be pretty

hard. Especially for some of the models, because these guys are young and impressionable."

Sterling chuckled in a way that sounded almost sinister. "Then they better grow up fast, Bentley. I think when we get downstairs, you should tell your guys not to stare and please, please don't ask for autographs. They need to act like they belong here. Are we on the same page?"

I nodded. "Yes, we are. I'll make sure they know. But it would have been better if I'd been told sooner."

"I told you your client was a very important man."

"Yeah, but never in a million years would I have expected that it was Seth Sinclair."

"The Emperor," Sterling said as he opened the elevator and disappeared into the crowded living area.

The huge room was packed and loud from all the voices and live music. I spent a few minutes searching for my models. Finally, I saw Godfrey and Bendal drinking champagne. They were older guys, so I hadn't told them they couldn't drink.

Godfrey was tall with a basketball build and absolutely beautiful brown skin that was the color of tobacco. Bendal was a football type, thick as a piece of corn bread, and made the cut because he was interpersonally generous. I knew he'd be a hit.

"Hello, guys," I said as I walked up to them. "I love the clothes."

"Whassup, Bentley!" Bendal said. "Man, this shit is off the chain. I ain't never been to a place or a party like this. Man, the only thing missing is some fly chicks."

"Well, that's not going to happen, guys."

Godfrey hit Bendal on the arm and said, "Remember, we're supposed to be gay."

"I thought Bentley said 'gay friendly.' "

"I did. Hey, fellas, let me talk to you a minute." I moved Godfrey and Bendal into a corner where no one could hear us.

"What's the deal, Bentley?" Godfrey asked.

"This is a bigger affair than even I suspected. There are some real high rollers here. Really famous people. So when you meet them, please don't stare. And above all, please don't ask for autographs."

"Is our presidential candidate here?" Bendal asked.

"Hell no," I said. "When I say important, I mean maybe you'll see some actors that you've watched in movies. When they introduce themselves to you and give you another name, just play along. Understand?"

"Sure," Godfrey said. "But man, I guess this is some real, undercover gay shit."

I gave them a serious warning look. "Yeah, and remember those papers you signed. These guys will come after you if any of this gets out. I've been warned. So if you see any of my guys that you know, make sure you remind them, too."

"Okay, we can do that," Bendal said.

"Have you seen any of my guys?"

"I met the flamer named Gabriel," Bendal said.

Godfrey laughed. "Yeah, what a jolt of sugar he is."

"I don't think we have to worry about Gabriel," I said. "He's been warned."

Bendal laughed. "Oh, I think Gabriel's gonna win most popular tonight."

I looked around for more models to warn as soon as possible. "Remember, no autographs, and if someone does something or asks you to do something that makes you uncomfortable, just decline in the nicest possible way."

"Don't worry, Bentley, we got the memo," Bendal said.

"Okay." I had to find Jah. As I strolled through the house, I saw so many familiar faces that I thought my eyes were playing tricks on me. I had to make sure the shock didn't show up on my face as I saw a few more actors, several leading businessmen, and even a politician or two.

Some guys were retired athletes. Several guys obviously didn't have the money to be members of PGC, but they had other attributes, if the gay Web sites were correct. The sight of a few porn stars — who were not sent by me — was a great relief. That lowered the chance of my guys getting propositioned for sex.

I had to find Jah, so I took the elevator back up to the floor where I'd met the Emperor. It opened onto a long hallway lined with closed doors. It was silent until I reached a room with double doors. I opened one.

All I saw was a tangle of nude male bodies. They were either old or very young. All over the floor and furniture, old guys were paired up with bois, engaging in various stages of sex acts. Moaning and groaning, they were too busy to notice me.

But at least Jah wasn't in that mix.

I tried to get that image out of my head as I hurried back down the hallway.

Downstairs, I walked outside to the pool area. A cool breeze from the nearby ocean whipped my face. Most of the men around the heated pool wore all-white pants and

151

jackets. Several guys were in the pool.

"Jah!" Finally! I was so relieved. He looked like he had a drink in one hand as he lounged on a pool raft, looking quite handsome in a yellow gold swimsuit. Several men were eating him up with their eyes, like Sterling had earlier. I suddenly wished he had his phone so I could text him and tell him to get his ass out of the pool, but I didn't have the opportunity to embarrass him.

"Damn, Bentley, you're right. There are some big ballers here."

I turned around and there was Godfrey standing next to me. He'd changed into a powder blue bikini swimsuit that left little to the imagination and could make some of the porn stars jealous. I looked down, but didn't linger. I took my gaze to Godfrey's face. "I told you."

I was pleased with myself for choosing Godfrey for this party.

"Man," he said, "I saw some of the guys I used to watch all the time. Now some of them are old enough to be my father, but this is some wild shit. Two of them got Gabriel in a corner, chatting him up real good."

"Does he look okay?" I glanced at Jah, who was obviously loving every minute of this surprise night of luxury.

Godfrey laughed. "Man, they all look like long-lost friends. But you might want to check on him a little later. He is throwing down the cocktails."

"Oh, shit," I said. "Where is he?"

"He's on the inside. But I'm sure he's cool."

"Where is Bendal?"

"He's getting his eat on. Some dude's been following him around like a little puppy, but my boi is handling himself correctly."

"Cool. So I guess you're going for a swim?" I took another look at Godfrey's impressive package.

"Yeah, I think I will. It's so weird being at a party without women. It's like chips without the dip. A burger without the bun. Popcorn without butter."

I smiled.

"Man, this is something none of my friends would believe. You sure they didn't invite some local strippers for later on tonight?"

"Trust me, Godfrey," I said playfully. "If strippers were invited, they're not the kind you're looking for."

"Let me just go jump into the pool. Who knows? I might leave here with a sugar daddy who can pay my way through law

153

school," Godfrey said with a sinister laugh.

I needed a drink, so I went to the bar near the pool. It was the perfect spot to keep an eye on Jah and Godfrey.

"Can I have a glass of merlot?" I asked the shirtless bartender.

"Sure."

Someone spoke so close to the back of my neck that it almost tickled. "There you are."

I turned around.

It was Warren, looking splendid in a pair of white, midlength swimming trucks.

"You been looking for me?" I asked coolly, refusing to look at Warren's bare chest as he stood beside me at the bar.

"You knew I would be." His eyes blazed at me.

"Where is your keeper?"

"Getting toasted."

"Really?" I glanced at Jah. "So are you a member of PGC?"

"Hell no! This is only my second event and it might be my last."

"Why is that?"

"Come on, Bentley, you know this isn't me."

"Then why are you here?"

"I scratch Radford's back and he looks out for me," he said as if it were a confession. "After we broke up, I ran into some

154

hard times and I'm still trying to work my way back to what I'm used to."

"I understand that. It's tough out here for everybody."

He gave me one of those penetrating stares that made it impossible to look away. "So can I see you tonight?"

"Are you serious?" The shock in my voice was sincere.

"Yeah, I'd like to spend some time with you."

"What about your benefactor?" I sounded mocking.

"He'll be asleep the moment I get him back to his hotel suite."

I loved the way Warren's bald head was shining in the evening light. But I refused to let lust distract me from the facts. "I know as an actor Radford works a lot," I said, "but I was told it cost a million dollars to join this organization. Is he making that kind of money?"

Warren glanced at the men in the pool as they laughed and splashed. "I don't know, but some of these guys, especially the ex-football and -basketball players, get free memberships. The first time I came, they offered me one, but like I said, this isn't my deal."

I could still feel the annoying presence of

Radford at Warren's side, even though he was nowhere in sight. "I guess he could be wealthy. He played on that show that's doing well in syndication. Hey, maybe you can tell him I'm a good guy and he'll throw some acting business my way."

Warren looked into my eyes and said, "You know I'll do whatever you ask me, Bentley. Are you still in business with Alex?"

I smiled. "Yeah, we're still partners. What happened to the young lady you left me for?"

Warren's broad shoulders rose up in a quick shrug. "She's still around, but we aren't as cool as we used to be. If I take the job down here, we'll be done for sure."

"Is that what you want?" I watched a gorgeous guy push Jah's raft up and down the length of the pool. Grinning, Jah saw me and raised his drink, as if toasting. Then his expression switched to "oops, I forgot!" and he tried to hide the drink behind his back.

Warren stepped in front of me, blocking my view of Jah. He stared into my eyes with a seductive look and said, "Let's talk about me and you."

I sipped my wine and said nonchalantly, "Why would I want to do that?"

His voice softened as he said, "Because you love me and you know I love you, despite some of my actions."

"So that was love?" I let a semidisgusted look shoot from my eyes.

"Come on, Bentley. Can I see you tonight?"

"Not tonight, Warren." It felt so good to feel in control and not cater to this man's romantic whims. "Now if you'll excuse me, Chef LaBron has cooked an excellent meal and I'm suddenly very hungry."

"Is your cell number still the same?"

"Why don't you find out?"

When the party started to wind down just before 3:00 A.M., I made contact with all of my models. Everybody seemed in good spirits and glad that they'd done the event.

"Good looking out, Bentley," Godfrey said. "I had a good time and made a few important connections. It feels good to be told how handsome you are all night. Females tell you once and that's it."

I smiled. "Glad you had a good time. Have you seen Jah?"

"Jah? You talking about the young kid?"

"Yeah."

Godfrey nodded. "I saw him in the pool, then I saw him when he left, getting into a silver Shadow that just appeared out of nowhere."

"Are you sure?"

"I'm pretty sure it was him. I haven't seen him since."

A panicky feeling shot through me. I had to find Sterling. I hurried into the kitchen, where he was sitting at a metal table and writing checks.

"Sterling, where is Jah?" My voice was urgent, but he didn't even look up.

"I think he got lucky."

"What?"

"Very lucky," Sterling said, ripping a check from the pad and starting another one.

"What are you talking about?" My angry voice echoed through the kitchen.

"He's fine." Sterling looked up at me like I was crazy for asking about Jah. "Don't worry about him. He's in good hands."

I took my cell phone out of my jacket pocket and dialed Jah's number. Voice mail clicked on before the first ring. Then I texted him: "Call me right away!"

I turned to Sterling and demanded, "Who did he leave with?"

"Let's just say, royalty." Sterling's playfulness really set me off. "He got the prize of the night or shall I say, he's getting the prize of the evening."

"That kid just turned eighteen. He's a virgin."

"So I heard," Sterling said with delight.

"How did you know that?"

"It seems it spread just like the caviar on toast points tonight." Sterling licked his finger to lift the next check, then ripped it off, and started the next one.

"Damn!" I almost shouted, hating all my thoughts about what Jah was doing right now. "I can't believe this shit! I thought you told me my guys weren't expected to have sex."

"I did." Sterling looked at me as he sipped a glass of ice water. "But we agreed they could all make adult decisions. I think fem boi Gabriel is going to be the star of another party at the Four Seasons downtown with two very rich, very hung older men."

"This is crazy. Who did Jah leave with?"

"Calm down, Bentley. He's fine. The last time I checked, eighteen is very legal. They can vote at that age, you know."

I ignored Sterling. I was mad and worried.

Who had Jah left with? And would he remember all the things I'd told him about gay men, and how to protect himself from the worst of them?

TWELVE

I was pouring cream in my coffee when I heard a knock at the door. After being up so late and now feeling so sluggish, I needed this caffeine jolt so badly, I didn't bother to turn on the lights in my modern, all-white kitchen. Even though I was only wearing pajama bottoms, I placed the creamer on the counter and dashed down the hallway lined with colorful paintings of athletic men.

When I swung the door open, the morning sunshine was painfully bright in my eyes. But it wasn't anywhere near as bright as the huge smile on Jah's face.

"What's up, B?" Jah walked in, wearing the same clothes that he'd worn to the party. "Man, what a night."

I closed the door and glared at him. "Where the hell have you been? I have been worried to death about your ass! Jah, where did you go?"

The dreamy look in his eyes let me know

he hadn't even heard the anger in my loud voice.

He stepped into the living room — no, he *floated* into the living room — and sat on the cobalt blue suede couch. "B, I had the most amazing night. I will never be able to repay you for taking me to that party. I got a life now."

I was too mad to sit, so I stood in front of the glass coffee table, glaring down at him. "What happened? I was looking all over for you! Why didn't you answer your phone or text me back?"

Jah sighed like he was slipping into a bubble bath. "I was falling in love."

"What?!" Alarm shot through my whole body ten times stronger than any cup of coffee could wake me up.

"I met the man of my dreams last night." Jah stretched his arms against the back of the couch and sat with his legs wide, like he was lounging.

"Who?"

"The Emperor."

"What?" I wanted to jump over the coffee table and shake some sense into him.

"Yes, I met him at the party in the pool. I've been floating on a cloud ever since."

"Jah, do you know who that is? He's married."

"In name only, B. And I think he feels the same way about me. Do you have some juice?"

"Come with me in the kitchen," I said, walking fast to vent my anger and digest what Jah was telling me. When we reached the kitchen, I sipped my lukewarm coffee and poured Jah some apple juice.

"So I need a favor," Jah said, sitting at the gray metal café table, where I served his juice and sat down as well.

"What?" For a second, I thought I could relax and just be glad that Jah had safely shown up at my door. But the twinkle in his eye hinted that he was up to something.

"B, can I leave my car here and can you give me a ride to the airport?"

"Where are you going? Don't you have school?"

He sipped the juice as if I were bringing up an irrelevant point. "It's okay for me to miss a few days. I'm going to Los Angeles."

"L.A.?" I snapped. Every word coming out of Jah's mouth was cranking me up to a higher notch of angry. "For what?"

"To see E." He sighed. "He flew back this morning on a private charter, but he called me from his plane and told me he had a ticket waiting for me. Isn't that romantic?" Jah's whole face was still brighter than the sun. "I wonder if the hotel we're staying at is going to be as nice as the one last night. I didn't know they had hotels like that in Miami."

"Jah, you can't do that!" I felt a pang of protectiveness over Jah like I'd never experienced.

"What do you mean, I can't go to see my man? I'm grown, B. I'm responsible for myself. I always have been."

"But what do you know about this man?"

"I know he makes me feel special like no one has ever done."

"All that after one night? Get real, Jah." Men like "E," as Jah called him, could buy and sell a thousand boi toys in a day. And they were masters at making their newest boi of the moment feel like a prince, the *only* prince.

Jah shot me a disappointed look. "B, I thought you'd be happy for me. You always say you want me to be happy. But now that it's happened, you want to become a hater?"

I shook my head. "Jah, it's not being a hater. You might be getting in over your head." I sipped my cold coffee, then shot up out of my chair and put it in the microwave.

"B, why would you say that?"

"That guy is old enough to be your father," I said over the low hum of the micro-wave.

"But he's not my father. Remember, I never had one of those."

"Is that what this is all about? You're looking for a father?"

"No. From what I do know, you don't make love with your father."

The microwave buzzed as if reacting to the alarm that Jah was setting off inside me.

"Jah!" I almost shouted. Jah had told me time and time again he was waiting for the right man. I had hoped that it would be with someone closer to his own age. Jah hadn't had intercourse but he'd told me about heavy petting, grinding, and I was pretty sure a little oral sex. "Jah, don't tell me you had sex with this guy!"

"Yes," he said, "and it was magical, just like you said it would be. E is so gentle. It didn't even hurt as much as I thought it would." Jah smiled. "Even though he's got a nice piece of equipment on him."

I had to turn away from his love-swept expression, so I opened the microwave and removed my hot coffee cup. I took a sip, then turned to face him. "Jah, please tell me you're making this all up. And his name isn't E or Emperor. His name is Seth Sinclair and he has a family."

164

Jah showed no reaction. "I know. But if that's what he wants me to call him, then that's what I'll call him."

I sat down and said, "Please tell me you used protection."

Jah looked away and took a long swallow of his juice, obviously to avoid answering my question.

"Jah, answer me. Did you use protection?" I gripped my cup so hard, my fingertips were burning.

"It all happened so quickly," he said. "I didn't go with him to have sex. It just happened. And by that, I mean we slept together all night holding each other and when we woke up this morning, it just happened. I promise to use protection the next time."

I slammed the cup on the table.

"Are you fucking crazy?" I shouted. "Did you at least ask his HIV status?"

"No, but I don't have to. Look at him. He's healthy. He's married and like you said, has kids. He's a movie star and if he had AIDS, don't you think it would be all over the Internet?"

I wanted to slap the naïve look off his handsome face. "That's your logic? When did you lose your brains, Jah?"

Jah looked at his watch, then at me. "Are

165

you going to take me to the airport and can I leave my car here?"

"What if I say no?"

"Then I'll just drive myself and park at the airport."

I shook my head. "Jah, are you sure you should be doing this? Have you even ever been on a plane?"

Jah stood, pulling his jangling keys from his jeans pocket. "No, but Seth said it'll be just fine. I'm actually looking forward to it."

I stood, looking at him with a pleading expression. "Jah, please listen to me and reconsider. If this guy is really for you, make him come back to see you. Once you get on that plane, then you're on his territory and he'll be in control totally."

Jah shrugged. "I don't care about that."

"You should."

"I've got to go. Are you taking me?"

I stared at him for a moment, thinking I'd already done enough when it came to this budding romance.

"I can't do it," I said.

"Why are you being this way?"

"Because I care about you."

"Well, you sure don't act like it. I guess I'll see you when I get back." He stormed toward the hallway.

"Will you text me when you land?"

"If you want me to."

"I do. Jah, please be safe and promise me you'll use protection. In fact, wait a minute. I have something for you."

I raced into my bathroom and located the tin canister where I kept my condoms. I took out three gold wrappers, then returned to the hallway and gave them to Jah.

"Make sure, if you engage in sex, to use these. Do I make myself clear, Jah?"

"I promise you, but I'm sure E will have some."

"You need your own. How long are you staying?"

"I don't know. Maybe just a couple days, but I'll let you know."

"Okay."

Jah gave me quick hug and walked swiftly out the door without turning around to look at me.

THIRTEEN

I almost had a wreck driving into the office. I couldn't get Jah off my mind. What was he getting himself into by becoming involved with Seth Sinclair? Had I done enough in trying to prevent him from getting on the plane? Or was I simply jealous that maybe this was going to turn out good for him?

When I got to the garage of my office building, my cell phone vibrated. I didn't even look to see who was calling and hoped it might be Jah.

"Hello."

"What's up, Bent?"

"Warren," I said, not sure how I felt about hearing his deep voice through my phone. "Are you still in Miami?"

"Yeah. Where are you?"

"I'm heading into my office," I said as I pressed the elevator button.

"You got a busy day?"

"It depends."

"On what?"

"What you call busy."

"I want to see you today."

"Now, why do you want to do that?" I asked, smiling at my reflection in the silver elevator doors.

"Don't make me beg, Bentley."

"I like having you beg." The elevators door opened. I stepped in and pushed eight.

Warren had a seductive tone when he said, "I'll do whatever it takes to see you." Damn, I forgot how sexy and persuasive Warren could be.

"I'm on the elevator, so I might lose you."

"But you'll find your way back to me, won't you?"

"I will." I was a little surprised the elevator hadn't dropped the connection.

"Bent, you still there?"

"Yep."

"So you didn't lose me," Warren said playfully, as if he loved the double meaning of what he said.

"Warren, what do you want to do?"

"Let's go to our place."

"Our place?" I wasn't in the mood for a guessing game. And I didn't appreciate how it seemed like he just wanted to get with me when it was convenient for him.

But Warren's voice had far more than lust in it when he said, "Let's go up to those little cabins on Lake St. Clair in Canada."

"That would take too long," I said.

"But I want to spend some time with you," Warren said.

"I know this place up at Clearwater Lake that has these really nice cabins; we can drive."

"That sounds good."

"Are you serious?" I smiled again.

"Yes, I am, boo."

I let my ears savor the sound of him calling me that again. "When?"

"Right now."

"I've got work to do," I said as I stepped off the elevator and into my office.

"Then after work," Warren said as I smiled at Laura in the reception area. "I've got a real nice rental car. I'll come and pick you up."

"Those words 'nice' and 'rental car' don't even go together, Warren."

He chuckled. "Wait 'til you see it. Are you game?"

"It might be nice."

"You *know* it'll be nice."

As I walked past Alex's office, she looked up from her desk and said, "Hey, Bentley." I must have been grinning because she stared at me, then smiled like she was glad I looked happier than I had in a while. A romantic getaway with this gorgeous hunk of man on the line was definitely boosting me into a better mood.

"I have to go back home and pack a bag."

"I can do it for you," Warren said, "or I can pick up some things for you. It looks like you still wear the same size."

My voice softened as I walked into my office and said, "You'll do that for me?"

"What else I got to do? Tell me where your office is."

"It's on Collins Avenue on South Beach right off Washington Road." I sat down, logging on for my e-mail and phone messages. I needed to check my Facebook page, or, as Alex called it, Facecrack.

"Okay, why don't I pack us a couple bags and pick you up around six?"

Excitement shot through me. The computer said 9:02. Nine hours to go. "That sounds good, Warren."

"It will be, boo. Just like old times."

FOURTEEN

Our cozy log cabin overlooking the lake had a stone fireplace, rustic furniture, and exposed beam ceilings. The deck in back overlooked a wooded area and a lake that reflected silvery moonlight.

"Where would you like your food?" asked the room service attendant with curly red hair.

"Put it over there against the sliding glass door," I said. I could hear water running in the bathroom, so I guessed Warren had decided to take a shower. Maybe there was hope or maybe Warren would remain true to form.

Warren never wanted to be seen sharing a room with me in a hotel. So whenever a member of the hotel staff would come to our room, Warren would suddenly disappear, but I knew he was hiding. Our cabin had two bedrooms, but that didn't matter to Warren. He was afraid of running into an old football fan or an attendant who would start asking questions.

Now, standing here with the room service guy, I had déjà vu about all my other trips with Warren. Some things about this relationship would never change.

The waiter lifted the silver domes over the plates to show me our dinner. "I have a turkey burger with fries, a club sandwich with coleslaw, and a bottle of Steven Kent pinot noir. Would you like me to open the wine?"

"Sure. Thank you," I said as I examined the bill. Damn, food and wine were getting so expensive.

The waiter poured wine and offered me a taste. I pulled the glass to my lips, took a sip, then nodded.

"Shall I pour one glass or two?"

"Two."

I signed the bill and handed it back to the lanky and pale white boi. He looked at the ticket, smiled, and let himself out of the cabin.

I took off my shirt, found my iPod, and picked up my glass of wine. Then I walked onto the deck, closing the sliding door behind me. Nightfall had arrived and a brilliant speckling of stars was hovering over the still lake. The cool night air caressed my neck as I listened to "I'm Gonna Be Ready" by Yolanda Adams. Stretching out on a cushioned lounge chair, I suddenly felt a sense of peace and believed for the first time in a long time that everything was going to be all right, whether Warren was in my life or he wasn't. Yolanda's voice had a way of soothing me.

"You gonna sleep out here tonight?" Warren asked. He startled me. I didn't even hear the door open.

"Oh, I'm sorry. I must have fallen asleep," I said, sitting up.

"Your food is getting cold." Warren wore only a pale yellow towel wrapped around the lower part of his body.

"Have you eaten yours yet?"

"I took a few bites."

I followed Warren to the dining-room table in the living room, where he had placed our meals. The light hanging over the wooden table was made of tree branches and metal, and it cast a soft glow over us. Warren's sultry gaze locked onto me. I acknowledged his smile with one of my own as I sat across from him and bit into my sandwich. I sipped the warm red wine and suddenly felt like I was on our first sleep-over date. Would I get lucky?

As I stared back into Warren's eyes, he got

up from the table, holding his wineglass. Maybe he wanted to get lucky, too. Still, I knew this wasn't about sex. It was about reestablishing our connection or deciding to move on for real this time.

But he did something very strange. Warren lay down on the pale blue carpet while holding the glass of wine. A sliver of the towel fell open, displaying the left side of his massive thigh.

Then I did something equally strange. I stood, kicked off my sneakers, and dropped my trousers. I picked up my glass of wine and placed it carefully next to Warren. Then I positioned myself next to him. I kissed him on the neck and he grabbed my hand, placing it on his chest with deliberate casualness. I wanted to start with a litany of questions about why we couldn't make it or give love another try. But I didn't. Instead I savored the touch of his skin against mine and enjoyed the silence that danced between us.

The moonlight shooting through the sliding glass doors woke us up.

"How did you sleep?" I asked after Warren had rubbed his beautiful hazel eyes for the second time.

"Okay, I guess," he said in the soft glow of

175

the light over the dining-room table. "I can't believe we fell asleep out here on the floor, especially when we have that big comfortable bed."

"Yeah, we did. I guess we both must have been really tired."

"Or maybe it was the wine," Warren said, turning on his side to rest on his elbow and gaze at me.

"Yeah, that helped. But it was nice. I'm glad we did this."

"Are you?" he asked softly.

I loved the way he was looking at me, like I was the only person on the planet who mattered. We felt a million miles away from the world and all its issues.

"Yeah," I said. "Aren't you?"

"It was nice to be in your arms again, Bent."

I turned on my side, resting on my elbow. "So, what's next?"

He drew his eyebrows together. "What do you mean?"

"The jobs with the new sports channel in Miami," I said, as if there were obviously nothing else to discuss. "Have you decided to take it?"

His tone was cool. "I'm thinking about it."

"Does the fact that I'm here increase

those chances?"

He shook his head. "Bent, I don't want to come in and mess up your life again."

Annoyance hardened my voice as I asked, "Who said you messed up my life?"

"I *know* I did."

"Warren, I'm a trouper. I know nothing is promised when it comes to gay relationships."

He looked annoyed. "Don't say gay."

"Why not, Warren?" I shot back. "That's what it is."

"Why can't you just say, we chill with each other? The term 'gay' makes my skin feel creepy. You know I don't see myself that way."

"And if your Facebook page is any indication," I snapped, "you don't want the world to see you that way, either. You have more pretty women 'friends' on there than the Miss America pageant, Miss Universe, and Miss U.S.A. combined."

Anger burned in Warren's eyes. "You're there."

"Yeah, but you ain't callin' me boo when you send me a message," I accused. "They call it Facebook for a reason. It's the *face* you're showing the world. It's fake. It's a grown-up playground where you can pretend and perpetrate —"

"Stop!" Warren's deep voice boomed through the silent cabin. "You wanna hang with Warren Stubbs? Then don't say gay. Don't think it, speak it, nothin'."

"And just forget you're layin' next to me butt naked under that towel, right?" I crossed my arms. My whole body was hot inside as annoyed thoughts shot through my mind.

Suddenly, lying here on the damn floor of this cabin didn't feel so cozy. All the frustrations and anger that I had felt years ago with Warren came rushing back. And I felt just as cold as I sounded. "So is that why you were at the party?"

His eyes took on a different expression, like he was trying to make me believe the lie that he was telling himself. "Bent, I was at the party because it was a way for me to make contacts. I still, at some point, plan to get married and have kids. I've always been up-front with you about that."

I sat up and glared down at him. "So what you're saying is that at some point in your life, there won't be room for me. Is that what you're trying to say, Warren?" I hated that this conversation was suddenly sounding like a repeat of what I'd told Kim, five years ago in my bed in Detroit.

Warren sat up, trying to cast that romantic

gaze back on me. "Bent, let's just take it slow. If I take the job in Miami, we'd see each other more. Then we could see what happens."

Deep down, unfortunately, I knew what would happen. The same old, same old. But seeing him again filled me with the same lovers' optimism that had put such a dreamy expression on Jah's face this morning.

It was odd how he'd written Radford out of the picture, so I asked, "What about the guy who you were at the party with?"

"I told you it was just a date," Warren said in a way that didn't convince me. "It means nothing."

"So what do you think about PGC?"

Warren let out a cynical chuckle. "You mean, what do I think of the Pretentious Gentlemen's Club?"

I laughed, loving the playful expression in Warren's eyes. I asked, "What do you think of them?"

"It's not a group I would be a part of. Why do you ask?"

I could have lain there looking at Warren's beautiful face — his broad jaw, the smooth ridge of his nose, his full, moist-looking lips — all day. But it really bothered me that he refused to face the truth about himself.

"Warren, I'm just surprised that of all the

179

places in Miami, that's where we see each other again. And how come I didn't know that such an organization exists?"

"Maybe because neither one of us has a million dollars to waste like that," he said with a tone like he was not impressed. "I guess if you married Kim, you'd be in that scene, too. Are you and your dad still not talking to each other?"

"No change."

"What about your mother?"

"I haven't talked to her in a minute, but it's not because we're upset with each other." I paused, not really wanting to get into all this. I thought we'd come here to get away and relax.

"What is it, B. D.?"

"My mother's very busy," I said with an annoyed tone. "She's got her charitable work and her young boyfriends."

Warren looked surprised. "So that's still going on?"

"As far as I know." I looked at his beautiful face wishing I could enjoy it in silence or by making sounds that weren't really words.

Warren asked, "How do you feel about that?"

"My mother doesn't comment on my sex life and I don't comment on hers."

Warren chuckled. "I feel you on that. I think it's funny that your mom is getting her swirl on with a young nigga."

It was time for us to get back on the subject of us and whether we had a future, so I asked, "Do you want to move in with me if you take the job?"

"Maybe for a couple of days," he said, "but I think we ought to keep our own places. If I'm going to become the star I envision, I'm going to have to be out in the Miami party scene."

Was that his way of saying he wouldn't have time for me? Or that he couldn't be seen with me? Or would he just have to see me on the sly to keep our secret from his benefactor? "Is Radford going to help you break into the movie business?"

Warren's deep voice vibrated through me as he said, "I don't want to talk about Radford. This is about you and me, boo."

"What about us?"

"I wonder if I can ever make you completely happy," Warren said.

"I think you can," I said as I moved closer to Warren and laid my hand across his naked stomach. Warren looked at me and gave me a sexy smile that softened his face. He placed his head on my stomach and I liked the warmth of his face against my skin.

"What do you really want, Bentley? What would truly make you happy?"

I didn't look up at him. I just said out loud, "That every night I could be next to you and that when we went to sleep we dreamed the same dreams. That would make me happy."

For a moment Warren remained silent. I knew he was thinking I had gotten him by saying something deep yet romantic.

"Ain't no way I can top that shit, Bentley."

"I know, Warren. Advantage, Bentley."

I woke up the next morning to find that Warren had fallen asleep with his head on my thigh. His lips were slightly parted and his left hand was placed under his face, making him look so peaceful. He reminded me of a baby, and I had the impulse to stroke his cheek, to run the back of my hand across the early-morning whiskers along his jaw. Instead I lay there motionless, savoring the silent intimacy between us and telling myself that this was one of life's moments to hold on to. Something to remember him by always, especially down the line if things went south.

Suddenly, there I was, preparing myself for disappointment again. Would I ever be able to let go of my fears that a seemingly perfect setup had to have a shelf life? Lord knows those fears were born out of good reasons. When Warren left me the first time, I was surprisingly devastated. I told myself karma was a bitch and turnabout was fair play, since I'd done the same thing to Kim. But Kim wouldn't be single for long and hopefully I wouldn't, either.

Now here I was with the man I felt I could love the rest of my life — but would he be able to love me with equal measure? I told myself not to get ahead of things for once, as I gently lifted Warren's head from my lap, taking care not to wake him.

This seemed like the perfect time to take a long hot shower and try to relax. I crossed the bedroom into the wide double shower and turned on the water. I stepped in and reached for the expensive skin conditioner the hotel supplied. Standing there all lathered under the steady spray of warm water, lost in my thoughts, I realized this was my first alone time in a few days. Being alone suddenly felt like a luxury. It had never occurred to me during my years as a single guy that being all by myself would ever feel like anything but loneliness. But those few minutes in the shower already felt like a sanctuary from something. I guess it was that "something" that made the difference, and he was just outside the door. I smiled. Solitude wasn't such a bad thing when it was yours to choose.

Once my shower was finished, I reached for one of the huge white towels and began drying myself. My thoughts turned immediately to Warren and what I ought to have waiting for him for breakfast. That was a nice feeling, too — having breakfast waiting for someone you love. But my day couldn't start without spreading cocoa butter all over my body. As soon as I finished, I slipped on some boxers and the new black warm-ups Warren purchased for me. I took a look at myself in the mirror at my cashew brown skin, which was smooth and solid, so I decided not to shave. I put a light cream in my hair, then I finally stuck my head into the bedroom to check on Warren, who was sleeping like a baby bear.

It was a wonder the loud cell phone ringing didn't wake him up. I leapt to the bedside to grab the phone from the night table when I saw that it was Jah calling. Closing the bedroom door behind me, I went onto the terrace to take the call.

"Hey, Jah. How's it going?"

"Everything's going *great,* B."

I was surprised to hear a smile in his voice. "When are you coming back?"

184

"I wish I didn't have to come back. I love it here. You should see the hotel suite I'm set up in."

I shook my head. I hated that he was so easily impressed and naïve. I hated to think that Seth recognized that and would take full advantage of Jah as a result.

"But you have to come back! What about school?"

Jah sounded love-struck when he said, "Seth treats me so wonderful that I don't want to leave."

"So it's all about Seth now." I wanted to tell Jah that you never take men like Seth Sinclair seriously. As I stared out at the lake, five baby ducks swam in a straight line, following behind the mother duck. That reminded me of Jah, following Seth across the country and doing exactly as he ordered.

"Yeah, B, but I can only call him Seth when we're alone. He's real strict about his privacy. But I don't mind. You should see the way he takes care of me. He had a driver come and take me on a shopping spree. I got some really nice clothes. I got some Paper Denim jeans, three pairs of sneakers, and some Ed Hardy T-shirts. I'll be the best-dressed man on the FIU campus."

"Did you use what I gave you?" I couldn't believe the number of young gay men I met

185

who didn't use condoms. When would we ever learn?

"Only one, but that's because we've spent a lot of time talking and just laying in bed. Can you believe that? I didn't know that it could be like this."

I snapped, "Know *what* could be like this?"

"Love!" he declared with perfect sincerity. "I think I'm falling in love."

"After two days?" I heard myself taking a chastising tone that I immediately realized wasn't going to get through to him, so I tried a subtler approach. "Listen, Jah, it thrills me that you're in love, but please take your time. You just met the guy. Getting to know someone is part of the process. These things take time. If it's real, he won't run away."

Jah sighed. "I'll try to go slow, but I think it might be too late. I think we're already in pretty deep, if you know what I mean."

Considering my own ambivalent situation with Warren, I knew exactly what he meant. How was it that I was advising someone in an area that I had so many uncertainties about? All I could come up with in reply was, "Be careful."

"Okay, but, hey, I need to run. Seth just texted me on my new BlackBerry to say he's on his way up to the suite. Everything is so top secret, but I guess that's how life is going to be from now on."

"I guess so," I said, wondering how long Jah could hold on and how badly he might get his heart broken. The first time was always the hardest. Unfortunately, getting hurt was something I had no control over, but you could be sure he'd be at my door when it was time to pick up the pieces. I told myself I was jumping ahead again and pushed the thought out of my mind. "Well, Jah, let me know when you're on your way back. I'll take you to lunch or dinner and we can catch up."

"I'd love that. In the meantime, take care, Bentley. I'll call you when I get back to Miami."

I snapped the phone shut and stood there a minute, processing our exchange while taking in the sweeping view of the golf course and lake. The sky looked like a rich blanket of blue velvet.

"So, you checking in with your other boyfriend?" came a sleepy voice.

Warren joined me on the terrace. He wore only his boxer briefs. Maybe it was the morning light making the hills around us look fresh and newly born, or maybe it was simply being caught off guard, but watching

Warren stroll up to me with a big, childlike grin that was at odds with his powerfully built adult male body, I'd never seen him look more handsome.

It was as if something so perfectly formed had stepped right out of nature itself. As if he were another one of God's gifts to mankind, just like the hills and lakes in the distance. I was incredibly turned on, but equally overcome by feelings of doubt. Where exactly did we stand in this relationship? Did I dare broach the subject?

Instead I struggled for words. "I don't have a boyfriend, you know that. So you finally woke up, huh?"

Warren now stood just inches away. He wrapped his massive arms around me. He followed through with a soft kiss on my lips. "Hmmm, that bed felt great. How did you sleep?"

"I slept well," I said, trying not to be swept away.

"I'll tell you this much: from now on, we do less sleeping and more of something else. That bed is made for more than sleeping." He embraced me tighter and kissed me once more, this time more hungrily. I returned the kiss with equal hunger, unable to prevent myself from being aroused by the thought of a marathon lovemaking session with this wall of muscle.

Warren at last rested his chin on my shoulder and whispered in my ear, as if to prevent the birds from listening, "We got all night for that. So what do you want to do until then?" I held my breath in anticipation of the come-on, which failed to materialize. "Are you up for golf?"

No, I *wasn't* up for golf. As much as I was holding back, I still wanted to see where our love scene on the terrace might lead. "I didn't bring my clubs," I said in the hope of squashing his plans.

"I'm sure we can rent some at the club."

How to get out of that? "Why don't we get some breakfast?"

"Room service or do you want to go out?"

Playing it cool in an attempt to mask my interest in sex, I answered offhandedly, "Either way."

"Okay, let me get dressed." He grabbed my ass and slapped it before heading back inside.

"Sounds good," I said, following him into the room. "I think I'm going to make some coffee. You want a cup?"

"Yeah, that will be right on time, boo boo."

I stopped and turned, shooting him an incredulous stare. "Boo boo? So I'm your boo boo again?" I loved the way that sounded.

"You'll always be my boo boo, Bent. You know that," he said with a wink as he dropped his boxers to the floor and strode toward the walk-in closet.

That evening, our last one on the lake, Warren and I did a five-mile run on the jogging trail. It had been a long time since we'd run the six miles around Detroit's island park, Belle Isle, along with joggers, cyclists, and Rollerbladers. Now, shocked by the exertion, we returned to the cabin exhausted. I was determined to beat Warren to the shower because I felt like a sweaty mess and didn't want him touching me — or me him, at least not in that condition. It didn't matter how drop-dead beautiful the man was — some things came first. While he poured himself a tall glass of orange juice, I headed to the bathroom.

A golden sunset filtered through the small bathroom window as I lathered my body. There I was for the second time that day, lost in my thoughts under the steady pressure of the shower. After about five minutes, I was getting ready to step out when Warren surprised me by sliding open the frosted shower door.

"How about I join you?" he asked. "Or do I have to wait for an invitation?"

I fought like a madman not to melt at the breathtaking sight of Warren's hard nakedness. "Come on in," I said casually. "I'm all done."

Before I could exit, however, he'd already stepped inside. "Would you like me to wash your back?"

"Thanks, but I'm cool."

"There must be something else I can wash," Warren said as he enveloped me from behind with those powerful arms once more. He began to nibble on my ear and very slowly run his erect, fat dick across my ass. As if responding to a dinner bell, my own dick quickly swelled until it swung before me like a pendulum. Warren gently rocked me back and forth, and I felt myself losing ground fast. I was unsure that I could stop what had started so suddenly, but also unsure that I *wanted* to stop what had started.

"You taste so good that I could eat you up, starting right about here," he said, circling the sensitive area beneath my right ear with his tongue. I stood frozen with my eyes closed, happily paralyzed by the chills running down my neck from the touch. "Yes, sir, you know I could eat *all* of you up, from top to bottom. But I got something that tastes just as good that's waiting on you," he added, lightly poking his dick against my asshole to underscore his point.

I inhaled and opened my eyes, determined to change course. "I bet you do. But why don't we wait until later for that," I said, slipping out of his wet embrace. "I'll meet you in the living room and we can talk about plans for the evening."

He looked puzzled, not quite hurt, but he appeared to be feeling his way through what had just happened.

Although I'd managed to resist Warren's fabulous touch and my own desire for a big throw down of lovemaking without condoms, that wasn't the end of it — not by a mile. Warren wasn't the type to take no for an answer, nor did he have a body that would elicit a no from anyone he chose to fuck. I therefore really shouldn't have been surprised when suddenly I noticed him in the mirror behind me as I stood shaving. He smiled devilishly at my reflection, as if to say, "I know what you want, and I'm about to give it to you." Instinctively I pulled my towel tighter around my waist — as if that might hold him off!

But this was a man full of surprises. Rather than have his way with me right there, he produced a bath towel and began to dry my still wet skin with long, lingering strokes. An almost uncomfortable silence hung in the air, since we were playing this by ear. I didn't think either of us knew what might follow. Once he had dried my entire body, including my feet, he took me by the shoulders and turned me around to face him.

He looked at me tenderly and said, "You know we're going to work this thing out, don't you?"

"What thing?" I asked, knowing precisely what he meant but wanting to hear it from him. I felt myself on the verge of melting inside, with love, lust, and longing for a real future with Warren.

His voice was so tender when he said, "You and me, boo."

"You think so?"

"I *know* so."

I tipped my head forward toward his chest, unable to face him. I wasn't sure what to believe. "But how, why . . . ?"

"Because at the end of the day, you're like that Eric Benet song."

"What song?"

" 'You're the Only One.' "

"Oh, yeah?" I said, looking up so he could see my tears starting to form. "Is that really what I am to you? The only one?"

"Yeah, that and a whole lot more, Bent."

"But we have to do everything out of the public eye," I complained. "How long do you expect me to live this way? Does it *have to* be like that?"

"For now," he said so quietly that I had to strain to hear him. "Can you handle it for now?"

I looked around the room as I attempted to formulate an answer. Did I even have a choice? "I don't know what to say, boo. It's a lot to expect. You and I got more issues than a magazine company."

"We can work them out," he said, pressing his forehead against mine. "Can you stick with me 'til I work things through?"

The question was so big that I didn't know how to reply. When I didn't answer, Warren planted a deep, desperate kiss on my mouth, almost as if he were trying to communicate through a kiss what he was unable to put into words. I could no longer resist this man, nor did I feel I needed to anymore. Whether he ever delivered on his plans or I was able to stick with him until he did, suddenly didn't matter to me. I needed Warren like nobody's business.

I threw my arms over his broad shoulders, which only further ignited our smoldering kiss. He stuck his big hand down the small of my back until he'd worked his way under the towel, which dropped to the floor. My rock-hard dick pressed against his swelling manhood. I reached between the folds of his towel and took him in my hand, stroking his fully erect, foot-long member.

"What do we have here?" I asked.

"You remember him, don't you?"

"He feels awfully familiar."

"Why don't you taste him and see if it's the one you remember."

"You mean the one I miss?" I asked. I knelt down and admired this beautiful piece of man meat — the same one I'd fought so valiantly to resist. I licked the palm of my hand and started to massage the length of his dick. Warren threw back his head, his mouth forming a silent O. When the first dribble of pre-cum bubbled up and neither of us could stand the wait any further, I took him in my mouth in one swift swallow. The taste of that man's sex drove me over the edge, propelling me to suck long and deeper. Finally Warren cupped the back of my head, his muscular thighs shuddering with excitement.

"Oh, fuck, baby," he cried out. "Nobody can do that like you. Shit, get that bad boi as hard as you can make him. I got plans for us."

I took his dick out of my mouth and

looked up. "What else we gonna do?"

"I feel like laying some pipe. Do you need some pipe in your life?"

"I always can use some good pipe in my life," I said, trying to hold back the laughter.

"You must have forgotten, boi."

"Forgot what?"

"My motto," Warren said with a sexy glint in his eyes.

"What motto?"

"That I got more wood than Home Depot."

"For real, for real?"

"Hmmm, how about we go into the bedroom and I fuck you so damn long and hard that I tear that ass of yours wide open."

"You promise?" I asked with a grin.

He took my hand. "Follow me and I'll show you just how good I can keep a promise."

FIFTEEN

"So what do you think of Seth Sinclair?" I asked Warren as he took a bite of his bacon. We were sitting at the dining-room table after ordering room service. Both of us wore the thick white robes with the resort's logo embroidered in gold on the breast.

Warren looked at me like my question had come out of left field. "What do you mean, what do I think of him?"

"I mean, I was really surprised to see him there," I said. "Everything I've read about him, his family and career totally contradicts what PGC stands for."

Warren dropped his bacon onto the plate, where it drowned in a small pool of maple syrup around his pancakes. He sounded irritated. "There you go with that waving the flag thing, Bentley. Just let the man live his life the way he wants to. He's done a lot for the African American community, especially in Hollywood. You don't have to like him."

I hated that Warren was defending Seth, but considering Warren's belief that fucking the shit out of another man didn't make him gay, I don't know why I was the least bit surprised.

"I didn't say I didn't like him," I snapped. "I only got to spend a few minutes with him. I just wonder what would happen if all his fans knew about that side of him."

Warren stabbed his fork into his eggs. "What would anybody think about a lot of men like Sinclair and men like me? I don't like how I've seen him treat people, but money is power and he has a lot of money."

The way he said that made me think of Jah. "What do you mean by that?"

Warren swallowed, then said, "I just get the feeling — and I've heard — that he thinks he can own people. Like a sort of modern-day slavery, if you will. He tried to hook up with me when I first met him, but I like to be in control. Besides, I heard he has some strange sexual tastes."

"For real? What have you heard?" I suddenly felt concerned about Jah and what Seth might be expecting from him.

Warren lifted a forkful of pancakes. "Look, I don't want to get into that over my breakfast. Sinclair doesn't have anything to do with either you or me. The man knows how to throw a good party and that's all I prefer to know."

I had lost my appetite. "How well does your friend know him?"

Warren shrugged. "They're tight. He said Sinclair has made a lot of calls on his behalf. Hey, boo, let's change the subject. So, am I going to beat you at tennis or golf today?"

I smiled. "Take your pick."

Warren chuckled and sounded so damn sexy and masculine. "You the one that's going to take the beating, so I guess I can at least let you pick your ass-whipping."

"Let's do tennis," I said, forking up some eggs. "That way I get to see that beautiful body in tennis whites."

Warren flashed me a sexy smile. "Hey, I might even put on a white jock for you. I know how you always liked that."

"Where did you get that from?"

He looked at me like, how could you forget? "I remember how you stared at me when I wore a jock. You didn't think I saw how mesmerized you were when I put this big old dick in a jock that can barely hold it?"

"Don't flatter yourself."

"Why should I when you do, Mr. Dean?"

"You think I'm trying to flatter you?"

"Maybe you keep me around to keep your

little fantasy going?"

"What fantasy would that be?"

"Having control over a professional football player," he said. "Even though your dad is still upset with you. Do you miss him?"

"Of course I miss him." I took a sip of hot coffee.

"I guess I messed that up for you. If you two guys aren't talking, then I know there's no way you'll ever get ownership of his football team."

"My mom owns the football team."

Warren smiled. "Then maybe there is a chance one day you'll be the owner and you can hire me to be your general manager."

"Wouldn't that be a hoot, two gay men controlling a football team," I said with a laugh.

Warren wasn't smiling.

"You know I don't consider myself gay, Bent. You know I don't like that."

I felt like it was impossible for me to pretend he wasn't gay when he was. "I'm sorry. And stop being so sensitive. So if I did get the team, you'd come and work for me?"

Warren nodded. "I'd consider it. I always said that if I couldn't be big in show business, I wouldn't mind being in professional football. But only in a management or

200

ownership capacity."

I had a sassy tone when I said, "Well, since you're not gay and we can't get married, you could only work for me. Now see if we were married, you could have me killed off and then you'd own the team."

Warren's face tensed. Anger filled his eyes. "Stop it, Bentley!" he shouted. "That shit's not funny!"

Warren shot up from his chair and stood there visibly shaking.

"Warren, dude. What's wrong with you? Stop trippin'! You know I was only joking."

"Killing someone is not something you joke about."

"Chill, dude, I know you would never kill someone."

"Do you, Bentley? How well do you really know me?"

"I know you well enough to fall asleep in your arms every night if you let me."

Warren didn't respond; instead he sulked until I went over and took his hands into mine.

"I'm sorry."

"How could you say that? I could never hurt somebody I loved."

I looked at Warren seriously for a moment. Was he about to say he was in love with me? I waited for him to say it. But he didn't.

"I need a nap, dude," he said. I followed him to the bedroom and we got in bed. We spooned. I loved his strong hands around my waist as I listened to his nervous stomach grumbling, but I never heard him say "I love you, Bentley."

SIXTEEN

It was election day and I was more nervous than when I ran for student body president of Detroit Country Day School. Back then, during my junior year, I was one of the few black students at the prestigious private school. And my blond-haired, blue-eyed opponent was the son of one of the Detroit Tigers. Not only did he have major name recognition, but he had a superstar reputation on the tennis court to boot.

But Bentley L. Dean III had charisma and a solid platform to improve some things for students, both academically and socially. Plus, I was always nice to everyone, whereas the other guy had a reputation for being snooty to anyone whose parents didn't have a certain net worth.

So, no surprise, I won, and went down in school history as the founder of the annual Bentley Ball, which we hosted in the ballroom of our home. The price of admission?

Two toys, one used and one new, for homeless children.

Back then, I loved feeling like I was making a positive difference in the world. And this morning when I voted, I had the same feeling about Barack Obama. His life mission was to make America better. But was America really going to elect its first African American president? As far as I was concerned, there could be only one answer to that question. So I just kept telling myself, "He'll win, he'll win."

I repeated that for the two hours I stood in line at my precinct. I was shocked when I arrived at 7:00 A.M. at the high school where I vote, and the line was snaking around the building, down the street. Two hours later, I cast my ballot for America's first black president. I needed "change" in just about every area of my life, and I prayed that an Obama administration could help make that happen.

When I got to the office around nine thirty, I didn't get a damn thing done all day. I was too busy watching CNN, MSNBC, or any TV reporter willing to give me information about the election.

And I'd soon celebrate at Mitch's election-night party.

Right now I was in my car on a barge for

the three-mile ride across Biscayne Bay to his condo on Fisher Island. Of course I had the radio on, for constant reports about the election. After the financial stress at the agency, I was hoping that it was prophetic of good fortune to come that I would enjoy this historic night on the private island. Fisher Island was where the superrich "wintered" in mansions and condos that made the places on *MTV Cribs* look like shacks.

I'd been there with my parents, so the first time I visited Mitch, I wasn't impressed with the fancy homes or their even fancier owners. He had invited me to a dinner party about a year ago, where a chef prepared Kobe beef that melted in my mouth.

Now, as the sun was setting over the ocean, I remembered how my father drew the connection to Detroit's Fisher Body factory and the Fisher Building, where my family would see Broadway plays on Sunday afternoons in the Fisher Theatre. Turns out, the building and the island were named after the guy who founded the automotive parts company back in the Motor City.

When the barge reached the island, I was counting the minutes until I could get to Mitch's condo and watch election results on TV. But for my viewing pleasure here in the car, several handsome, dark-skinned brothers sprayed my vehicle with a water hose as I drove off the barge and onto the island.

Minutes later, I was riding the elevator to a high floor in Mitch's building. I rang the doorbell and an attractive white guy in a butler's outfit greeted me at the door.

"Good evening," he said over the chatter of dozens of people and live news reports on flat-screen TVs. "You are?"

"Bentley Dean."

"Welcome to the victory party, Mr. Dean. I will tell Mr. Proctor you're here. What can I get you to drink?"

"A beer would be cool."

"Would you like imported or domestic, sir?"

"Why don't you choose," I said as I walked down a long hallway into a sea of handsome white and Italian men. The rich-looking crowd was about two-thirds women, but I could tell immediately that this party had a gay victory vibe.

I scanned the crowd for Mitch and familiar faces. Some guys had Mitch's agency country-club rich-boi look, while others wore business suits or had that superhip, overgroomed metrosexual style. The gorgeous, muscular men who were obviously models were sporting everything from jeans to tailored suits. As I studied the guys I assumed were models I wondered if Mitch and I would ever really compete against each other. The women ranged from fashionista models to banker-lawyer types to preppy. Almost everybody I saw in this sea of pale people was wearing "Obama for Change" buttons.

But I didn't see a single African American face. I wondered what the mood was on South Beach or, better yet, Homestead, where the community was mostly African American.

Here, almost everybody I made eye contact with made it a point to smile. If it was a woman, it seemed like they were pushing out their breasts so I could see the button they were wearing.

But I was more interested in the flatscreen TVs showing live election coverage in every corner of the enormous space. The outer walls of Mitch's three-bedroom condo were floor-to-ceiling windows that led to a huge outdoor terrace where even more people were eating, drinking, and talking.

But I couldn't look away from the TVs, even though I suddenly felt nervous again. The polls were closing on the East Coast in thirty minutes. Soon we'd know whether we'd be saying "President Obama" for the next four to eight years.

A waiter brought me a beer on a silver platter.

As I took it, Mitch popped up out of nowhere. He kissed my cheek and stepped back to look at me. Wearing a pin that said "Change" on the breast of his pink button-down shirt, Mitch wore crisp khakis and a white sweater over his shoulders. He nodded approval at my black linen hook-up with man sandals.

"Bentley! I'm so glad you came. It's a historic night." He took my free hand and pulled me through the crowd. "Come on in, get something to eat. I have several people I want you to meet. A lot of my models are here. It's great to have eye candy at your party for free!" Mitch let out a hearty laugh.

"What's the latest on the election?" I asked as several people looked at me curiously. "Have they said anything new?"

"No, but not to worry. The gays, the blacks, and it seems like people of all colors are going to give this country what it needs."

"I'm not worried." Of course that was a lie. I suddenly had the desire to be back in Michigan with my family watching the returns. We'd have dinner and then retire to the family room to talk the pros and cons of the election. But that was not to be. My dad was most likely at the country club or with some of his golf buddies drinking beer. My mother was most likely unaware that anything aside from her bridge game was going on. Anna and her husband were likely putting the kids to bed early so that they could watch the election results.

Mitch led me into the dining room, where the table held a beautiful buffet of food. In the center was a huge ice-sculpture bust of Barack Obama. All around that were towers of exotic cheeses, tropical fruits, a basket of gourmet breads, seafood, fresh vegetables with dip, and pasta salads. Nearby, men in chef uniforms stood at carving stations, serving lamb, turkey, and prime rib. In the corner was a giant cake with Obama's face, the White House, and the word "change."

"No egg white omelets served here, buddy," Mitch said playfully. "Indulge. Party like it's 2010."

Mitch stood by me as I piled my plate. As people streamed in and out of the dining room, they greeted him and he introduced me. Was I the token black man? Had he invited me to show his friends just how "liberal" he was or was I being an ass?

With my plate of boiled shrimp, oysters,

and mushrooms stuffed with crabmeat, I headed to the terrace with Mitch in tow. People stood at the railing with drinks and plates, while others sat at tables.

"Mitch!" called a George Hamilton–type man in a navy blue pin-striped suit. He was sitting with a middle-aged blonde who reminded me of Cindy McCain.

"Richard!" Mitch exclaimed, taking my arm to guide me to their table, which had a view of the sun setting over the Atlantic Ocean. "Meet my friend, Bentley Dean. He owns a modeling agency on South Beach. Bentley, this is Richard Mayer and his lovely wife, Linda. Richard is chairman and CEO of the company that owns the world's largest cruise ship line."

Richard stood and shook my hand. His dyed black hair remained perfectly combed back as he nodded and said, "It's my pleasure to meet you, Bentley." A piercing look from his gray eyes stunned me for a minute. This man definitely had serious charisma. "Join us, please."

"Thank you," I said.

"Do you guys compete against each other?" Richard asked.

"Almost never," Mitch and I said in unison without even trying.

Linda, who wore a white St. John suit with

silver trim, shook my hand and smiled. "Delighted to meet you," she said.

Mitch leaned over and whispered to me, "Doesn't Linda look like she's going for her interview as Miss Valdosta Feed and Grain?" I tried to suppress my smile as I thought of the *Designing Women* episode.

Mitch pulled out a chair for me and I sat. I'd hardly eaten all day, thanks to my nervous stomach, so I really needed some dinner. I raised a stuffed mushroom to my mouth. I took a bite and savored the delicious flavors.

"Tell us about your modeling agency," Linda said. "That sounds like so much fun."

"He used to model in New York," Mitch said proudly. "He's so gorgeous, you can see why. But with all the brains behind the beautiful face, good old capitalism was calling his name to open his own business."

Richard nodded approvingly. "You know, we often have fashion events on our cruise ships. Perhaps we could employ some of your models for our events. Not only does it pay very well, but they'd get a chance to see the world and meet people from every continent."

His offer to do business with me, and the delicious taste of shrimp and pasta salad, plus the slight buzz from my beer on an empty stomach — not to mention the overwhelming excitement of this historic day — well, I was feeling like everything was just about perfect right now. The only thing that would make it better would be to hear that Barack Obama had won the election. But we still had several hours to wait for that.

"That sounds like the opportunity of a lifetime," I said to Richard. "Thank you. I'd never even thought about hiring my models on cruise ships."

Linda raised her glass of champagne. "I'm loving that idea!" She laid her fingertips on my forearm and leaned closer. "Bentley, take it from me, the ladies absolutely love the male fashion shows. And since you're on a cruise ship after the show, the guys just can't escape all that adoring female attention."

Mitch raised his beer. "Cheers to new opportunities, new friends, and a new president!"

We all clinked our drinks together and I sipped my beer.

I hadn't felt this great in a long time, so I made a point to stay in the moment and bask in the festive mood of this historic night.

"Mitch!" exclaimed a female voice in the

crowd as we were mingling in the dining room. He turned toward the living room. A stunning sista in a slim-fitting designer dress was dashing toward him. An attractive brunet man in an impeccable business suit followed close behind.

"Annette!" Mitch said happily. She took his pale, chubby jaw in the palms of her elegant brown hands and kissed each of his cheeks. Her huge diamond wedding ring sparkled and her long, cocoa-hued fingernails almost touched his ears.

He glanced at me, as if this greeting had just earned him some much-needed points on my "cool white guy" scale.

"Mitch," said the brunet man following the only other brown face in the room. "Thanks for having us. Annette and I have been making the rounds. So many parties. But our final stop is Fisher Island."

Mitch smiled. "It's an honor to have you both. Annette, Brad, this is my dear friend Bentley Dean. He owns a modeling agency." Oh, so now he was tailoring his introduction of me based on whom I was meeting.

"We own a boutique," Annette said proudly, smiling and shaking my hand before her husband did the same. "I do the women's fashions, and Brad handles the men's clothing. Our store is called Black,

White, and Gray. We're on Washington."

Suddenly I felt happier than I'd felt all evening as I recalled the funky displays I'd seen in their storefront windows. I always thought that whoever had come up with that store concept and their displays had to be cool people.

"Everything in the store is black, white, or gray," Mitch said proudly. "Brilliant concept! We use their clothes for shoots all the time."

"What is your agency?" Annette asked.

"Picture Perfect," I said, equally proudly. "We specialize in African American men and women. My partner oversees our female models."

She turned to her husband. "Why have we never used his agency?"

"Tonight is all about change," I said, handing them each a business card.

"Change, yes," Brad said. "We're excited that our new president is biracial."

"Don't jinx it," Mitch warned. "The votes aren't counted yet."

Brad looked at Mitch and repeated, "We're excited that our new president is biracial."

"He will win," Annette said. "My grandmother in Africa had a dream. She saw Sasha and Malia playing on the lawn of the

White House, and Michelle reading to kids at a school as the first lady."

I turned to Mitch and said playfully, "Don't challenge an African grandmother and her dream."

"Oh, I've heard all about Gramma," Mitch teased, looking at Annette. "She's a superpower unto herself."

Annette smiled, taking Mitch's hand. "If this guy is your friend, then you're our friend as well." She took my hand and raised both my hand and Mitch's. "Victory tonight! For everyone!"

"Especially our kids," Brad told me. "We started the store because we wanted to play up the metaphor about our children."

"We don't believe they're black or white or even in the gray area between," Annette said. "They're a colorful mosaic of both of us. His allergies, caramel skin, my temper, my nose, his ears —"

"A penchant for debate," Brad said, "that one comes from Annette. Just a warning."

I smiled.

"Another warning," Mitch said. "Don't say their kids are exotic. People walk up in the grocery store and say, 'What *are* they?' like Lily and Leland are exotic pets. It's so obnoxious."

Annette said, "We celebrate our children

for their character and their intelligence. Physical beauty is simply icing on the cake."

Brad put his arm around Annette. "You're proof of that, my queen."

"Well, we're all about the icing on the cake," Mitch said, "seeing as we both own modeling agencies." He turned to the couple. "Annette, Brad, I think we should talk about how Bentley's models can show Black, White, and Gray's sizzlin' hot fashions to the world."

They nodded at me. "I think you're right."

Cha-ching! I thought as I nodded back and smiled.

But for now business was the last thing I wanted to deal with; I needed to find a television and get my fix on the latest reports about the election.

I felt like I was floating.

My ears were still ringing from the cheers that had almost shattered the windows when Barack Obama's victory was announced. Now, the crowd was so quiet, you could almost hear people's hearts beat as we watched his acceptance speech.

I was enjoying the party, and had gotten my fill of delicious food and even a piece of cake that would keep me on the treadmill extra long tomorrow.

But deep down, I felt empty.

This historic moment should have been shared with family or a lover or a best friend. There, in that sea of unfamiliar white faces, I decided that inauguration day would be different. Maybe I would even go to Washington. Or perhaps I'd watch it on television. Regardless, Bentley L. Dean III was going to enjoy the most historic day of the millennium with one of the above. Family, a lover, or a best friend.

Now, President-elect Obama's face blurred as tears stung my eyes. I heard sniffles all around me, so I knew other people were crying, too. Mitch appeared out of nowhere and put his arm around me. A short time later, he and I stood on the terrace, drinking beer and staring at the sparkling Miami skyline across the black bay.

"Did you ever think we'd live to see this day?" Mitch asked.

"I'd like to say yes, but no, I didn't, Mitch."

"Tomorrow the sun is gonna rise on a whole new era," Mitch said. "One of my wishes is that right now, your dad is wishing you were with him. My first election night wish came true — we just watched it on live TV. My second wish is that you don't end up like me."

217

"Mitch, what do you mean?" Was he referring to his HIV status?

"I mean fatherless and robbed of a chance to make up before he died," Mitch said. "That's all I could think about tonight, that I wish Dad were here to see this. If America can change in such a profound way, with millions of white people voting for a black man, then why couldn't my dad change enough to love his son again?"

Mitch's lower lip quivered like he was about to cry. So I hugged him and let him rest his cheek on my shoulder. He didn't sob. But he was shaking. I felt overwhelmed with sympathy for him. And I hoped that his wish would come true for me, too.

SEVENTEEN

A big surprise was waiting on the other side of my door when I opened it.

"Mother. What are you doing here?"

Her black leather pants, sky-high heels, and gold lamé blouse were so inappropriate for her age. Her jet-black hair framed her face, which was made up like a hand-painted portrait. Yet her expression announced she didn't give a damn what anybody thought.

"I'm here to see you," she said with that tone that was both ladylike and domineering. "Are you going to invite me in?"

I stepped back to let her pass through the doorway. "Of course, Mother. Come in. I didn't even know you knew where I lived. Or that you were coming to Miami."

Her White Shoulders perfume breezed around her as she whizzed past me, looking around like a housing inspector. "I got your address from your sister. This is a nice place for someone in the middle class. You do own this place, don't you, Bentley?"

Closing the door, I said, "I don't own it yet, but I'm purchasing it."

"Where is your artwork, hon? A Jonathan Green or some nice prints would brighten up this place."

"I can't afford artwork, Mother."

She ran her perfect red manicure over my bar and said, "I bet if you hadn't made your father mad, you could be living someplace nicer. Even though I'm sure you're going to fix this up." Her disapproving expression made me almost wish she hadn't even found me. "How is that little business you started going?"

"It's tough all over, but we're hanging in there. The economy is really rough."

"So I heard," she said, dashing into the kitchen. Her wrists full of gold bracelets jangled. "Are you still in business with that girl?"

"Alexandria? Yes, we're still in business." I followed her.

"That's good," she said, inspecting the contents of my refrigerator and cabinets. She was like a little tornado that shimmered with a diamond necklace that looked like a huge tennis bracelet at the base of her neck, which looked like a crinkled paper bag stretched over her throat. Maybe Botox and whatever else were keeping her face looking decades younger than her real age, but her neck left no doubt.

"Bentley, dear, I was worrying when you decided to become gay that you wouldn't have that female influence in your life. I assume you're still gay?"

Half of me wanted to laugh. The other half wanted to cry.

"Yes, Mother, I'm still gay. Now I know you didn't come down here to ask me that. I could have answered that over the phone or in an e-mail. What are you doing in Miami?"

She stood still for a second and looked at me. "Tyrone is down here training and trying out for another football team. And I want to do some shopping for the inauguration. Are you coming to D.C. for the swearing in for our new president?"

I chuckled. "Do you know how sad and funny that sounds? And I don't think I can afford to make the trip in January."

"What sounds?" she snapped.

"That you're dating someone named Tyrone. There's something very wrong with that picture."

She stepped toward me, looking up with a scolding expression. "Listen, I don't tell you who to date and you don't get to tell me. Tyrone takes good care of your mother when I can get him away from the computer games and the gym. Even though I like the results the gym provides me."

I sighed and shook my head. "That's way too much information, Mother."

She glared. "Maybe you think it's funny because *you're* dating someone named Tyrone, too." She gave me a sly smile. "Bentley Dean, you know my middle name is Independence. And I apologize to no one for my sexy young lover."

I shook my head, still smiling. "Mother, I hope I have half your spunk when I'm your age."

"Are you on Facebook, Bentley? If not, you should be."

"I'm on Facebook, Mother, but it takes up too much of my time."

She ran her fingertips over my cheek and looked at me like I was the most beautiful thing she'd ever seen, the way she looked at me as a child. Then she spun away just as quickly, looking around my breakfast nook.

My tone got back to business, too. "Mother, where are you staying? I know you don't want to stay here."

She pulled a BlackBerry from her designer purse and scrolled through messages. Without looking at me, she said, "I got a suite at the Four Seasons on Brickell. I really didn't want to be near the beach. I know I look good for my age, but I'll be damned if you think I'm going to be strolling through the sand in a swimsuit."

I smiled.

"Bentley, you need to come over there and have lunch or something with Tyrone and me. I need to remind you how the other half lives. Then maybe you'll reconsider this gay thing and get back in your father's good graces."

She said it like I could turn straight as easily as I could just flip an on-off switch or dye my hair from black to blond. "How is he doing?"

"I don't know. I hear from Anna that he has a new girlfriend. I guess when this one runs through his money, he'll get another one. Old fool. I did sell him his football team back. Didn't you always want to manage that?"

"Now is that the pot calling the kettle black?" I laughed. "I thought about it, but Father won't let me get near his football team."

"What are you saying?" My mother's brows arched dramatically.

"Not saying a word, Mother. As long as

you and Father are happy, then I'm ecstatic. He can keep his football team. Who is he dating?"

She crossed her arms, which made a diamond ring on her right hand glimmer. "I don't know who he's dating and I don't care. So how is your love life?"

There was no way I would tell her about my love life. "I'm doing just fine. Do you want something to drink, Mother?"

"No, I won't be here long. I have a driver waiting on me. Later in the week we're going to some steak house called Prime 112. My girlfriend Greta told me it's the hottest restaurant in town. Would you like to join us?"

Subjecting myself to several hours' worth of this was not my idea of a nice time. Yet I said, "Yeah, I've heard 112 is really good. I'll try to meet you there. But I will definitely come over to the Four Seasons and have lunch with you. How many days are you here?"

"Don't know. I have no schedule and no one to answer to. It might be two days. It might be two weeks. It's been a long time since I've been here." She looked like her mind was racing forward to tearing up Neiman Marcus and Miami's expensive boutiques.

She looked more like she needed a hug from someone who really cared about her. I wondered if my mother stayed on fast-forward so she wouldn't have to think about anything. Was she happy? Did she wish she were still married to my father? I would probably never know, so I said, "I think we could have lunch in a few days if that fits your schedule. Just let me know."

"I'll make it fit my schedule, baby. You look good." My mother hugged me and kissed my cheeks.

"Thanks, Mother. You look good, too. I'm really glad to see you. I've missed you."

"And I've missed you, too, Bentley. Next time don't make me have to come find you or I'll give you a good whipping. I can still do that."

"I won't, Mother. Come here and give me another hug. I've missed those."

"And I've missed giving them out."

I squeezed my mother tightly and inhaled her scent, which was the same one I loved as a little boy.

EIGHTEEN

Another surprise came later when Jah strode into my office with two bags from our favorite sub place.

"That's so nice of you to bring my lunch, Jah. Have a seat and tell me about your trip."

"It's just a sandwich, B," Jah said as he took a seat in front of my desk. "I know you were a little upset with me for going. But see, I made it back in one piece."

"I see," I said, scanning his new jeans, a silver belt buckle, and a black, long-sleeved T-shirt that I'd never seen on him. "I was a little worried. So tell me what happened."

He opened the bags and handed me my sub as he said, "California was amazing. Seth got a suite in a beautiful hotel in Beverly Hills. It had two bedrooms and a private pool and garden. We ate our meals in bed and he treated me like I was the most special person in the world."

I smiled. "That's good. I'm glad you had

a good time."

"I did," he said, opening his sub, "and I can't wait to go back."

The turkey and cheese on sourdough tasted delicious. I swallowed quickly, though, and asked, "You're not going to miss any more school, are you?"

Jah looked at me like he was about to confess something. "I'm thinking about transferring."

"Where?"

"To UCLA or maybe Southern Cal. I just want to be close to Seth." That dreamy look swept over his face. It was obviously fogging up his mind, too.

I snapped, "What about law school?"

"There are plenty of law schools in California."

"What about modeling? I think you're starting to pick up regular clients here."

"I can do it in California as well."

"The competition is tougher," I said, taking another bite.

He sighed and said, "I know, but I just want to be with Seth."

"All this for Seth?"

"I miss him so much. We've been texting each other ever since I got back."

"So you really like him?"

"I do."

"Did he mention his wife?"

"No, and I didn't ask. Do you want some mustard for your sandwich?"

"There's plenty on here already. Does he want you to move to California?"

"He didn't ask me to, but I'm pretty sure that he does. I love California, even though I didn't get out much. It seems like a magic place with all the trees and beautiful houses."

I set down my sandwich and said, "I don't like California."

"Why not?"

"You'll learn why if you spend some more time out there. I find the people to be really fake and shallow."

Jah laughed. "You mean like the people in Miami!"

"There are only a few people like that in Miami and I bet they moved here from California," I said.

Jah hugged himself. "Oh, and Seth is such a wonderful lover. I could stay in bed with him all day. I told you he has a huge dick."

He smiled, but I looked down at the bag of chips, wondering if I wanted to indulge in all those calories. "Too much information, Jah."

"I'm sorry, but I'm just saying. What a way to get broke in."

"Again, too much for me while eating, young man."

Jah had hardly touched his sandwich. "Okay. You know what? Right before I left, Seth gave me two thousand dollars in cash and told me if I need more money, to just text him. I'm going to be able to finally save some money."

I gave Jah a serious look. "Why did he do that?"

"Do what?"

"Give you money."

"I don't know, B. Maybe because he's rich. Or he had a good time."

I shook my head and took on my protective big-brother voice. "Jah, that sounds like you're some escort or something. I don't like that."

He sat up straighter. "I'm not an escort and I didn't ask him for any money."

"Then I don't think you should take money from him. I mean, if you keep dating or spending time with him, I think it might be okay if he gives you a gift every now and then. But cash money just doesn't sound right. Do you understand what I'm saying?"

"B, it sounds like you're trying to turn this into something sordid and trashy."

I felt so frustrated by his expression —

naïve yet thinking he knew everything about the ways of the world. "Jah, that's not what I'm doing. I just want you to be careful. Seth is a very powerful man. You can't let him control your life with sex and money."

"He's not trying to do that."

"I just want you to be careful."

Jah sulked like the teenage boy that I sometimes forgot that he was. "I just think I'll keep what goes on between Seth and me to myself."

"Suit yourself, but still watch yourself, Jah. I'm going to try my best to not let Seth take advantage of you. Remember who cared about you first."

"I know, but I want you to be happy for me."

"I'm happy for you, if it's the right kind of happiness."

"Whatever," he said, rolling his eyes.

I took a bite of my sandwich. "Let's change the subject. My mother is in town. I want you to meet her."

"The one who dates the hot young football player?"

I smiled. "I only have one mother and that would be her."

"What's she doing down here?"

"Came to surprise me, I think. But yes, the boyfriend is with her."

Jah picked up his sandwich. "I want to meet him, and of course it would be nice to meet your mother."

"I'm going for lunch with her tomorrow at the hotel. If you're free, I can take you along."

"I love eating and sleeping in hotels."

"I bet you do," I said with a laugh.

Right before I was getting ready to leave work, Alexandria stuck her head in the door of my office. She offered me a piece of red licorice from the package she was carrying. If my clocks ever went on the fritz, I'd always know it was five o'clock when Alex broke out the licorice to get her through another hour or so of work. I smiled because she looked so badass businesswoman in her form-fitting black suit and stilettos, yet playful with the candy.

"Bentley, I saw your little friend and our client, Jah, a little earlier. He seemed like he was floating on a cloud and the moon. What's going on with him?"

I sighed. "Jah thinks he's in love."

"Good for him." Alex bit her licorice and smiled.

"Yeah, right. What does an eighteen-year-old know about love?"

"Party of bitter for one." Alexandria

laughed. "From my conversations with Jah, he seems pretty level-headed."

"Whatever," I said. "Let's see how long this love lasts."

"Do you have plans for tonight?"

I shoved some papers into a file to leave my desk looking halfway neat for the night.

"Not tonight. My mother is in town and I might be going to Prime 112 with her later in the week."

"Oh my, fancy, fancy. And how is Lucinda doing?"

"She seems fine."

"What brought her to town?"

"Guess."

Alexandria's face lit up. "To see her baby?"

"Guess again."

She crossed her arms with a playful smile. "Something to do with the young stud?"

"You got it."

She chomped more licorice. "So she's still doing the cougar high thing."

"It seems that way."

"Boy," Alex said, "I'd like to be a fly on the wall at that dinner." The thought of seeing Alex watch my mother while she made a fool of herself didn't sound like fun. I missed the charming, witty mother who made people laugh when she asked questions like "What's in a gin and tonic?"

knowing full well everyone would break out into laughter. As much as I loved my mother's independence and gall, the visual of seeing her with a guy younger than me, instead of my father, was just *wrong*.

"Speaking of dinner, I have plans with an independent producer from Los Angeles tonight. He's thinking about doing a film on South Beach."

"And don't forget, I leave for my West Coast trip tomorrow. I got a lot of meetings lined up."

"Sounds good. Don't forget you're going out there to work, lady. I don't think your party days are over like you say."

"It's all business, baby," she said, patting her stomach. "I'm about to become a mom, remember? When we get back, you're gonna look at those DVDs from the sperm bank with me and help me pick a baby daddy."

I laughed. "That just sounds so bizarre."

Alex wrapped up the candy. "Hey, I'm going to cast that role just like they do for Hollywood movies. Maybe I'll ask for some pointers while I'm out there."

I asked, "Hey, have you ever met Seth Sinclair?"

Alex smiled. "Mr. Actor, Producer, Director, and Mega-personality? No, I haven't. He probably got people in front of people to get to him. That guy is a major player and I just don't mean in black Hollywood. He is the real deal. Why do you ask?"

I played it cool. "Just wondering. I was reading this article about him and thought how great it might be if we could submit some people for his next project."

She chuckled cynically. "Yeah, and while you're at it, why don't we do the same thing with Steven Spielberg and Clint Eastwood?" Alexandria said. There she was going again with her somewhat dry sense of humor.

I shrugged. "It never hurts to dream."

"You know, Seth's wife and I modeled at the same time," Alex said. "I doubt she'd even remember me. She had a way of not really caring about anyone but herself. Diva with a capital D."

I asked, "Do you know anyone who might be able to make the connection?"

"I do have a friend," Alex said, "and I use that term loosely, that I used to model with who married some ballplayer who said she had become friends with his wife. She said they met while serving on some charity committee. But Lola is the kind of girl who you can only believe half of what she says, so I don't know. Maybe I'll call her while I'm out there."

"Yeah, there was a picture of his wife and

twins in the magazine article. Very beautiful lady, and the kids look like little angels."

"And you're surprised. Seth Sinclair is fine as hell and he got bank. Who else is he going to marry besides someone who's drop-dead gorgeous?"

I lowered my voice and asked, "You ever heard any juicy rumors about him?"

"Like what?"

"I don't know, but you hear stories about all the big players in Hollywood."

"No," Alex said. "I have to say I haven't. He must be as clean as new underwear or have a damn good publicist."

I laughed. "Okay, I hope you have fun tonight. And if I don't talk to you before you leave, have a safe trip."

"Will do, B. D. You stay out of trouble while I'm gone." She hugged me.

"Trouble don't even know I've moved to Miami, so you don't have anything to worry about, Alex."

NINETEEN

It was a beautiful day on South Beach, so I decided to do some scouting. I loved getting myself a butter pecan ice-cream cone and strolling down Lincoln Road, checking out the eye candy that might be the next hot model on my list. Sometimes I would do it at some of the malls outside the city, but usually had better luck here because everybody was either gay or gay friendly. I didn't get the strange looks I got when I approached guys with a card and the "Are you interested in being a model?" question that I sometimes got when I went to the malls.

Sometimes I would walk down one side of the large outdoor mall areas, then turn around and walk on the other side. If it was a nice day like today, I would give out at least ten cards. That would usually result in at least five calls from guys who were interested in modeling.

I purchased my single-scoop cone and sat

at a little table with a huge umbrella outside of the shop. I was enjoying my cold treat when my cell phone vibrated inside my long plaid shorts. I pulled it out. JAH flashed across the screen.

"What's up, boi?"

"Hey, B, are you busy?"

"Not yet. What's up?"

"I'm thinking of dropping out of school this semester."

I stiffened. "Why on earth you do that, Jah?"

"Because I'm just not focused this semester and I just got a text from Seth asking if I can meet him in Houston tonight. I want to do it, but I have a lab."

My tone hardened, sounding almost angry. "Don't do it, Jah. You need to give school a little more time."

Jah sounded like a love-swept teenaged girl. "But I want to see Seth and he wants to see me."

I shook my head, watching the hot sun melt my ice cream, which didn't even look good anymore. "I know, Jah. But you just can't drop everything and take off every time he calls. What if I need you for something?"

"You know I'll do anything for you, B. But you don't need me."

A group of handsome guys walked past. Maybe I could approach them later; they looked like the type that Mitch had mentioned for his Caribbean shoot. "Jah, what if I get a call from a client who wants to book you?"

Jah whined like a kid being told he couldn't have his treat. "I thought you said things were slow."

I snapped, "They'll heat back up."

"Then just let me know and I'm there, B. I still need to work."

"Think about this, Jah. What if you decide you want to go to school this semester, then you don't want to get far behind?"

A woman on another bench was checking me out. She was a hot sista in a business suit, clearly on her lunch break, scouting for a man. I smiled back, delighted to serve as her eye candy for the moment.

"B, I got friends I can get notes from. Maybe even the cute boi who looks at me all the time. I want to tell him he waited too late to make his move. I got a man now." Jah spoke like he was going to rationalize this situation from every angle to justify his decision to be at Seth's beck and call across America.

"Jah, promise me you won't do anything crazy like dropping out of school or moving without telling me." I spotted a trio of gangly guys with beautiful chests walking down Lincoln Road with a basketball. I needed to give them a card, but also didn't want to hang up on Jah, so I watched them as they stopped and did a little window shopping.

"B, I won't do anything without telling you. You've been good to me and I don't want you worrying about me."

"Well, it's too late for that." I dropped my mess of an ice-cream cone in the garbage. I told myself it was okay because that was several hundred calories less I'd have to think about later on the treadmill. "I always worry about you."

"That's nice to know," Jah said sweetly.

The guys started heading away. "Hey, I gotta run. I'm out doing a little scouting and I need to get back to the office."

"Okay. Talk to you later."

"Okay, do that."

I felt nervous, dashing toward the guys, business cards in hand. Sometimes guys thought I was coming on to them and ugly exchanges occurred. Other times, when it was a group, it might be one prized handsome guy hanging out with homely friends. Usually the good-looking one would be skeptical, while the not so attractive ones would have their tongues hanging out at the prospect of modeling. Very rarely would I see a group of three beauties.

When I got up close to the guys, I heard them talking about how tight the clothes in the window were and how one day they would have money to purchase anything they wanted on Lincoln Road. Out of the side of my eyes, I could see that two of the litter were really handsome. I couldn't tell about the third one because he was being blocked by the guy in the middle and was a little shorter than the other two.

"Excuse me," I said nervously. "Have you guys ever thought about modeling?"

Two of the guys started laughing while bumping fists with each other. I wondered what was so funny.

"Dude, stop trippin'," said the guy closest to me. "So are you gonna tell me you're some famous photographer who wants to take pictures of us in swimming trunks and maybe some nude shots if we trust you? Man, dudes be coming up to us all the time when we come to this spot. You think we stupid or something?" This guy had an amazing chest with sweat glistening around his lean neck. All three of them exhibited such over-the-top masculinity, they would have been big hits at the party or any sports casting.

I was all business as I said, "No, I'm not a photographer. But I do own a modeling agency on South Beach and I think all of you guys could model if you wanted to."

"No, we can't," the guy in the middle said.

"Why not?" I asked.

" 'Cause we Panthers."

"Panthers?"

The guys nodded as the middle one said, "Yeah, we play basketball for the FIU Panthers and holding a job is against the NCAA rules. We could lose our scholarships."

"Who's going to tell?" I asked.

One guy nodded and said, "Dude got a point there. How is anybody going to know? How much does that shit pay?"

"Depends."

"Depends on what?"

"The job," I said, envisioning how gorgeous they would look in sportswear, business suits, or casual attire. "Most of my clients go out for one hundred fifty an hour but sometimes you're paid more for swimwear and underwear jobs."

One guy shook his head. "There you go. I knew it was going to get down to us coming out of our clothes. Let me guess. You're gay, right?"

241

I subtly squared my shoulders and lifted my chin, maintaining my business tone of voice. "I have no reason to answer that. I'm offering you a legitimate business opportunity here."

"Yeah, dude must be gay," said the one in the middle with the deep-set hazel eyes. He was by far the most handsome of the three with copper skin and pearly white teeth.

I handed them my business cards with both my office and cell phone number on them. "Let me give you my cards. Call if you like. Also, I'm sure I can find a way around the rules since this would be considered a part-time job. I've had college athletes work for me before. I could also pay you off the books in cash so there wouldn't be any tracking system. Just think about it."

All three took a card, with the handsome one studying it, then looking back at me like he was trying to figure me out. I started to ask his name, but decided against it. If they were interested, somebody would call.

"Pay in cash?" the gorgeous one asked. "That's what's up. And you think we could really do this?"

"Yes, I do," I said as I concealed my triumph. I knew I was going to get at least one of them and possibly all three.

The gorgeous one looked skeptical. "And

folks ain't going to be trying to pull any gay shit on us?"

I shook my head and said, "That would be sexual harassment and I don't think any of my clients want a lawsuit from a college basketball star. That wouldn't be good."

The handsome one said, "Sure in the shit wouldn't be. I'll sue the shit out of a mofo if they coming asking me something about sucking my dick. Wouldn't be prudent, if you get my drift." He gave me a slow once-over. A smile curled the corner of his mouth.

My business expression masked my certainty that this guy would definitely be calling. "Okay, fellas, I'm going to bounce. Both of my numbers are on the cards. Think about it and give me a call if you change your mind or have any questions."

I turned around and walked up Lincoln Road toward Washington Street and my office, knowing I'd just scored at least one new model.

I decided to cure my wave of anxiety about Jah and Seth by calling Sterling. Maybe he could assure me that everything would be okay. I had saved his number in my phone; he must have done the same because he answered knowing it was me calling.

"Wow! Is this a surprise," Sterling said,

sounding raspy but glad to hear from me.

"Hello, Sterling. Did I catch you at a bad time?"

"No, matter of fact I just woke up from a nap. What's going on? You got some hot bois for the next PGC function? I hope so, because you got some hot guys."

My tone of voice was all business as I said, "I'm sure I can find you some good guys. Where are you guys going next?"

He chuckled. "Believe it or not, we're doing something in D.C., right around the inauguration. We changed our plans. Don't want to miss history."

"I hear that," I said. "And finding good-looking black men will be real easy, I suspect, in the Chocolate City."

It sounded like Sterling was moving around. "I hope so. It might be a two- or three-night affair for this party. It's a little harder finding suitable accommodations, but the Emperor has said that money is no option. That'll make it easy if I have to outbid somebody."

As much as I loved the sound of making more money for the agency and my models, my concern for Jah outweighed that a million times over right now. "I'm sure you'll find something nice. Sterling, I got a question and I hope you can help me out."

"Shoot."

"Do you know what Seth's intentions are with Jah?"

His voice deepened, sounding annoyed. "Jah? Who in the hell is Jah?"

I looked at my phone, not really believing that Sterling had forgotten Jah so quickly, considering how he'd drooled over him when we first got to the party.

"You met him at the party. Remember the young guy that came with me?"

Sterling's tone changed to playful. "Oh, yeah, that cutie." Then he sounded annoyed again. "What do you mean, intentions?"

I spoke in a way that was not threatening or accusatory. "Jah is still very young and impressionable and I think he's falling for Seth. I don't want him to get hurt."

Sterling spoke back like I was stupid. "You do know that Seth is married and has a family, don't you?"

I knew we were entering into a zone where Sterling would stick to the lie that Seth wasn't even gay, or if he was, it wasn't open for conversation. "I know that and I think Jah knows that, but he's not really paying much attention to that."

Sterling spoke as if the conversation were over and not worth having at all. "That's how the youngsters always do, but I assure you, the Emperor is not about to leave his family or career for any guy. Especially someone like Jah." Sterling said that as if I had nothing to worry about. But it didn't make me feel better.

"Then can you ask Seth to not lead him on? Jah had a rough life for someone so young and he might not take the rejection well."

"Look, Bentley," Sterling snapped, "I understand what you're saying but I've been working for Seth or the Emperor for over five years. One thing he made very clear to me was that he wasn't paying me for my advice, unless it's on what place to hold his function. I don't comment on his life outside his marriage."

"Then you have to help me out."

"How can I do that?" I heard him clinking around, like a glass on a counter, water running, and a door closing.

I asked, "Are you the person who makes the reservations or connections when Seth wants to see Jah?"

"I guess so."

"Then when he asks to see Jah, just tell him Jah can't come, that he has school or something."

He made a sound like what I said was ridiculous. "I can't do that and I don't always make the reservations. Matter of fact, until I got this call, I didn't even know Seth had seen the young man since the party. We don't talk about who he beds."

"Could he be serious about Jah?"

"I doubt it," Sterling said, sounding resigned to talk to me so that I'd drop it. "This is all a game for Seth and most of the members of PGC. These guys aren't interested in falling in love with these guys so much as they are in owning them for a minute, then throwing the bois out like soured milk. I thought you knew that."

That spiked my urgency to get Jah away from Seth. "Sterling, if you can't stop it, arrange a meeting for me to sit down and talk to Seth. Maybe I can convince him that doing that to Jah is not a good move."

It sounded like Sterling was brushing his teeth, but he stopped to say, "Seth will not talk to you about any relationship, serious or otherwise, that he's involved in. That's *not* going to happen."

I refused to hear that. "I can be pretty convincing."

"Then you need to convince *Jah* not to see Seth anymore."

Frustration tried to take hold of me. "I've tried, but he really thinks they have something special."

Sterling spit over the sound of running water. "And right now they might have something going on, but it won't last for long. Trust me on that, Bentley."

My tone was semithreatening as I said, "Okay, if you don't think you can help me, I'll have to try something else."

"I wish I could be of more help. Will you come to the function in D.C.?"

My thoughts went on fast-forward as I tried to figure out a plan B for getting Jah away from Seth. "I might. I need to start looking for guys."

"Let me know ASAP, because we do have a guy up there that we used before. He supplied us with some pretty hot guys, but I'm sure you can do the same."

I had such mixed feelings. Working for the Emperor and Sterling was a great solution to my financial problems, but their party was the root cause of all my worries about Jah.

"I'll give it a try," I said. "Thanks, Sterling. I'll get back with you in the next couple of days after I have a chance to run a few ads."

"Okay, Bentley. I'll talk with you later."

"That'll work." I hung up the phone and tried to think up another plan to keep Jah away from Seth. I picked up Jah's comp card and thought if I sent it to a lot of clients that maybe I could luck up on a modeling campaign that might take Jah out of the city or even the country for a minute. I didn't think he would turn down a great opportunity because he thought he was falling in love. The problem with that plan was that very few companies, due to the economy, were starting new campaigns. At least not the lucrative kinds that would make Jah miss an opportunity to go wherever Seth instructed him to meet him.

I thought of one of my clients — Wilson Starks in Chicago — who did a lot of catalogue work for department stores all over the country. Maybe he had something that could take Jah's attention away from trying to please a sugar daddy.

In a few seconds, I had him on the phone.

"Media Works, this is Wilson speaking."

"Wilson, how are you, sir?"

He sounded thrilled to hear from me. "Bentley Dean? Man, I thought you'd fallen off the face of the earth. How are you? And why haven't I heard from you in a while?"

The last time I saw Wilson was on a shoot with some of my guys. He'd taken me to a really nice restaurant on Michigan Avenue and after a bottle of wine, we ended up in my hotel suite doing the nasty. I was a little tipsy, and the next day regretted the move. I hoped Wilson wasn't going to hold this against me, but I didn't want him to think that I was a whore, even though at that point that might have been an accurate description.

"Just been real busy, Wilson, but that's no excuse."

He sounded relieved. "I thought maybe I'd done something to offend you, man. I like you and enjoy doing business with you."

"I feel the same way and I'm sorry for not getting back, but I just got real busy."

"No problem. You're calling me now, so we have a chance to reconnect. When are you coming back to Chicago?"

I stared at Jah's picture on his comp card, praying that Wilson might be a solution to all this anxiety I was feeling. "I don't know, but hopefully real soon, which is one of the reasons why I'm calling."

"I'm listening."

I sounded all business as I said, "I was just wondering if you had any campaigns, or even just a two-day shoot, where you can use a really hot guy. Matter of fact, you saw him in my book before. You thought he was attractive, but too young."

"Hmmm," Wilson said, as if trying to jog his memory.

"His name is Jah and you remember, he

was the kid from the foster home I told you about. And if you thought he was cute then, you should take a look at him now. He's turned into quite the young man."

Wilson sounded agreeable. "I think I remember him. Send me his comp card. But I can't promise you anything for sure. Business up here has taken a dive. Even my bigger clients are using stock photos now."

I felt hopeful. "I understand, but I might just need you to create a job, and don't worry about sending me a check."

"What? I don't understand."

I sighed. "Wilson, I'll be real honest with you. I'm trying to keep this young man from making a big mistake. I need to get him out of Miami for a couple of days, even if it ends up costing me money. I think if I tell him he has a chance to shoot with you on something big, he might come to Chicago. I just need a real big distraction."

Wilson had a sympathetic tone as he said, "I hear you and I could certainly shoot him. Hey, wait a minute. How does his body look?"

"Jah has an awesome body," I said.

"Cool," Wilson said. "Send me a couple of recent shots of him in underwear or swimwear. There's a young man I'm working with here in Chicago who's doing a line

251

of sexy underwear and swimwear for men. He doesn't have a lot of money, so he hasn't been able to get glossy photos of men in his underwear that he can use in his catalogue or on the Net. I think once people see this stuff, it's going to explode."

My voice sounded a little higher, with excitement that perhaps I'd solved the Seth problem. "I can send you a couple of pictures of him as soon as I hang up." On my computer, I called up some recent shots of Jah that I could easily e-mail to Wilson right away.

"Okay, do that. I'll show them to my client and see what he thinks. If he doesn't like him, maybe we can just make up something to get him here."

"Thanks, Wilson. I hope we can make this happen. This means a lot to me."

"I hope I can help out, Bentley. Great talking to you."

"Same here." What a relief. And I was glad that Wilson hadn't broached the subject of when he'd get to see *me* again.

A couple of hours later, Wilson called back.

"Bentley, this is Wilson. Dude, you was right. Oh, boi is hot! I sent his pics to my client and he agrees with me. We want to use him. Will he wear real sexy underwear?

252

And I'm talking sheer and see-through stuff?"

I chuckled. "He'll wear whatever you tell him to put on."

"Great. How quick can you get him up here?"

"Is tomorrow soon enough?"

"That works fine. Are you coming with him?"

"I don't think so, I got a big casting coming up."

"Okay, don't worry," Wilson said. "I'll look after him and make sure he's all right. And since we're doing this on a small budget, he can just stay here at the studio." Wilson laughed. "I promise to look and not touch."

For a second, I wondered if I were saving Jah from one shark and sending him to another. But Wilson and Seth were nothing like each other. If I had to trust one, it would be Wilson. I said, "I'll either call you or e-mail his flight information."

"Good," Wilson said. "Looking forward to meeting the young man. It would be nice to see you again soon."

"I'll try and make that happen," I said, grateful that Wilson was willing to help with Jah.

"You promise?"

"For sure. Bye, Wilson."

TWENTY

The following morning, after my first cup of coffee, I checked my e-mails. Amid the usual spam stuff, I spotted an e-mail address that looked familiar. It was from Wilson:

> Bentley, it was good talking to you yesterday. Believe it or not, you cross my mind a lot. I guess I didn't put it down like I needed to when I got the chance. Please rest assured that if I'm ever given another chance, I won't have to wait so long for a call.
>
> Now about your young friend. Let me know his flight information and I'll meet him at the airport.
>
> — Wilson

I called Jah instead.

After one ring, Jah answered, "What's up, B?"

"I got some great news!"

"Oh, yeah? What?"

"I just booked an underwear campaign for you. When can you go to Chicago?"

"What! That's great news. Who is it with? Calvin Klein?"

"No."

"Papi?" Jah asked, naming a hot designer.

"No, it's a new designer," I said. "I sent them your comps and some of the underwear shots I had and they just went crazy. Said you were the guy they'd been looking for. They want you to be the face and body for the company."

"That's good news, but I hope it can wait for a couple of days."

"I'm sure it can. Are you worried about missing school?"

"Not really," Jah said with a nonchalant tone. "I just got to the airport and I'm about to get on a train to my flight."

Anger surged through me because I knew right away that the Seth travel saga was continuing at the expense of Jah's schooling and ultimately his emotional well-being. Not to mention, the Chicago shoot with Wilson would be impossible. "Where are you going, Jah?"

"To Denver."

"Denver!" I snapped. "What's going on in

Denver?"

"Meeting Seth," Jah said, unfazed and excited. "He's up there scouting locations for his next movie. He called me this morning and told me he had a ticket waiting. And don't worry, I talked to some classmates and they'll let me borrow their notes. I only have two classes today, anyway."

I felt like my blood pressure spiked. My face felt hot. But I controlled my voice so he wouldn't just hang up on me for sounding so mad.

"Come on, Jah! This is getting ridiculous. This man calls you and you jump every time. He's going to take advantage of you. Can't you just tell him no, one time? This is a great opportunity for you. I made sure you were the only guy from the agency that I submitted. Now I'll look stupid."

An uneasy silence came between us over the line.

"Jah, are you still there?"

"Yeah," he almost whispered.

"Are you sure you ought to be going to Denver?"

"I don't want to disappoint you, B, but I want to go." His voice sounded tight and emotional, like he was about to cry. "I'll be back in a couple of days."

I exhaled loudly. "Only a couple of

257

days, right?"

"Maybe. I don't know."

"Okay, Jah, do what you must. Call me when you get back. I can't promise the job will still be waiting." I hung up.

"Damn it!" I shouted. How could this boi be so stupid? He was still very much a boi, playing an adult game. I wanted to throw my cell phone across the room, but instead I took a deep breath and dialed Wilson number.

"So I see you got my e-mail," Wilson said.

"Yeah, I got it, Wilson. Thanks a lot. And trust me, you will get another chance."

Wilson chuckled in a semiseductive way. "That's good to know. So when do I get to meet our new superstar?"

"Looks like it's not going to happen as soon as I would have liked."

"What happened?" Wilson sounded disappointed. "Don't tell me he's not interested."

I hated that Jah was dissing my plan and that I had to explain it all to Wilson. "Oh, he's interested, but right now I think he's hornier than he is hungry. You know how young bois can be."

"Yeah, unfortunately I do know."

I spent a few minutes telling Wilson about Jah and why I was worried. But I didn't give away the identity of his suitor or how I was responsible for the meeting.

"You need to tell him to be careful," Wilson said with a warning tone that disturbed me. "Especially if he's powerful like you said and has a family." He paused, making me feel even more worried. "Black people have started to act like they're in the mafia when it comes to protecting their secrets."

"What do you mean?"

Wilson lowered his voice and said, "I have a friend, Wentworth, who's been in a coma for more than three months. I'm convinced his married boyfriend got some goons to beat him up. I can't prove it, but hopefully he'll come out of it and be able to help the police."

My thoughts spun in all the wrong directions, thinking about Jah in a situation like that.

"I mean," Wilson said with emotional rawness in his voice, "my friend lives in a doorman building on the Magnificent Mile here in Chicago and they still got up to his apartment. He never told me who his boyfriend was. He just said that he was really powerful and that if he called his name, I would know."

This was sounding hauntingly familiar to Jah's situation. "How did he meet him?"

"At some private party," Wilson said, "like

your friend. He tried to get me to go and I did. But when I got there, my name wasn't on the guest list and I wouldn't sign some piece of paper. So they turned my ass around, out the door."

He could have been describing a PGC party. "Were they all black men?"

"I don't know," Wilson said, "because I didn't get in. But I'm guessing they were because that's all my friend dates. My friend dropped a few hints and I think I know who it is. But Wentworth wouldn't confirm it, even when he got a little high."

"Wilson, do you think —"

My call waiting beeped. A 305 area code for Miami and a number that I didn't recognize flashed across the phone.

I clicked over. "Hello?"

"Is this Bentley Dean?" The voice was so deep, I felt wet and weak.

"Yeah, whom am I speaking with?"

"DeMarco Leon."

"Where do I know you from?"

"We met a couple days ago on Lincoln Road."

Bingo! I grinned. "Are you one of the Panthers?"

"Yeah, that's me. Hey, I think I'm interested in that modeling thing you were talking about. And I ain't scared of getting naked in front of nobody. I just can't do no film of me being naked."

I felt electrified at the idea of laying eyes on this gorgeous guy once again. It would be strictly professional, but this was one of the perks of my job. Thug eye candy galore, all who thought they had what it took to model. Sad thing was many of them thought a fat dick and an ass shaped like two volleyballs were all that it took to be successful in this business. "That isn't even necessary, DeMarco. When can you come and see me?"

It sounded like he was in a school hallway with students' chatter behind him. "Maybe later on today. I got class this morning and then practice, but I'm free after seven."

"Can you meet me at my office?"

"Sure, I'll meet you at your office, house, or whatever."

"Okay. Hey, I'm on another call. Can I call you back at this number?"

"Yeah, that's cool, but if I don't answer, remember I'll be in class. You can text me. My teacher don't like us texting in class, but I do it all the time without getting caught. You feel me?"

"Yeah, DeMarco. I'll call or text you. I look forward to seeing you again."

"Yeah, that's what's up. Take care, Bentley Dean."

"Good-bye, DeMarco."

I clicked back over to the other line and told Wilson I would call him when Jah returned. Then I'd know if Jah was still interested in doing the shoot.

"That's cool, Bentley. Don't forget about your promise."

"I won't."

TWENTY-ONE

I got home after being stood up by De-Marco and was looking in the fridge for something to eat. Just as I located some cold chicken, I got a text message. At first I was excited that it was from Warren. Until I read it:

"Hey, sexy Sheila. What time you cumin'?"

"What?" I texted back.

"My bad," Warren texted me.

That fool was so busy chasing women, he couldn't keep his booty-call text messages straight. Before I could feel annoyed, my phone rang. It was my mother.

"Hello, Mother."

She spoke in that scolding tone as if I'd been a bad boy and hadn't done my homework. "Bentley, where are you? You said you would try and meet me and my man for dinner."

I stared at the empty shelves in my refrigerator, realizing I could have been dining on steak and lobster right now. "Damn. I forgot, Mother."

Her voice softened. "Forget your dear mother? Bentley, that's not like you."

"I'm sorry, Mother. Is it too late?"

The buzz of restaurant sounds — silverware clinking on china, people talking — shot through the phone with her voice. "No, we haven't even been seated yet. This place must be really popular. We had reservations and they're still saying we have to wait thirty minutes."

I heard the beep. DEMARCO flashed across the phone.

"Hold on, Mother. I have another call." I clicked over. "Hello, DeMarco."

"Already got me locked in," DeMarco said playfully. "That's what's up."

"What happened to you?"

"Practice went a little long and I didn't have my phone with me." I hated lame-ass excuses. I didn't care if he was a college student and fine as hell. Standing me up for a job opportunity was just plain unprofessional.

"You couldn't text me?"

"Naw, man. I'm sorry. I can come now."

"I'm not at the office."

"Tell me where you live. I'll come to you."

My inner voice told me not to let a

stranger come to my place. Then again, I could Google DeMarco Leon and see if he was a player for Florida International University. If he wasn't, then I wouldn't see him. Besides, spending the evening interviewing a handsome young man sure did sound better than watching my mother make a fool of herself with her young lover.

"Let me call you back," I said.

"I can be there in fifteen minutes if you let me take a shower at your place. That way you can take a look at the goods and see if I'm what you looking for."

My inner voice announced that DeMarco was all about a scheme. Shocked at how open and forward he was being, I snapped, "For what?" Was this boi trying to set me up? "Let me call you back."

"Okay, I'll be waiting. But get back with me quick, before my girl starts ridin' my jock."

"I will."

Clicking back over, I said, "Mother?" I started to hang up.

"Bentley, are you back yet?"

"Yes, Mother. Hey, look, that was one of my clients. It looks like I can't make it. Maybe you and I can have lunch tomorrow or the next day. I have someone I want you to meet."

She sounded excited. "A young lady?"

"No, Mother."

Her bad-boy scolding tone returned as she said, "Okay, I understand your clients are more important than your mother."

"I got to make some money, Mother. I'm not independently wealthy like you." It was times like this when I really missed my father. He could get Mother to stop talking instantly without her even knowing. He was real good that way. In fact my father was good at most things without even trying.

"Huh," she huffed. "You could be if you tell your daddy you're going to get married and give him some grandkids."

I rolled my eyes, not in the mood to hear all this again. "Have a nice dinner, Mother."

"Bentley! Don't take that tone with me. I'm still the mother."

"Sorry, Mother. Have fun."

"I will, son."

I texted DeMarco my address, warning him to be on time. Then I went to my computer and Googled him. His name popped up immediately: *DeMarco Sean Leon, Westlake High School, Atlanta, Georgia. Mr. Georgia Basketball 2005, Top Five Point Guard, Five Star on all recruiting services. Picked Florida International University over Duke, Georgia, Kentucky, and Arkansas. Son of Lucy and Kevin Leon.*

I suddenly felt safe and thought maybe I should take a shower and order some food for my guest.

DeMarco bounced inside my condo like he'd been there before. He was wearing a navy blue on light blue sweat suit and a white T-shirt. He was the biggest of the bunch, but not the pretty one. Still, he had a casual handsomeness about him with strong teeth and full lips.

"You give good directions. Nice place," DeMarco said as he looked around my living room.

"Would you like something to drink?"

"You got any beer?"

"Are you twenty-one?"

"Yeah, you want to see some ID?"

"I should, but I trust you."

I went to the kitchen and got a beer and a bottle of water and walked back into the living room, where DeMarco was inspecting my framed photographs.

"Why no pictures of females?"

"Maybe they're in my bedroom," I said, ignoring what he was implying.

"That's what's up. So tell me how this modeling thing works," DeMarco said as he gulped down the beer.

"What do you want to know?"

He looked at me like it was obvious. "How do I make the money? What I got to do?"

"Well, first we'd need to get a book for you," I said, launching into autopilot to explain something I'd said a million times to new models. "That means have you do shoots with several photographers who might be willing to shoot you for free."

"That's what's up," DeMarco said, chugging more beer and staring intently at me.

"Once we get your book done, then I'll look over the requests I have for guys that fit your description. After that, you'll be sent on what we call in the industry a go-see, which means you go see the client and they look at your book. Then they might take some shots of you or just ask to see your body."

DeMarco held the beer bottle close to his mouth and asked, "Will they want to see me in the nude?"

"Most likely not," I said, knowing there was much more on this boi's mind than modeling. "But if it's that kind of job, you'll be told in advance. Otherwise I would advise you not to do it. Some of the photographers I know only do nudes. Others do catalogue shots or sports modeling, which is where I see you fitting in."

"Sports modeling, huh? That's what's up."

Something told me to keep my guard up with this boi.

"So you're a senior?"

"No, I'm a junior. But I'm skipping my senior year and going to try out for the league."

"The NBA?"

"Yeah."

"So you think you'll get drafted?"

"Depends on what kind of season I have, but I should be a lottery pick."

I pretended I was confused and needed him to school me on sports. "A lottery pick? I think I know what that means?" Making him think he knew more about sports than me would make him feel more comfortable.

He laughed, as if he were excited to explain something to me. "It means I would be one of the first players picked."

"Oh, I understand."

He set the beer bottle on my coffee table. "So you want to see what my body looks like?"

"You think I should?" I continued to play coy. Of course I wanted to see the goods! Damn, maybe I even wanted to touch the goods.

"I ain't got no problem with that," De-Marco announced. "I like my body. Which

269

way to the shower? I want to get it all nice and clean for you."

"The guest bathroom is back there," I said as I pointed to the hallway. "There are some clean towels in the cabinet."

He cast a seductive look at me. "You not gonna show me which way?"

"You're a big guy. You can find your way."

But he didn't move, as if he really wanted me to head back to the shower with him. "Okay. So you trust me in your house? You don't really know me. I might be some mass murderer or something."

"I get a good vibe from you. I think you're probably good people."

"You think so?"

I stepped toward the kitchen. "Yeah. Why don't you take a shower and I'll get my digital camera and snap a few shots of you so you can see how you look on film."

"Okay." DeMarco walked toward the bathroom. Before he reached the hallway, he'd removed the warm-ups to reveal a nice pair of tight-fitting boxer briefs covering a plump, muscular ass. Right as he reached the door, off came the jacket and T-shirt.

Damn, that boi was hot and he knew it.

While DeMarco was taking a shower, I went into the kitchen and poured myself a glass of wine and took a few sips. I figured this would give me a little more courage. I was about to return to the living room when my phone rang with an unfamiliar Miami number.

"Hello?"

"Is this Bentley Dean?" a male voice asked.

"Yeah, this is Bentley. How can I help you?"

The guy said, "I think I might be able to help *you*. This is Ramon Meeks. I met you on Lincoln Road a couple days ago. You gave me your card."

He must have been one of the guys who'd been window shopping with DeMarco. "Okay, Ramon. So you're interested in modeling?"

"I might be," he said, sounding serious, "but I need to warn you about something."

"Warn me about what?"

"My homeboy that was with me, the tall dude. His name is DeMarco."

I peeked around the corner to see if DeMarco had finished showering. "What about DeMarco?"

"I think he's going to try and set you up."

"How?"

"He a cool dude," the guy warned, "but he already got two babies and he needs some money to hold him over until the draft."

"Ha!" I said. "So he thinks he can get some money from me? I ain't got that kind of money, Ramon."

The young man on the phone sounded sincere. "Then you need to keep your distance from him. He told me that he was going to come and see you and try and get you to make a pass at him, then threaten to sue you unless you gave him some money."

"Blackmail?" I asked, remembering the warning from my inner voice earlier this evening. "So he's going to try and blackmail me?"

"I guess you could say that."

Was Ramon a hater who was trying to ruin DeMarco's chances for a modeling gig? Or was he telling the truth? "Ramon, why are you telling me this? You don't know me or owe me anything."

"I don't know why."

"I appreciate it, though."

"That's cool," he said.

"So are you the good-looking one?"

He sounded excited. "You think I'm good-looking?"

"You were the one on the end?"

"That's me."

"Yeah, you were the best-looking one of

the group."

"Dig that," he said.

"So why don't you give me a call tomorrow and let's try and get together and talk about modeling."

"I might do that."

I clicked off the phone and took another sip of my wine. I walked back into the living room just as DeMarco was walking out. He was wearing a white towel wrapped loosely around his body.

"How was your shower?" I asked.

"It was straight."

"How much do you weigh?"

"Two hundred and thirty-five pounds."

My eyes moved down his coal-colored, lineless face encased in six foot five — I guessed — two hundred and thirty-five healthy country boi pounds with a solid meaty look. He noticed this and very clumsily dropped the towel. He looked at me, stroking what looked like nine plus inches of dick. He smacked his lips.

"You want to take a picture of this?" he asked seductively.

I looked at him and could see "schemer" written all over his face. "I think I should take pics of you in clothes or, at the very least, underwear."

"You sure?"

"Yeah, I'm sure. Let me get my camera."

I went to the den and got my digital camera. When I came back in the living room, DeMarco was sitting on the sofa with his legs gaped open, stroking his now hard dick.

"You got any lotion?"

I knew what he was hinting at, but my voice and my expression let him know I wasn't about to bite. "What kind of lotion?"

"I don't care. I can make it harder."

"I'm sure you can," I said, unimpressed. "Would you like me to give you a pair of underwear or swimming trunks to put on?"

"Don't you want to touch it?"

"Touch what?"

"The dick, dude. You know you want to touch. And most likely do even more if the price is right."

"I think you read me wrong, DeMarco," I lied. Under normal circumstances I would have been on him so fast, DeMarco wouldn't have known what had slurped him up. I was proud of my oral skills and always had them coming back for more.

"You ain't gay?"

"I told you I wasn't going to answer that." I looked at him as if he were wearing a business suit and sitting across my desk from me in my office.

He sounded almost pleading. "Ain't no-body got to know what we do."

"No worries," I said, "because ain't nothing going to happen here."

He sounded harsh as he said, "You must got a dude."

"DeMarco, are you interested in modeling or playing games?"

"Why can't we do both?"

"I think you need to leave," I said firmly.

"You sure?"

I looked at the massive piece of manhood he was stroking and thought about how good it might taste. But just as quickly I thought about Ramon's call and how no dick, no matter how big or beautiful, was worth having to give up my hard-earned money.

"I think you need to leave, DeMarco. If you get serious about modeling, give me a call. I'm not going to get myself into a situation with someone who might look like a man but who is obviously still very much a kid."

"You think I'm a kid?"

"You just proved to me you are. I'm going to go into my bedroom and allow you to get dressed. You can let yourself out."

I turned around and walked very slowly toward my bedroom, leaving the massive mound of manhood alone. I wasn't in the mood to defend my own manhood or end up the headline of the *Miami Herald* with the caption SOUTH BEACH BUSINESSMAN FOUND BATTERED. If DeMarco needed money for his first boi-boi sex experience, he was going to find another way to do it.

TWENTY-TWO

The next morning I had my coffee and got on my treadmill for forty-five minutes. Before going into the office, I called my mother to see what time she wanted to meet for lunch. I could tell by the shrill tone in her voice that something was wrong.

"I can't meet for lunch, Bentley. I'm sorry, but you should have come last night."

"I told you something came up, Mother. Is everything all right?"

"Sure, everything is all right." She sounded sarcastic and was talking like a tape recorder on fast-forward. "Why would you ask me that? Why does something have to be wrong? My life is fine. Just fine. I just said I couldn't meet you for lunch. I do have my own life. Long gone are the days when my life centered around your father, Anna, and you."

I felt tired just listening to her. And worried. Had Tyrone done something to upset her? "Okay, Mother," I snapped. "I didn't mean to touch a nerve. I just thought we were going to get together. That's all! And I'm glad you have a life."

"Sure you are. I finally found a dress for D.C. and I've decided to get back to Detroit later on today."

I picked up my car keys and my coffee to go, heading for the door. "So you're leaving today? I thought you said you might stay as long as a week or two."

"I changed my mind," she said, sounding like she'd had too many cappuccinos. "A woman can change her mind. If you want to see me, you know where I live. It's the same place. I guess if I hadn't come to your little condo, I never would have seen you. But I understand. You and Anna don't need me anymore."

I closed and locked the door, stepping out in the humid sunshine. "Now you know that's not true, Mother. We'll always need you."

"That's what you say."

"Would like for me to come and go with you when you pick up your dress?"

"Why would you want to do that?"

"So I can see you. And since I'm not going to D.C., I want to see what it looks like." I got into my car, thinking about driving to

278

her hotel to give her the hug that she sounded like she desperately needed.

Her hard tone shot through the phone. "I'm sure my dress will make somebody's society page or, at the very least, the Internet. And if not, I'll have Anna take a picture and send it to you."

I started my car. "Anna's going with you? I didn't know that."

My Usher CD started to play; I turned it down as Mother spoke. "Yeah, I forgot to tell you that. She and that husband of hers are going. So I guess you see that your dad is still giving her money. I mean, how else would she be able to afford a Danish nanny for my grandkids?"

"I know, Mother, and you don't have to rub it in. I'm doing okay for myself. I'll be just fine."

Mother's voice was half angry, half worried as she said, "Bentley, I worry about you and that lifestyle you've chosen. I hear about bad things happening to gay people. AIDS. Haters. Discrimination. Violence."

"Mother!" I snapped, driving past the pastel-colored art deco hotels and buildings that characterized South Beach. "You saw me. I'm healthy and happy. Nothing bad is going to happen to me. Plus, I live in a place where it's comfortable to be out. I'm doing just fine."

She huffed. "Bentley, if you were doing so fine, you'd be living on Fisher Island or Star Island where you belong. Not on the outskirts of South Beach! Living like you're so *common*."

I wanted to hang up. I didn't need to hear my mother insult me or my lifestyle.

"Bentley, now don't get me wrong, there are some lovely parts of South Beach. Did I tell you that when you were younger your father and I came down here for a little vacation and I tried to get him to buy some property on South Beach, but he wouldn't listen to me?"

I exhaled, resigned to listening to whatever else she had to say. Besides, I was still worried about her state of mind. "No, I didn't know that. But, Mother, I'm already in the car. It wouldn't be anything for me to run over to your hotel and see you. I can at least get a hug before you leave."

"No, Bentley, don't do that," Mother said. Suddenly there was a sadness in her voice and if I was hearing things, I could have sworn that I heard some sniffles.

"Are you sure you're okay?"

"I'm fine. I'll see you soon. Bye, Bentley."

"Bye, Mo —"

Click.

Something was wrong. I didn't know what, but I was determined to find out. I called my sister. Some lady with a slight accent answered the phone and inquired about who was calling.

"It's her brother, Bentley," I said.

"Please hold, sir, while I secure Miss Anna."

A few minutes later, my sister, sounding bubbly as usual, was on the phone.

"What a pleasant surprise!" she squealed. "How are you doing, brother dear?"

"I'm doing okay," I said, wishing I could feel that excited to just be alive. "Hey, do you know if everything is okay with Mother?"

Anna sounded calm. "Why do you ask? I'm sure things are okay. But I haven't talked to her in a couple of days."

I watched a tall, skinny woman with a chubby man cross the street in front of me at a red light. They each held a leash for a Bouvier that was pulling *them* across the street. "Did you know she was down here with that alleged boyfriend?"

"Down where?" Anna asked.

"In Miami. She showed up on my doorstep a few days ago."

Anna spoke like she was figuring something out. "So that's why she wanted your address. I assumed she was sending you something. Did you meet the boyfriend?"

I explained what happened. "I swear she sounded like she was crying."

Anna's bubbly tone suddenly gave way to frustration and impatience. "That doesn't sound like our mother, but to be honest, Bentley, she hasn't been like our mother for the last couple of years. It's like she had a stroke or something and didn't tell anyone."

My sister exhaled. "But when I see her, she seems happy. She does have a different group of friends. All younger than her, but I guess that's because all of Father's friends sided with him in the divorce. It's okay for him to have younger girlfriends, but they treat Mother like she has some plague because she got herself a hottie. It's such a double standard."

I rolled my eyes, pulling into the parking garage at my office. "Well, I didn't call to talk about the black bourgeoisie. I'm just worried about my mother. Do you think this young guy is doing something underhanded to hurt her?"

"Like what?" Anna asked.

"I don't know. You see her more than I do."

My sister sounded like she was ready to end this conversation. "Bentley, I'm sure you're making more out of this than need be. I'm going to Washington, D.C., with her for the inauguration and I'll be around her and the boyfriend. I'll call you while I'm there and let you know what I think. Is that cool?"

"Sure, Anna, please do that. Are you taking the kids?"

"Oh, no!" she exclaimed playfully. "This is supposed to be fun, honey."

"But, Anna, you got a nanny."

"And your point is?"

I got out of my car and headed toward the elevator. "Don't let me get into this. I'm obviously not a parent, so I guess I can't comment on parenting issues."

She laughed, sounding the same as when she was a little girl. "Wise move. How's your business?"

"It's slow like everybody else, but I'm hanging in there."

"I'm sure you'll be just fine. Let me know when one of your models gets a big job or something. Are you still doing movie business as well?"

"We're trying," I said, riding up in the elevator. "But it's a tough nut to crack. Alexandria is out in Hollywood right now trying to drum up some business."

"How is Alexandria?"

"She's doing great."

"Tell her I said hello."

"I will, and kiss my niece and nephew for me."

"I will. I love you, Bentley."

"I love you, too, Anna. Please check in on our mother and let me know what's up. Also tell me what you think of this guy."

"Trust me, I will. And I promise to call and let you know what's what."

"Thanks, sis."

"Bye, Bentley."

"Talk to you later, Anna."

It was nice talking with Anna, but somehow I got the feeling she was too frustrated or naïve or annoyed about our mother to give an objective answer. Why hadn't she met Mother's newest boyfriend? And why was she so unconcerned when I implied that something might be wrong?

TWENTY-THREE

I was so relieved when I walked into Dr. Fenton's office. The way she looked at me and talked to me in such a nonjudgmental way, and the sense of security and confidentiality I felt within the walls of her office, put me at ease to unload everything that was weighing so heavily on my heart and mind.

When I first sat down, I must have talked for five minutes straight about Jah, the party, and Seth.

Dr. Fenton listened, nodding. Then she asked, "Why are you so worried about your young friend, Bentley?"

I shook my head, remembering Sterling's comment about Seth and his crew tossing out young bois like spoiled milk. "Because I don't think Jah realizes what he's getting himself into."

"And you do?"

The way she asked me that made me

wonder if I was letting my imagination get the best of me. I almost felt defensive about it, because I had no evidence of anything bad. Just a hunch.

"Dr. Fenton, it's hard to put my finger on it. But my intuition tells me, I just don't think this guy is right for Jah. I don't think this guy has the right motives in mind."

"Because he's rich and famous?"

"No, because I think he uses the fact that he's rich and famous for power."

"Don't most people?" she countered. "Doesn't that sound like what your father did to you?"

I stiffened. I loved Dr. Fenton's direct style, but that rubbed me the wrong way. I snapped, "What does my father have to do with this?"

She took off her half-glasses and looked hard into my eyes. "I'm just thinking about the time you said you didn't like the way he used his power."

"But we were talking about Jah."

"I understand. Do you feel guilty?"

I flinched. "About what?"

She raised her eyebrows as if it were obvious. "Well, Bentley, you're the one who brought him to the party. If you hadn't done that, this wouldn't be happening."

Whether I believed that or not, I didn't

want to hear it. "But I needed an extra guy to complete my contract." My heart was racing. Maybe that *was* my problem, that I felt guilty for putting Jah in this mess in the first place.

Dr. Fenton asked, "So now you don't want your friend to be happy?"

I felt like I was about to break out in a sweat, despite the air-conditioning. Maybe to her, that's what it sounded like. That I was almost hating on Jah for what — so far — sounded like his personalized fairy tale. But I just didn't want the clock to strike at midnight, leaving him with a broken dream, out on the street with nothing but a pumpkin.

"Dr. Fenton," I said too loudly. "Do you think that's what this is about? Me not wanting Jah to be happy? I would love for Jah to be happy. When he told me some of the stories about growing up in the foster care system, my heart just hurt so much for him. That's why I helped him get his own apartment and into college. It's why, a month after meeting him, I took him on a shopping spree for clothes. The reason why, when I buy myself a pair of sneakers, I will get a pair for Jah."

She looked puzzled. "Why do you do that?"

"Why?"

"Yes, Bentley." She had that blunt New Yorker tone when she asked, "What are your motives in regard to Jah?"

I crossed my arms and glared back at her. "Are you implying that I have some romantic interest in Jah?"

"Do you?"

"First of all, he's a kid," I said, not even trying to hide my annoyance. "And the answer to your question is no. Hell naw."

She looked skeptical. "Then why does this have you so worked up?"

"Look, I love Jah like a little brother. I look back on my childhood and how my sister and I didn't have to worry about anything. Ever. We were spoiled, but my parents always told us, 'To whom much is given, much is expected.' My sister and I have always reached out to help those who didn't have as much as we did."

She still looked like she wasn't buying my story. "But, Bentley, that's all been taken away from you."

I shook my head. "But I'm working hard to get it back. Jah never had any of that."

Dr. Fenton said, "It sounds like his new friend might provide some of that."

"But at what cost?"

She drew her eyebrows together as if she

were worried. "Do you think he could be in physical harm?"

I didn't even want to put into words what I really thought. "This guy is way too much of a public person than to try and hurt Jah. I think."

Dr. Fenton looked at me like she was waiting for me to explain that. "Then are you worried about the emotional toll? If so, someday soon, someone will break this young man's heart. It's how we learn to live with heartbreak. Remember how you talked about when your lover left you?"

Thinking about that heartache did nothing to make me feel better. I hated that therapy was so hard because it forced me to confront things head-on. And I loved Dr. Fenton's style, even though today it seemed like her every question and comment was just cranking me up another notch toward worried, annoyed, or sad.

I sounded more excited than I intended when I asked, "Did I tell you he was at the party?"

"No. Did you talk with him?"

"Did I talk to him? We did a little more than talking, Dr. Fenton."

She smiled. "So it was a good meeting?"

I thought for a moment about her question and the time Warren and I spent at the lake. I smiled.

"I guess that means you were glad to see him."

"And he was glad to see me."

"Are you going to see him again?"

"I don't know. I'm sure I will if he moves down here."

"And if he doesn't?"

I exhaled, feeling the brief happiness of my smile give way to disappointment. "It'll make it a little harder. Look, I know I love Warren, but he's made it perfectly clear that he'll always live life behind closed doors. I might be able to do it now, but I don't know about forever. Besides, I basically gave up my family for Warren and then he dumped me. Not good! I don't know if I can ever forgive him for that."

She spoke gently as she said, "Bentley, it's not too late to reconcile with your father. He's probably wishing for that just as intensely as you are."

I shook my head. "I just don't see how that could happen."

"You can make it happen," she said. "As simply as picking up the phone. Or passing on a message through your mother and sister. You still have a relationship with them."

"Yeah, I do but . . ."

"But?"

Suddenly the image of my father popped into my head. For an instant, I was really sad. I missed him and the relationship we had shared. My thoughts flashed back to the first time he'd taken me to a University of Michigan football game and a Detroit Tigers baseball game. I thought about the days we'd spent out on Lake Michigan on his boat, just the two of us, father and son, talking about how we were both responsible for changing the world. So many times during the recent election, I wanted to pick up the phone and call him and talk about the issues. But I was so afraid that he would say something mean, which would damage our relationship further.

Dr. Fenton's voice snapped me out of the daydream. "Are you still with me, Bentley?"

"Yeah, I'm here."

"What are those tears about?"

"What tears?" I asked as I used my arm to wipe my damp face.

TWENTY-FOUR

When Jah got back from Denver, I talked to him but didn't see him. This morning, right after I'd had my first cup of coffee and shaved, Jah called again.

"B, I'm outside your condo. Please come out right away."

"What's going on, Jah?"

He sounded as happy as if it were Christmas morning. "Just come outside, B. I got something I want to show you."

"Okay. Give me a couple of minutes."

I walked into my closet and picked out a pair of black warm-ups with a white stripe running down them and put on a pair of red sneakers. I tucked my T-shirt in and walked outside. When I looked to my left, there was Jah smiling and leaning on a beautiful silver Porsche. I walked toward him. When I got close, Jah started clapping like a young kid.

"Can you believe this? Isn't this the most

beautiful car you've ever seen?"

"It's nice, Jah. Is this yours?"

"Seth had it waiting for me when I got back. It was waiting at the airport for me. He is the greatest guy ever. I feel like Cinderfella. Finally things are going so well for me."

"I'm happy for you, Jah," I whispered as I gave him a hug. I was not completely convinced that I *was* happy for him. "Nothing in life is free," Father used to always tell me as a warning that things that seem free often come with a huge price tag. What price would Jah have to pay for accepting this car? And being Seth's boi toy of the week?

"Are you really happy for me?"

"Yes," I said, because that's what he wanted to hear. I didn't want to seem jealous or any of the negative things Dr. Fenton and I had talked about. "That's a whole lot of car for an eighteen-year-old."

"You keep saying that. But I'll be nineteen soon and before you know it, twenty."

"Did you ask Seth for this car?"

"No, that's the beauty of it!" Jah explained that he'd told Seth this was his dream car when he saw it in a magazine while they were together in Los Angeles. "No one in my entire life has ever given me such an amazing gift. I feel like I'm in a dream."

"It's certainly dreamlike," I said as I stuck my head in to inhale the new car smell that I hadn't sensed in a long time.

"Get in. Let me take you for a spin."

"You know, Jah, can we do that later? I have a meeting and I can't be late." That was a lie. Maybe I wasn't happy for Jah.

He offered to take me to the office. I promised him he could when I had time. Jah looked disappointed, but perked up when he asked, "Did you hear any more about the gig?"

I told him I'd talked with Wilson and that the deal was postponed. "Are you still interested?"

"Of course, and why wouldn't I be?"

"Looks like Seth is going to take pretty good care of you." I really didn't know what I was feeling right now. Did I secretly wish that someone would come along and sweep me off my feet and shower me with beautiful gifts? Had my relationship with Warren jaded me so that I believed that romance was dead because everyone had some sinister motive? What if Seth really did want to do the right thing with Jah? What if I really was jealous?

Jah leaned on the car. "Yeah, Seth is taking care of me. But you're always telling me that I need to be able to take care of myself. I still want to work. I'm not some trophy boi."

"Really, Jah." As soon as the words came out of my mouth I felt bad, but Jah didn't react. He hadn't heard me because he was too busy caressing his new toy.

I was trying to figure out answers to Dr. Fenton's questions and understand my reaction to Jah's new car as I reached the reception area of my office.

"Hold on, please, he just walked in," said my assistant, Laura, into the phone with authority. She put the call on hold and said, "Bentley, there's a Ramon calling for you."

Laura looked so cheerful in her turquoise dress and sparkly earrings, her hair swooped up in a ponytail.

"Okay. I'll take it in my office." I stopped. "Laura, good job. You're not making everything sound like a question anymore."

She smiled. "Thanks to you."

As I walked to my office, I thought about how so many things seemed like nothing but questions in my life. I sat behind my desk and picked up the phone. "This is Bentley Dean."

"Hey, dude, what's up? This is Ramon." It sounded like he was in a gym, with deep

voices echoing, whistles blowing, and bas-
ketballs bouncing.

I turned on my computer. "Hello, Ramon.
What's going on?"

He had an accusatory tone that I really
didn't like as he asked, "How come you
didn't tell me my dude DeMarco was there
when I called you?"

I logged on to check my e-mail. I really
didn't have time for Ramon's childish
chitchat. "I don't see why that is important."

"I thought I was looking out for you."

"And I appreciate that, Ramon. But to be
truthful, he was already there, so you did
look out for me. You were right. He was trying to seduce me."

I read an e-mail from Alex saying she had
arrived safely in Los Angeles and was
preparing for her meetings.

Ramon said, "But dude ain't gay. I don't
think he would have gone all the way. I think
he wanted you to make a move."

I sent an encouraging e-mail back to Alex
as I said, "I know, Ramon, and I would have
known that without your help. So thanks a
lot."

"I did it for DeMarco as well. Who knows,
you might be some powerful man who could
have made life real hard for our teammate.
We need DeMarco. He's our point guard

and makes our team click."

I read an e-mail from Mitch about the modeling gig in the Caribbean. "It never would have gotten to that. Trust me."

"So are you still interested in seeing me?"

"If you're interested in modeling."

Ramon paused. "I am, but I want to make sure I won't get into trouble. Maybe I should wait until the season is over."

I scrolled through spam and deleted it. "Whatever you decide, I'm with you, Ramon. I really appreciate what you did for me, so you know I'll look out for you. But if we meet, it needs to be in my office and both of us need to keep it professional."

Laura brought in a stack of mail and messages, along with today's *Miami Herald*. I couldn't read another article about the recession or foreclosures or unemployment. And that's all I saw on the front page. So I put a stack of comp cards on top of the paper on my desk. I needed to concentrate on keeping the Benjamins flowing into my business. Hopefully with more athletic hunks like Ramon.

He asked, "What do you mean by professional?"

"You don't have to worry about me coming on to you," I said in a matter-of-fact voice.

"Dude, I can take care of myself. I wasn't worried about that. But I understand you wanting to meet in your office and that's cool."

I was ready to make an appointment and hang up when he said, "So what are you going to do about DeMarco? If he calls again?"

I scanned my favorite Web sites for scouting new models. "I'll see him if it's about modeling. Of the three of you, DeMarco and you really could have a career in modeling if you really wanted it. I'm just trying to do what I can to help."

Ramon sounded surprised. "You'll help dude, even though he was trying to set you up?"

" 'Trying' being the operative word, Ramon," I said, sounding confident and professional. "You see, I'm a grown-ass man and I know when somebody is trying to run a game. I've been in this business a long time." Even though it would have been easy to give in to DeMarco's delicious-looking temptation.

"I hear you," Ramon said. "Okay, I gotta go to class. I'll call you when I'm ready."

"That's cool," I said, scanning my online calendar for any meetings today that may have slipped my mind.

Ramon said, "Hey, I know some football players you might be interested in. Do you give anything for referrals?"

I logged on to the agency's bank accounts. Seth's party had been a huge help for our bottom line, but money was starting to dwindle. I thought about Sterling's request for models for their inauguration party. Did I want to reach into the shark-infested waters again to pull out another treasure chest of cash?

"Ramon, we'll talk about referrals later. Let's get you and DeMarco in the fold first. Then I'd be happy to talk to any guys you send my way."

"Cool. You a'ight, Bentley."

"Thanks, Ramon. I feel the same way about you. I'll talk with you. Have a good day."

"Yeah, you do the same."

What if I sent Ramon and DeMarco into the feeding frenzy of handsome young meat? Would they both end up as some rich guy's boi toys, just like Jah? In Washington, perhaps a powerful lawmaker would impress them with gifts and fancy hotel rooms. Did I really want to do that again, even in exchange for a huge amount of cash?

TWENTY-FIVE

Jah and I had just ordered Kobe beef burgers at an upscale burger joint off Washington Road. We were at our table and Jah was still wearing the Cartier sunglasses that Seth had bought for him. He'd worn them through a dramatic comment outside when he was so impressed with himself. When we pulled up to the valet, he threw the guy his keys. I smiled, amused at Jah's playfulness. I had to admit it was a nice car.

I ordered a beer and Jah ordered a Coke.

"Jah, you can take off your glasses now," I said playfully amid the bustling restaurant noises.

Sitting across from me, he took them off and gently set them on the table. When I looked directly in his eyes, I noticed they were really red and glassy.

"Jah?" I asked, trying to sound calm. "Are you okay?"

"Sure, I'm fine. Why do you ask?"

Either he'd been crying or he hadn't slept in three days or he'd been doing something illegal.

I leaned closer. "What's wrong with your eyes? They're red as apples."

"I'm cool," he said, wiping his eyes as if he could make them clear. He sipped his Coke, then made a face like he was in pain.

I shook my head and demanded, "What's up, Jah? Are you on something?"

Jah tilted his head and snapped, "Something? What are you talking about?"

My voice was deep and demanding. "Are you doing drugs?"

Jah looked away. His face might as well have been stamped with a giant yes.

"Jah, answer me!" I whispered loudly so that no one at the surrounding tables would hear me. "Are you doing drugs?"

He exhaled. "Seth and I did a little blow when I was in Denver. I like it, okay? And before you start giving me lectures, B, don't worry. I'm not hooked on coke or anything."

Anger shot through my whole body. We could have both been dead or in jail right now.

"So that's why you're doing it in the middle of the day? And driving me here! Do you know how dangerous that is?" I glared at the naïve look in his bloodshot

301

eyes. "I should knock the shit out of you. Not only are you playing with your life, you're messing with mine. And that's not cool, Jah."

He stared back with a sad expression. "I'm sorry, B. My bad. I promise not to do it again and drive."

That upset me even more. "Jah! You need to promise me you won't do any more drugs. Period! Jah, I'm serious."

"I don't want you to be mad at me, B, so I won't." Tears glazed his tomato red eyes. He sipped more of his Coke and made that painful expression again.

"What's wrong?"

"My throat feels irritated. Maybe I'm catching a cold —"

I remembered how some of the models back in my New York days used to stay high for days on coke. Then they'd always be sniffling and complaining about a raw throat because their sinuses were draining. "It's the cocaine," I said, staring at him with questioning eyes. I didn't even want to think about what sexual acts Seth might have done involving Jah's throat.

"And I'm driving us home. If we get stopped, both of us will end up in jail." I wondered what the hell else Seth was exposing Jah to. Unsafe sex? Porn? Weed?

Jah yawned. "That's cool if you drive. I'm tired anyway. I guess I must be coming down." He looked worried.

"What is it, Jah?"

He leaned close and whispered, "How do I know if the things Seth wants me to do in bed are normal?"

I felt like a thermometer, and all the red mercury was shooting up to the top and exploding out because it was too damn hot — with anger. I inhaled to stop myself from going off.

"What do you mean, Jah?" I asked as calmly as possible.

He shifted on the chair and made that pained face again. And he ran his hands over his wrists, as if to massage away the pain. "I mean, sometimes the things he does" — he looked down at the table — "it hurts. But —"

"Jah!" What the hell had I done? Tossing this troubled young man into the ruthless jaws of a sex freak, all in the name of making money for the agency. "Love is not supposed to hurt. Making love is not supposed to hurt!"

He sighed, looking at me with pleading eyes. "B, I just don't know if it's because I've never done these things, or —"

"Tell him to stop! If it hurts, or you're not

comfortable, tell him to stop, Jah!"

He wiped his nose on the back of his hand. All of a sudden, that reminded me of a junkie I'd seen on the corner in the drug- and prostitution-plagued Cass Corridor. Our parents had driven me and Anna there once, after our middle school friends were caught with marijuana. Mother and Father wanted to show us what happened to people who got hooked on drugs. They ended up living on the corner, selling their bodies to anyone, so they could get more drugs.

I was horrified at the thought of Jah turning into the luxury version of a Cass Corridor crackhead. The elements were the same: sex, money, and drugs. Even though he was driving a Porsche, fucking a rich, powerful man, and snorting coke in expensive hotel rooms. It was still wrong, sleazy, and dangerous.

I cast a sympathetic look at him as my brain raced to figure out how to get him away from Seth. "Jah, you don't have any drugs on you, do you?"

The waitress delivered our expensive gourmet burgers. But suddenly I was too mad to enjoy this treat.

"No," Jah said. "Seth made me promise to only do them in the privacy of my home or when I'm with him. It's just that when you called and invited me to lunch, it sounded like a great plan."

I was not going to let this ruin my delicious lunch. "It seems like Seth is planning your every move, Jah."

"He's just concerned about me."

"So he gets you started on drugs." Jah was sounding like some dumb schoolgirl who wanted to please her star athlete boyfriend by fucking not only him, but his friends as well. I started to tell him this, but I could see he felt bad enough.

"I could have said no," he said softly.

"Then why didn't you?"

"We had a nice evening. A great dinner with wine and stuff. I just wanted to try it once."

"Sounds like you did it more than just once. And this is the first you mentioned about the drinking."

"It was just a little wine."

"That's how it gets started, Jah. Drinking and doing drugs makes it hard to stay alert — and safe. Did you use what I gave you?"

He cast his gaze down at the floor.

I angrily cut my burger down the middle and picked up half. "Do I need to take you to the AIDS ward so you can see what happens? Just because someone is famous and rich and looks healthy, doesn't mean they're negative, Jah!"

I inhaled deeply and closed my eyes. Ranting and raving at Jah was definitely not going to make him hear me. Hopefully, I would say a few things that would make him think and decide on his own that this relationship with Seth just wasn't right for him.

"Jah, I'm sorry," I said softly. "I feel like your big brother. And big brothers are protective."

"It's okay, B," he said softly. "I'm glad you care."

I nodded toward his plate, which he hadn't seemed to notice. "Jah, you need to eat. And you need to stay focused on school and doing the things with your life you've always told me you want to do."

He slowly ate a French fry. "And I will. I just got sidetracked. I promised to make you proud, B."

"You need to do it for yourself, Jah." I took a bite and savored the juicy, flavorful burger.

Jah did the same, chewing in the awkward silence. "I feel like I disappointed you," he said, looking at me with those sad, bloodshot eyes. "I want you to be happy with me as well."

"I'll be happy," I said, "when you get your

head out of the clouds and think about what's best for Jah, not Seth."

TWENTY-SIX

I was watching the *American Idol* audition show with all the bad singers when my cell phone rang. It was Warren and I suddenly realized it had been about a week since I talked with him.

"Where you been, stranger?" I asked.

"I guess you don't miss me."

I closed my eyes, loving the sound of his deep voice shooting through the phone into my ear. "Why do you say that?"

"You haven't called, Bent, so I must not be on your mind."

I turned down the volume on the TV so I could concentrate on Warren's sexy voice. I said, "The same could be said for you. That works both ways."

"I've been real busy," he said, launching into one of his famous cat-and-mouse conversations that sometimes frustrated the hell out of me.

"Me, too."

"So what are you doing?" he asked seductively.

"Watching television."

"Alone?"

"Of course," I said.

"What you got on?"

"Nothing."

"Come on, silly B, I know you're not sitting up butt-ass naked watching television."

"Since you're not here," I said, "you can't know that."

Warren countered, "You might be sitting on the sofa in your drawers with no shirt, but that's it."

I smiled. "You act like you know me."

"I do, boi."

"So when you moving here?"

"Don't know," Warren said with his trademark air of mystery. "My station made a very nice counteroffer."

"So you might be staying in the Motor City." I shifted on the couch, feeling warm and cozy in my black sweat suit.

"Yeah, I might. I would do the main sportscasts and get the Lions as my beat."

I laughed. "And that's a good thing? The Lions are horrible."

Warren became playfully defensive. "What are you talking about, Bent? They had a perfect record."

"I know. They lost every single game. I bet that locker room is full of gloom."

"It won't be if I'm reporting from there live every day."

"Oh," I said with a sultry tone, "let me get that image out of my mind because I might be naked for real in a minute."

Warren groaned. "Now I like how that sounds. Why don't you move back home?"

"For what?"

"For me."

"My business is here."

"You said it wasn't going that well."

"At least I got a roof over my head."

"All that real estate your folks got up here and you think you wouldn't have a place to stay."

I stared blankly at the television for a minute, stunned by the irony of Warren talking to me about my parents' houses in Detroit. All of which I lost because I fell in love with his noncommittal ass. "What if I wanted to stay with you?"

"We could talk about it."

"That's your way of saying, 'not on your life.'"

Of course I wasn't surprised when he snapped back, "Let's change the subject. I really wanted to hear your voice. I was hoping you'd need a little tune-up soon and I'd be hearing from you."

I knew it was pointless to push the topic of a real relationship. But it sure was fun to flirt. "I always need a tune-up, Warren."

His deep voice shot through the phone so strong that I almost shivered as he asked, "So, when you coming to sit on this dick?"

"When you gonna bring that dick?"

"Soon."

"You promise?"

"Now you know how I am with promises, boo."

"I do." My voice got serious and I thought of Jah in the restaurant. "I got a favor to ask you."

"What up, baby?"

I clicked off the TV and asked, "Can you find out when the next PGC function is and where?"

Warren agreed, then asked if I'd talked with Sterling. When I said yes, but he wasn't much help, Warren asked what I wanted to know.

"I need to get in front of Seth Sinclair."

"What for?"

"A little business matter."

Warren had a warning tone when he said, "Seth, I hear, is a shrewd businessman."

I let my irritation harden my tone of voice. "Are you saying I'm not? I can handle my business, Warren."

"I'm sure you can," Warren said with that tone like he didn't really want to take the conversation to a serious place. "Hey, it's almost time for me to get ready to go on air. I was checking in with you. I'll see what I can find out about your boi Seth."

"Thanks, Warren. We will see each other real soon."

"I know we will, boo. Whack that dick off and think of me."

"You ain't said nothing but a word, boi."

TWENTY-SEVEN

I had just ordered a venti coffee drink at the Starbucks on Lincoln Road when I heard a familiar voice behind me.

"My, my, fancy meeting you here." The feminine male voice was equally friendly and bitchy. "I was going to call you today."

I turned around and discovered Gabriel standing a few feet away. He was the feminine gay guy I'd recruited, at Sterling's request, for the party. I smiled, remembering Gabriel's grand entrance, posing in the crowd as if he were Diana Ross.

"Gabriel, how are you doing?" I asked, wondering what dramatic antics he was going to pull off here in Starbucks. He wore a purple sweater with a matching scarf that was wrapped around his head, like women in the 1950s who were taking a ride in a convertible and didn't want to mess up their hair. His white-rimmed sunglasses and gold hoop earrings were causing a few folks to look up from their lattes for a double take, to figure out if he was male or female.

Even here in Miami, Gabriel was so flamboyant — especially the way he switched his slim hips in those jeans — and spoke too loud, I thought he made a spectacle of himself on purpose.

"I'm doing fine as can be," Gabriel said, stepping to the counter beside me, "considering this fucked-up economy. A girl might have to go sell some pussy if things don't get better soon. That's why I was going to call you today."

"For what?" I asked, shocked. For a moment I wondered if this was the type of conversation I wanted to have in Starbucks, so I looked down the counter to see if my drink was ready. When the clerk called out my order, I took it and invited Gabriel to join me outside on one of the cement benches.

"Let me get my carrot loaf and I'll meet you in a few."

"Okay."

I walked outside and spotted an empty bench. I sat down, sipping my coffee. There was a fall-like nip in the air and the drink warmed me. After a few sips, Gabriel joined me with his pastry and what looked like orange juice in a plastic bottle.

"It's a nice day, isn't it?" Gabriel said, sitting a few feet from me on the bench. Why had he dusted off the chair in my office with his scarf before sitting down, but here on an outside bench, he just sat down?

"Yeah, a little chilly," I said, gripping my warm cup.

"That's what I love about Miami. I bet it's cold as crap in South Carolina."

"Is that where you're from?"

"A little town outside of Columbia," he said, nibbling his carrot loaf. "I don't ever want to go back there, Bentley."

"Small towns can be tough on gay people."

"Hell yeah. Especially black gay people. Miami is heaven compared to that hellhole."

I hated to admit that I'd left Detroit for the same reason: intolerance. Except rather than a whole town, it was from the one person who mattered most, my father. But I wasn't about to bare my soul to Gabriel. I needed to keep it strictly professional.

"So, Gabriel, you said you were going to call me. What about?"

He sipped his juice, then dramatically balanced it on the upper knee of his crossed legs. "How well do you know those people from the party?" The negative way he said "those people" made me wonder if he'd gotten into some trouble.

"What do you mean?"

Gabriel inhaled as if he were about to launch into a long story. "I knew to get in contact with a couple of the gentlemen. One of them said he could help me find work, but the nigga gave me the wrong number."

I felt relieved that he hadn't said anything about violating the nondisclosure agreement. That would be very bad business for my agency. "Oh, I'm sorry to hear that."

Gabriel play-swatted my arm. "Don't look so worried, Aunt Mildred. I'm a big girl. I can handle myself. Even when I get played like a baby grand piano."

I tried to laugh, but if something had gone wrong at the party, I needed to know whether it might affect the agency.

I asked, "Do you remember his name?"

Gabriel snickered. "I think he said Don, but I don't think that was the truth. I should have looked through his wallet like I always do with men like that."

I sipped my coffee. "What do you mean, men like that?"

He looked at me like "duh!" and spoke the same way. "Bentley, I'm sure you know what I'm talking about. Typical married closet case. But I'm not interested in their wives. He promised to help me while I was sucking his dick, but I guess he forgot once he and his friend came."

I must have winced a frown because Gabriel got angry and told me not to pass judgments against him.

"I'm sorry," I said. He was right about what I was thinking.

Gabriel snatched off his sunglasses and glared at me. "I don't know why guys like you think you can treat us fem guys any way you damn please. I'm just as good as you."

I tilted my chin upward. There was no way I was going to justify that b.s. with a response. "I'm sorry, Gabriel. I'm just not used to talking to someone I barely know about such intimate matters."

The truth was I felt sorry for Gabriel because he was so bitter. It was like he had a point to prove to the world, but it backfired because he was so negative and abrasive.

"You know me," he accused. "That's why you picked me for the party. You knew I'd deliver what the party guests were looking for, more than those so-called straight bois you booked. Let's not fool ourselves; your clients were looking for sex. I knew that when I took the job."

I was ready to stand up and leave. "That's not why I picked you, Gabriel. And I was not asked to provide guys for sex. I'm not running an escort agency."

Gabriel twisted his hand in the air, dismissing what I said. "Modeling agency, escort service. Trust me, they're the same thing."

"I'm sorry you feel that way," I said, knowing that Gabriel loved to get under my skin. He was, but I didn't want to give him the satisfaction of knowing it. "I didn't have anything to do with what happened after you left the party."

Gabriel nibbled his pastry. "What about that young kid? Did Seth Sinclair get him a job?"

"I don't discuss my friends' business," I said flatly. Little did I know my response would be like striking a match for Gabriel to explode at me.

"Oh!" he spat. "So, he's your friend and I'm not because I wear my clothes too tight, maybe switch too much for your liking? Yes, I'm a sissy and I don't give a damn what anyone thinks." Two teenaged girls walking past stared at him like he was a lunatic. "I've been a sissy since day one and no one, and I mean no one, is going to change me. Do you understand that, Bentley Dean?"

I didn't know how our little midday snack had turned so confrontational. Why was Gabriel so angry? I was stunned and just stared at him.

"You don't have to answer me," Gabriel said, "but I'm going to find that bastard and he's going to do what he promised me. If he doesn't, I will find Mister Seth Sinclair and blow his little cover unless he helps."

I shook my head and spoke calmly, even though his threat set off a panic inside me. "You can't do that, Gabriel. You signed a nondisclosure."

"Do you think that little piece of paper means anything to me? I need some money or a job. They can pick."

Where was this leading? Did I need to alert Sterling Sneed about this? Maybe not. If Gabriel was so hard up for money, surely he didn't have money to spend on a plane ticket to California.

"Why are you so bitter, Gabriel?"

He stood and glared down at me. "I'm a bitter bitch because of people like you. Self-hating gay men who get mad at people like me because I accept who I am."

He was so wrong. But how could I convince him? I stood and faced him. "Has it ever occurred to you that I'm happy with who I am? There is no typical gay man and just because I don't act like you, doesn't mean I hate myself. That's crazy. I'm sorry people have disappointed you, but I think you're directing your anger in the wrong direction."

Gabriel crossed his arms so hard he huffed. He glared at the street, where luxury cars and beautiful people were streaming past. "Those men think because they have a little money and power, that they can treat me just like yesterday's garbage. Men like that make me sicker than people like you, Bentley."

I stiffened. This guy was really whack. Maybe he was capable of doing something crazy regarding Seth and whoever lied to him after the party. "Gabriel, what do you mean, people like me?"

He looked me up and down. "Not only are you one of those self-hating gay men who most likely was born with a silver spoon in your mouth, but you think you're better than anyone."

I shook my head. I wanted to just walk away, but I was too worried that Gabriel could become a problem with Sterling and Seth. And I didn't need anything interfering with the mess I was already trying to clean up with Jah.

"Wrong again, Gabriel. But I want to help you. Do you want me to see if I can get you some more modeling jobs?"

He looked at me like I was stupid. "Like the party or legit stuff?"

"The party was a legit job."

"Keep telling yourself that."

I looked at my watch and told Gabriel to reconsider my offer and give me a call when he did.

I was about to step away when he asked, "What are you going to do when they ruin your little friend?"

"What are you talking about?"

He shook his head. " 'Cause you know it's going to happen. Men like Seth Sinclair have young bois like that for breakfast. So if you really are a friend, you'd warn him. But you only see that kid as a piece of meat. You modeling people are the new, modern-day pimps."

My fingers balled into a fist, crushing my coffee cup. I threw it in a nearby garbage can and started walking toward my office.

Behind me, Gabriel yelled, "You haven't heard the last of me, Bentley Dean!"

TWENTY-EIGHT

Jah and I were in my kitchen, opening a just-delivered box of pizza, when his face lit up with excitement.

"B, I got some news for you, and I hope you're happy for me," Jah said as he pulled a piece of pizza from the box. I just looked at him as he picked the tiny mushrooms from the cheese. I always forgot that he didn't share my taste for mushrooms.

"Jah, why do I think this has something to do with Seth Sinclair?"

He was about to bite into the slice when he smiled. "It does."

"I'm listening."

He put the pizza down. "I'm moving to Hollywood!" he announced. "Seth has gotten me a condo. He said he wants to be able to see me whenever he wants."

I showed no reaction. "He's been doing that since he met you, Jah. What about school?"

Jah shrugged. "I'll pick that up next year. Seth said I can go wherever I want, although he said I should consider Pepperdine. Have you ever heard of that school?" He picked up the slice and took a big bite, making a playful face and saying, "Mmm-mmm."

But for me, here he was again, saying something over a meal to ruin my appetite. "Yes, Pepperdine is a very good school, Jah, but so is Florida International."

Jah wiped his mouth. At least the whites of his eyes were white today. "I know, but I need to just make sure I don't have to spend a lot of time studying because I think Seth is going to be spending a lot of time with me."

Since prior conversations of me blowing up and lecturing Jah about his relationship with Seth hadn't worked, today I was taking a different approach. Maybe I would let Father Time do the job for me, and let familiarity breed the contempt that made it famous. All that time together, surely Seth and Jah would grow tired of each other, right? Then Jah would come to his senses and return to Florida.

I casually bit into my pizza and shrugged just like he'd done. "Jah, if this is what you want, then I'm happy for you."

His eyes grew big with surprise. "B, do

you mean that?"

"I mean it, Jah."

Jah jumped from his seat, came around the table, and hugged me. "Thank you, B," he whispered.

I looked into his eyes and said, "If this really is going to make you happy, then I say do it. Doesn't mean I won't miss you."

Happiness glowed on his face. "Oh, B, I'll miss you, too, but Seth said I'll be getting an allowance and I'm sure I can use some of it for tickets back here. And I can fly you to California when you have some free time. I'll finally be able to pay you back some of the money you've loaned me."

I was still blown away at how Jah seemed to be fitting into a perfectly orchestrated plan where every detail was covered. I shook my head.

"Jah, I gave you the money because you needed it. Don't worry about paying me back." He sat back down and we both ate for a minute. "If you feel compelled to do something, then find some young kid like yourself that needs help and give it to them. I'm sure you'll find a lot of them in Hollywood."

Jah smiled. "Good idea, B! Why didn't I think of that?"

I poured us both some root beer and

asked, "When are you moving? What about your car?"

"Seth said we could ship the car or he'd buy me another one when I get there."

I laughed at the idea of having so much bank that he could just buy another Porsche on a whim and forget about the one here in Florida. My voice was dry and flat when I said, "It must be nice to have that kind of money."

"Yeah, right," Jah said, gulping down soda. "But I remember what you told me, that Seth's money isn't mine. I guess maybe God is finally making up for all the shit I took as a child in foster care."

I shook my head. "I don't think God operates like that, Jah."

That dreamy look swept over Jah's face. "I know, but it's kind of amazing what has happened to my life since I met Seth. I really should be thanking you."

My stomach cramped. He had no clue how guilty I felt about this, or how much I'd been worrying about the downside of this fairy tale. "Don't give me credit for that, Jah. I'd really like to see you with someone your own age."

He made an annoyed sound. "Guys my age are so immature. I don't know how I could ever consider them as partners."

I just shook my head and forced a smile.

"What's up with the fake smile, B?"

"As you always say, Jah, whatever." My thoughts fast-forwarded to Jah living in California. Then I'd rarely see him and have no influence on what he was doing.

"B, you want the last piece of pizza?"

"I'm cool."

"Then I'll eat it," he said, holding it in front of his mouth. "Seth wants me to gain about five pounds. I think he likes bois with big asses."

I sipped my soda. "Well, we both know whatever Seth wants, Seth gets."

"But that only applies to me."

"And his wife," I corrected, casting him a hard look.

"B," Jah whined, "are you saying that to be mean?"

"No, Jah, but you can't forget she's there."

He shrugged and chewed. "I don't care about her."

I raised my eyebrows. "What about the kids?"

"I'm getting ready to go."

I reached across the table and held his hand down so he couldn't get up. "Jah, it might feel like a fantasy with Seth. But there's reality to think about, too. And it won't go away just because you don't want to talk about this. You can't just run away from your problems."

Jah's eyes filled with anger and hurt as he stared at me over our last supper together in Florida. "They aren't my problem!" he snapped. "I'm very happy right now and no one is going to spoil that. Not even you, B."

Jah stood up and grabbed his keys from the counter without even a good-bye.

TWENTY-NINE

I started my morning by calling Wilson to tell him that Jah wouldn't be flying to Chicago and to thank him for his help. When he picked up the phone, I detected sadness in his voice.

"Is everything okay, Wilson?"

He sighed and he sounded like he'd been crying. "Not really, Bentley. I just got some really bad news." He exhaled loudly, as if he was trying to compose himself. "But I appreciate you calling and giving me an update. You don't have to thank me for offering to help."

I wished I could give him a hug. "Is there anything I can do?"

"Just pray for my friend's family."

"What friend?"

Wilson blew his nose. "Remember the one I told you about who was messing around with somebody real famous? And that he got beat up really bad and was in a coma?"

I grimaced, leaning back in my chair. That recent conversation with Gabriel, and of course Jah's situation, came to mind. Everything was a dream when they were doing what the powerful man wanted. But what happened when the boi or fem got sassy? Angry? Defiant?

Could Wilson's friend have been messing with someone as rich as Seth?

"Yeah, I remember that," I said. "Has there been any change?"

Wilson paused for a long moment, then he told me that his friend had died late last night.

The words echoed in my head. All I could think about was Jah, taking up residence in the shark's luxurious nest on the other side of the country, far away from me. I had to find out if Wilson's friend had any connection to the PGC or Seth. If so, this would, unfortunately, confirm my fears about just how viciously they tossed out their used bois like spoiled milk. If not, then I could breathe easy for a minute. Maybe.

"Oh, Wilson, I'm sorry to hear that. Is there anything I can do?"

Wilson sighed. "We might be setting up a fund at Freedom Bank to help with funeral expenses because I know his family doesn't have a lot of money and they were not that supportive of his life. I'm sure we can use any money you want to donate."

I logged on to my computer. "Just e-mail the address when it's set up and I'll do that. Are the police treating this as a hate crime?"

I almost shivered as those words passed over my lips. Gay bashing was one of the things that terrified me most after hearing reports in college of a gang of straight guys who'd roam the streets looking for a lone gay guy to beat up.

Wilson sighed. "I don't know if it can be a hate crime if other gay men did this to him."

That set off an alarm inside me. "What makes you think gay men did this?"

Wilson's cynical laugh didn't make me feel any better. "In Chicago, there's a gang of gay thugs, if you can believe that. I've heard that sometimes ex-lovers or people trying to get back at some of the kids have been paying these bullies to rough people up. I can't prove it, but it's really what I think."

I had to ask him and find out if Seth Sinclair could be behind that. "Wilson, do you have any idea who might be giving the orders to the gang?"

Wilson sniffled. "My friend was too afraid to tell me, even from the beginning. He just said the guy was one of the most famous people on the planet. They'd go on these weekend getaways in fancy hotels. And all of a sudden my friend showed up with a Porsche."

My heart pounded. This was sounding way too close for comfort. "Wilson, what happened to end the relationship?"

He was quiet.

"Wilson?"

Wilson cleared his throat. "My friend was too scared to tell me. He just said when he refused to do certain things, he got the boot. Literally."

I had to breathe deeply to stop myself from applying all this stuff to Jah's situation. So far, it was smooth sailing. Jah said he was happy, and I'd have to just stay calm with that thought.

"Wilson, have you told anyone about this?"

He sounded defeated as he said, "No one will listen to me."

I spoke with authority. "I think you should talk to the police. Somebody in Chicago has got to know who these people are."

He sighed. "I'll think about it. Thanks for being so supportive, Bentley. I hope we get the chance to see each other real soon."

Now I wished more than ever that I could give him a hug. "Yeah, Wilson, me, too. Now

you take care and stay strong. I'll check on
you in a couple of days. Call me if you need
me."

"I will. Take care."

"Bye, Wilson."

I hung up the phone and shook my head
as I muttered, "Gay thugs. Yikes."

Thirty

My session with Dr. Fenton couldn't have come at a better time, because after talking with Wilson, my head was a horror strip of worries about Jah. He'd been gone a week, and I was spending too much energy on trying to convince myself that he was okay.

"Bentley," Dr. Fenton said with worry in her eyes, "you look like you haven't slept all month."

The relief of being in her office made me slump into the couch and grasp the leopard print pillows. I loved that this was the one place where I could just unload, no matter how crazy it sounded.

"Dr. Fenton, every time I lay down at night, all I can think about is Jah's fantasy turning into a nightmare," I said. "Wilson's dead friend in Chicago, the gay bashers, Gabriel's warning and threat —"

"Wait, stop, Bentley," she said. "Explain, please."

I told her about Wilson's dead friend, the gay thugs, Gabriel's angry threat about exposing Seth, and his warning about how Jah would get used, abused, and tossed out.

"Let's step back and separate the reality of all this," Dr. Fenton said. "It's all very dramatic and scary. But how much of it is truth?"

I almost smiled. Dr. Fenton was about to deflate my fears.

"Bentley, who's to say that this relationship for Jah couldn't become a long-term affair where he truly does get the love and care that he's wanted all his life?"

I nodded. "That is a possibility, but —"

"But what proof do you have that could apply other people's problems to your friend's arrangement?" she asked.

I hated that it seemed like I was sounding paranoid. But I loved that she was making me look at the facts.

"None," I said, "but my parents always said, if something sounds too good to be true, then it is. And nothing is free."

Dr. Fenton nodded. "Very wise. However, we could say that Jah is already facing a downside of it, and perhaps that's the extent of it."

I didn't understand, and my face let her know that.

"Look, this guy is married with a family, and has a reputation to uphold for the whole world as a straight man, right?"

I nodded.

"So the downside for Jah is that the most exciting thing that's ever happened to him is completely secret. When you're in love, don't you want to stand on a mountain and shout it to the world?" She laughed softly. "Metaphorically, anyway."

I couldn't help but smile. What if that were the extent of it?

"Bentley, do you think as a straight woman, I'm being naïve?"

Damn, she burst my bubble of relief and hope.

"Yes," I said without hesitation. "I just have this fear of Jah throwing a tantrum if things don't play out like he wants. Whether it's freaky sex or drugs or who knows what. And what does Daddy do when his boi throws a tantrum?"

"He gives him a spanking," Dr. Fenton said.

All my fears flooded back.

"I think this is far more complex, Bentley, than you realize," Dr. Fenton said. "You're so upset by what Gabriel said at Starbucks. Why?"

"He was basically calling me a snob."

"Are you?"

"No."

She raised her eyebrows in a way that questioned my honesty. "Are you sure? You did grow up in a privileged background."

I was not about to let her lay a guilt trip on me for how I was raised. "That doesn't make you a snob!" I said too loudly. "Our parents were always reminding us a lot of people were less fortunate and a lot would be expected from us. We always took old toys and clothes to poor neighborhoods in Detroit. In college, I always tutored kids that were less privileged. I know how lucky I was to have the childhood I enjoyed."

She nodded. "But I think Gabriel touched a nerve in terms of sexual politics."

I exhaled, feeling annoyed. "What does *that* mean?"

She took off her half-glasses and used them to pull her hair from her face. "I don't think he doesn't like you because he sees you as a snob as much as identifying with you as a gay man."

"I'm not in the closet," I said, "but I'm not leading the parade, either."

"How do you feel about feminine gay men?"

"What do you mean?"

"Do you have any feminine gay friends?"

I looked at her like I still didn't get it. What did this have to do with Jah or Gabriel or me? "If you're talking tops and bottoms, then I have friends from both groups."

She gave me a super-analytical look. "But a bottom, from my understanding, can sometimes be very masculine as well. What do you consider yourself?"

I sighed, not feeling like this was getting anywhere. "I don't like labels, but I would most likely say 'versatile.' 'Bisexual' in the gay world."

She looked at me as if I'd said the magic word. "Okay. I think Gabriel was pointing out that as a feminine gay man, he's most likely going to face double discrimination. First from society as a whole, then within the gay community."

I snapped, "He could bring it on himself when he acts like that. I know he's just acting out."

"Aha," Dr. Fenton said. "But maybe he's being himself. I think his anger comes from the fact that when people meet you, they don't know you're gay unless you tell them. You can pass in and out of the straight world without much problem."

I crossed my arms over my chest. "That's not my fault. I didn't make up the rules."

"That's a cop-out, Bentley."

The lightbulb lit up in my head. "You know, I never really thought of it that way. I just figured people like Gabriel were looking for attention."

Her voice had a hard edge when she said, "Attention that could bring them harm."

I felt confused. "Harm?"

"From gay bashers," she said. "Studies show that a danger or beating because of sexual orientation is more likely if there are clear signs that a man or a woman is obviously gay."

My eyes widened as I connected the dots. "Whoa, I never thought about that."

Dr. Fenton leaned forward. "Bentley, why do you think you've always been involved with guys who are hypermasculine?"

I thought about my men. "Like —"

"Warren?"

"That's just my type," I declared. "Sometimes I see a softer side of Warren, but not often."

"Why is that?"

Wherever this was going, I felt it was unnecessary. We needed to get back to the things I wanted to talk about. "I don't know, Dr. Fenton. But I'm not a snob! And if I am, I guess I did pick up some of those clues that people were different from my father."

338

Her eyes widened as if she were shocked to hear this true confession from me. "So we should blame *him?*"

"That's not what I'm saying." Suddenly an image of my father and me when I was a little boy clouded my thoughts. It was a happy memory.

"What is that smile about, Bentley?" Dr. Fenton asked.

"When I was a little boy, sometimes on Saturdays I would go with my dad as he tried to make payment plans with his customers who were behind on their car notes. He would do everything he could to prevent sending the repo man to get one of his cars. Most of the time people had good excuses for not being able to make a car note and I saw the kindness in my father that I didn't always see when he dealt with business matters."

Dr. Fenton nodded. "You sound happy recalling that."

I nodded. "Sometimes after we'd make the rounds, my father and I would go to have a cheeseburger, fries, Coke, or sometimes a milk shake, at White Castle."

I leaned forward playfully and almost whispered, "Now this was our little secret, because both my mother and sister thought restaurants like White Castle and Church's

339

Chicken were set up for poor people. Not only were they cheap, but they served food that we knew wasn't good for you. I mean, we had a family cook and sometimes my mother would get on her for frying chicken, even though everyone in the family loved it."

Dr. Fenton smiled. "So this was a little secret between you and your father?"

My throat burned with sadness. "Yes, and I miss those times more than I care to admit."

"You could call him."

"He wouldn't answer," I said. "And if he did, he'd hang up when he realized it was me."

"Why is that?"

"Because my father is ashamed of who I've become."

She sounded shocked. "Who you've *become?* I thought you felt you were always gay."

"Looking back, I most likely was, but not acting on it kept me safe." I sank deeper into the couch, remembering the feeling as a kid of curling up on my parents' laps and feeling safe and loved. Oh, what I would do right now to feel that kind of love and comfort. Damn. That was probably the feeling that Jah got from Seth. The feeling that every human being ached for, and tried to get by any means necessary. The feeling that I got from Warren, when the mood was right.

Dr. Fenton asked, "Do you think your father loves you even though he might not really understand your life now?"

"It's black and white with my father. Either you're with him or you're against him. He's sees my sexual orientation as being against him."

Her voice hardened. "You didn't answer my question, Bentley. Do you think your father loves you?"

I thought about Dr. Fenton's question for a few moments. "I don't know, Dr. Fenton. You would have to ask him that."

After several attempts, I finally reached Jah on his cell. He quickly explained that Seth had gotten him a new cell phone with a Beverly Hills area code and that was the one he'd been using. When I asked him why he hadn't sent me the number, Jah said he'd texted it to me, which I didn't believe for one second.

"B, I'm sorry we haven't talked," he said, really fast with excitement. "I've been so busy trying to find my way around Los Angeles. It's so big, but I love it out here.

There's the weather and, of course, I see Seth an awful lot."

He sounded great; I felt relieved. Maybe Dr. Fenton was right. Maybe the only price that Jah had to pay was the secrecy of the relationship. At least that's what I told myself to keep this feeling of relief that he was safe and happy.

"That's good, Jah," I said, sitting at my desk, where I'd been unable to concentrate on anything but reaching Jah. A stack of bills was calling my name to the right, a long list of e-mails was beckoning on the computer screen, and I needed to talk to Mitch about the Caribbean shoot because he'd left a message saying he had more details and definitely needed my models. "Jah, I was just a little worried about you."

"Oh, don't be, I'm fine," he said. "You should see my condo, B. It's awesome! I never thought I'd live in a place like this. I have a doorman and we have a lady during the day and an older man in the evening who'll run errands for us."

"A concierge?"

Jah giggled. "Yeah, I think that's what Seth calls him. I have a terrace and I can see all of West Hollywood from my bedroom. I don't have to clean or do anything. It's just wonderful. All Seth wants me to do is to spend two hours a day in the gym and get a facial at least once a week."

"You're young, Jah. Your skin will be fine." My voice sounded flat and sarcastic because I was lost in the idea of Jah's luxury lifestyle. That sounded like a dream right now, with all this work in front of me. What if all I had to do all day was go to the gym, get a facial, and wait in my condo for my man to come over and make love to me? I couldn't even imagine.

Jah's voice snapped me back to attention. "I'm thinking about checking out some modeling agencies out here. Do you know anyone I can talk to?"

I logged on to my online database. "Let me check. I'm surprised Seth will let you do that."

Jah said, "I haven't mentioned it to him."

"Are you going to?"

"Sure," Jah said. "We don't keep anything from each other."

I rolled my eyes, thinking about Mrs. Sinclair, the children, and the public image that was so different than the secret side that Jah was experiencing. Suddenly now that I knew Jah was safe and being treated like a prince, I'd heard enough.

"Okay, Jah, now that I got your new number, I know where to find you. Take care of yourself and don't forget if you need me, I'm only a phone call away."

Jah sounded happier than ever when he said, "I know that, B, and I appreciate that. I love you, Bentley."

"And I love you, Jah. Take care of yourself."

THIRTY-ONE

Instead of lunch, I went to the gym and pushed through a ninety-minute workout. On the way back to the office, I picked up a protein shake and some fruit from the bustling market around the corner. When I got back to Picture Perfect, Laura greeted me in the reception area with one of those black-and-white-striped boards that film-makers use to mark the start of each scene.

She made the top slam down as I entered and said, "Act one, scene one, Alex returns from Hollywood."

I smiled. "She must have some good news with all this."

Laura showed me the slate. "I've always wanted one of these. Next time someone goes on my nerves, I'm gonna hold it up and say, 'Cut!' "

I laughed, hurrying into my office to drop off my healthy lunch. Then I dashed into Alex's office, where she was typing furiously

345

at her computer.

"How was the trip?"

She shot up from her desk, beaming and smiling. Wearing a sleek, beige pencil skirt and tailored cream blouse with man-killer pumps, she hugged me.

"You know," she said, "if you'd asked me about the trip thirty minutes ago, I would have said it was just okay. But thanks to a phone call I just received, I have to upgrade it to an awesome trip!" I had only seen Alex look so excited when she scored big modeling jobs, so that had to be great news.

"What happened?" I asked. "Who called?"

I sat down as Alex explained that her good fortune started the first day of her trip, during lunch at a beautiful restaurant on the beach in Santa Monica. Alex took the chair beside me, in front of her desk, saying that she was with her friend from school and her catalogue modeling days.

"Well," Alex said, "she brought one of her friends with her. Her name was Katie Parker and it turns out that she is the personal assistant to Trinity Sinclair, Seth Sinclair's baby sister, who works for him running one of his production companies."

I secretly tripped on the idea that I had just spoken with Jah about Seth's very personal life, and now Mr. Sinclair's professional life was crossing paths with our agency.

"Katie and I hit it off," Alex exclaimed, "and I just mentioned what a big fan I was of Seth and how I was trying to get a meeting with him to see if we could send him candidates for small roles and walk-ons in his films."

I listened, smiling, loving her excitement. Was this fate? Coincidence? "Wow," I said, "what are the chances of that happening?"

Alexandria smiled. "Thanks to my phone call, very good. Katie calls me today to say, not only are we getting business, but that Seth himself wants to meet with me personally."

That could mean huge money for the agency, but I was just not impressed with that man's character. But I couldn't put my finger on exactly why, other than the fact that he was living a lie, and helping all those men in the PGC live out their lies, too.

"That's great," I said to Alexandria. "When is this going to happen?"

She exhaled. "It sounds like pretty soon and I think you should go with me."

I shook my head. "You think so? Can we afford two tickets and hotels for another trip? Besides, who would run the office?"

She leaned forward and grasped my

hands. "Bentley! This is Seth Sinclair! It could be huge! The answer to our prayers. Even in this tough economy, his movies still do big box office."

I squeezed her hands, not wanting to burst her bubble on this career coup. "I know, Alex, and I would definitely welcome the business. But this is your contact. Maybe you should involve me only if he insists. I'm sure Seth Sinclair is not going to do business with just anybody and will most likely check us out."

"Yeah, you're right," she said with a bit of disappointment.

"Alex, I'm proud of you, girl!" I exclaimed, smiling. "Sounds like you're taking us to the big time!"

She smiled, squeezing my hands. "Thanks, Bentley. I always knew we'd get our lucky break. So how's everything else? Any luck in finding new clients or models?"

I told her I had a really great-looking kid from Florida International that I was talking to. He was an athlete, so I told her we had to make sure we weren't breaking any rules. Then I told Alex that I had some photos of a fitness instructor who wanted to model.

"She's very pretty," I said, "reminds you of Tom Joyner's wife, Donna, and she is

348

great in person." Then I reported that I planned to check out Model Mania later this afternoon to see if any new hopefuls had posted pictures there.

Alex stood up, heading back to her computer. "I'm almost finished with putting our Facebook listing up. I think that will help a lot, especially with college kids."

I chuckled. "High school, as well as I can understand. I can't believe our old asses are going to be on Facebook."

She cast a playful glance across her desk. "Speak for your own old ass because I'm not old, don't feel old, and will never use that word to describe myself."

I stood, thinking about the pile of work on my desk. "You know what I mean, Alexandria. Do you ever miss being on the other side of this business?"

"Ha!" She laughed. "If I never have to go on another fitting or a go-see it will be too soon. Does that answer your question?"

I glanced down at myself, feeling trim and firm under my navy blue slacks and mock neck shirt with a belt and loafers. "I hear you. I just got back from an intense workout because I wanted to do it, not because I had to."

Alex shot an approving look at my physique, then looked down at herself, saying

349

she'd be heading to the gym after work.

"Oh, yeah," she said, "I didn't see it, but one of my friends told me Miss Georgia in Miss America this year is a very pretty African American girl who is really fit and toned. I'm going to watch clips from the pageant tonight and see what I think. If she's not represented, then maybe we can get her."

I hadn't heard anything about that. "Did she win?"

"No. She was first runner-up. America has made strides, but ain't no way they're going to have a black president *and* Miss America," Alex said with a hearty laugh.

It felt good to laugh with her. "Yeah, I bet white folks are saying, 'Hey, America, let's not get it twisted.'"

"Or as my mother would say, 'Ain't that the truth, Ruth!'"

Even though Alex had just told me about a deal with Seth that could bring huge money to the agency, I was still brainstorming other ways to get paid. Did I not believe her connection with the Sinclairs would result in a deal? I headed toward the door, not sure how I felt.

"Alex, do you think we should do another calendar audition?" This was one of our most successful recruiting tools. It seemed that everyone in Miami thought they had a good enough body to pose in swimwear on the beach for the camera.

"Hmm," Alex said over the clicking sound of her fingers on the keyboard. "What photographer could we use and who might do it for free?"

"I'll look through my contacts." I stepped into the hallway.

"Uh, Bentley?" Alex called in a way that sounded like she was about to tell me something awkward, like my fly was down or I had toilet paper stuck to the bottom of my shoe. I turned around, scanning her face for clues.

"I don't know if I should say anything, but —"

I cast a playfully disgusted look at her. "Well, now that you've said something, spill it."

"It's about Kim," she said.

I shrugged. "Kim Boston? Okay, and . . . ? I hope she finds her Prince Charming and lives happily ever after."

Alex stood and perched on the edge of the desk, crossing her arms. "When I was in California, my college friend had the 411 on your girl."

I laughed. "She's not my girl."

"Well, according to gossip, she's found her

351

Prince Charming all right," Alex said with a sly tone. "And he ain't who you'd think. *At all.*"

"Let's see, Detroit, Detroit, who would she go after in the Motor City? Who could possibly fill my shoes?"

Alex smiled. "Hint, hint. It's someone who would remind her of you."

I looked at her blankly. "Just call me clueless."

"Here are some clues," Alex said. "He's successful, prominent, handsome."

Just for the fun of it, I thought of Warren, who was way too much of a player to lock down with one woman. Even though he said he wanted to get married and have kids someday. Plus, he wouldn't do that to me.

"Who's that gorgeous sports reporter?" I pretended. "You know, he used to play football, now he's a commentator for one of the local TV stations?"

"Quit playin'," Alex said. "How am I supposed to know who's on TV in Detroit?"

"Then it's not him," I said. "Okay, who?"

She shook her head. "Nah! This one definitely classifies as TMI. Too much damn information." She giggled nervously with an expression like she was hiding a juicy secret. "And my name is not Snitch."

"No, not Snitch. Your name is Tease!"

We shared a laugh. As I headed into the hallway, I thought about how I really didn't care about Kim's love life, except that I hoped she was happy and that she'd gotten over the trauma that I'd inflicted on her by being honest.

But who could be so big and bad that it had Alex looking so mischievous? I stopped in my tracks, turned around, and went back to her office.

"Who is it?" I demanded, sticking my head in the door.

Alex, back to work at her computer, shook her head.

"Nope!" she said. "You'll have to play detective on your own. One more clue. They have a common bond through you."

That made me even more confused.

"Bentley, let's just say she's rebounded very nicely from you."

"Good for Kim. She deserves somebody nice."

Alex exhaled and looked at me more seriously. "Okay, I hear you. I didn't get all the details because you know me and I don't like to gossip, but I understand her new beau is very wealthy."

"Hey, thanks for sharing. Maybe if things really get bad I can hit Kim up for a loan," I said with a sneaky grin.

"I don't think we should count on that, Bentley. Let's hope Seth Sinclair comes through."

"You're probably right, Alexandria."

I walked away, my brain spinning with clues about who could possibly be *all that* for Kim. I wondered if it was anybody I knew.

THIRTY-TWO

It had been five days since I'd heard from Jah and I was a bit concerned. I was coming out of the gym looking for Jah's new cell phone number when my cell phone vibrated.

"Hello?" I answered without looking at the screen.

"B," Jah said with a frantic edge in his voice. "I need to talk with you. I'm scared." His voice was rushed and I could tell something was wrong.

My heart raced. I prayed that he was not about to confirm my fears about Seth.

Instead of opening my car door, I leaned against it so I could find out what was wrong with Jah. I pressed my finger to my other ear to block out a police car siren, a honking cab, and the bass beat from a car full of teenagers rolling past.

"Jah, I'm here. What's wrong?"

"If you love someone," Jah asked, "are you

supposed to do whatever they ask you to do?"

"No, Jah. Why would you ask me that? You don't just do what someone asks you in a relationship unless it's something you want to do. Tell me what happened."

Jah exhaled. His voice sounded shaky. "Right after we talked the last time, I had a visitor."

"Who?"

"It was that Sterling guy we met at the party. He told me Seth had sent him over to make sure that I was okay and see if I needed anything. I didn't think anything about it because I knew he works for Seth and so I let him in."

"Okay," I said. "And?"

"When I told him I was doing fine, he started making comments about my body and how good I looked. I thought he was just being nice. But then he tried to kiss me. When I stopped him, he got crazy and started asking me, 'Who do you think you are?' Then he shouted, 'All of Seth's boyfriends take care of me, too! Especially when Seth is busy working on some of his deals or movies.' "

I forced myself not to think about all the bad outcomes that could have resulted from that scene. "Jah, what did you do?"

Jah huffed as if it were obvious. "I told him I wasn't that kind of guy and that I was only sleeping with Seth."

I nodded with relief. "Good, that's what you should have told him. Did you tell Seth?"

Jah groaned with disappointment. "I did, and that's when the problems started."

Police sirens roared past me, along with a bus that needed a new muffler. I got in my car to escape all the noise. "What do you mean?"

"I called Seth and it took him almost two days to call me back. When I told him about Sterling, he told me it was no big deal. He said I shouldn't be so uptight."

I hoped this was enough to convince Jah to get on the next plane home to Miami.

"Don't let those people use you, Jah. We both know you're not that kind of person. You might care about Seth, but don't let him talk you into anything you don't want to do."

I closed my eyes, hoping that Jah would see past all the luxury and realize this whole setup had nothing to do with love.

"B, I told Seth I wasn't that kind of person and I haven't heard from him since." Jah sounded shocked and frantic. I couldn't help thinking about Wilson's friend in

Chicago who'd been beaten up and died when things went wrong with his powerful gay lover. I prayed that Jah would stay safe and come home.

"Then this morning," Jah said, "some guy I've never met showed up at my condo, basically asking me for the same thing that Sterling guy wanted. He told me that he'd been sent by Seth and that I was supposed to be nice to him."

I stiffened as anger pumped through my whole body. "You're kidding, right?"

"No, B, I wish I was. Now I can't get in contact with Seth. What do you think I should do?"

I forced myself to sound calm. "Jah, you need to get on a plane and bring yourself back to Miami. Now. I don't like how this sounds."

I hated the whiny sound in Jah's voice as he said, "I want to hear from Seth first. Maybe both of these guys are lying and just trying to get rid of me."

I shook my head, wishing I could shake some sense into that boi. "But you said Seth told you to stop being so uptight. He could be behind it, Jah."

"He loves me and wouldn't do that to me."

"Jah, get on a plane and come back

home!" The fantasy was over and we needed to let the curtain fall before somebody else wrote a tragic final scene.

Jah whined again, "I don't have an apartment anymore."

"You can stay here until we find you another one."

"I need to see Seth and find out what's going on."

"Jah!" I almost shouted. "Why are you putting yourself through this?"

"Because I wanted to be loved, B." The sadness and desperation in his voice gave me goose bumps.

"You *are* loved, Jah. More than you know. I love you."

"I know," he sighed, "but I'm talking about a different kind of love. You're like a big brother to me."

"Jah, you said you were scared and I think you have reason to be. Come home, Jah."

"Oh, wait a minute!" He sounded excited. "This is Seth calling me. I'll call you back, B."

"Jah!"

No Jah. Just the dial tone.

I waited about an hour before trying to call Jah back, but I didn't get an answer. I thought maybe if I went and got something to eat, the meal might take my mind off Jah. I grabbed a light jacket and as soon as I opened my door, I had a guest standing there. For a second I didn't recognize him, but the afternoon in my office on the desk came back into my memory quickly.

As I stared at his gorgeous face and his huge, athletic body, I flashed back to the erotic encounter we'd shared a few months ago. It was Daniel. He was the model who had no condoms but made me cum like a teenager from just humpin' on my lap.

"Daniel," I said with surprise and delight, "what are you doing here?"

He smiled. "You remember my name. That's a good sign. What's up?"

"I was getting ready to grab a quick bite. I wasn't expecting a guest."

He devoured me with his eyes as he said, "I started to call, but I thought a surprise might be better. Can I come in?"

"Sure, I'm sorry."

Daniel walked in, looking very dapper in all white. I led him to the living room and offered him a seat. He plopped down on the sofa like he'd been to my house before.

I sat down on the couch, glad that Daniel was distracting me from my worries about Jah. "So why haven't I heard from you before this evening?"

Daniel looked down at the glossy magazines on my coffee table as he said, "I had some out-of-town business and I didn't have your number in my cell phone. I'd got a call the day I met you and left your info next to my bed."

I smiled as he looked back up at me. With a seductive voice, I said, "Sounds like a good place for it. Is everything okay?"

"What do you mean?"

"With your out-of-town business."

Daniel flipped through a magazine. "Yeah, I had to take care of something in Chicago." Then he made eye contact and asked, "How's the modeling business?"

I noticed how large and beautiful his hands were. "Things are still slow. The industry needs a little stimulus like everybody else."

He pressed his hand to his flat stomach and asked, "So where were you going to get something to eat?"

I told him I had decided to get in the car and just drive until something caught my eye.

"Cool," he said. "Looks like I came at the right time."

Just as I was getting ready to see if Daniel wanted to join me for dinner, my cell phone rang and Warren's name flashed across my screen.

"I need to take this," I said as I stood and walked near the wall unit. I heard Daniel tell me to take my time. I nodded at him and watched him pick up one of my photographic art books from the coffee table.

"Hey, Warren, what's up, guy?"

"Just thinking about you and thought I'd give you a call."

"That's cool. Where you hanging these days?" For a split second I thought about taking the call in another room. After all, Daniel was a stranger, even though we'd simulated the wild thing on my desk.

"Right now I'm out in California on business."

His boyfriend at the party appeared in my mind. I'm sure I made a snarling face. "Is that business in the form of your actor friend?"

"I might see him while I'm here, but I came out here for a couple of meetings with agents."

"How's that going?" Daniel had now closed the book.

"It's cool. I'm thinking about making the move out here."

Why was I not surprised? Warren was king of mystery, a moving target. "So it looks like I'm going to lose out again."

"Don't talk like that, boo. Besides, if you really want me, you could always move out here."

"My business is here, Warren." My inner voice was whispering that I shouldn't have this conversation in front of Daniel, but the rest of my brain was telling me I was being overly cautious because my imagination was running wild about Jah's safety.

"Nothing is final, Bent."

"Cool," I said, knowing that this conversation would go nowhere except in frustrating circles. "Hey, can I ask you something?"

"Sure, boo boo."

Daniel was perusing one of Miami's glossy lifestyle magazines. I turned my back to him and lowered my voice: "Do you think you'll see Seth or any PGC members?"

Warren answered, "I don't know, why?"

"I'm a little worried about my young friend that I was telling you about. He moved out there and I want to see if you can find out if he's all right."

Warren sounded eager to help. "What's his name again?"

"Everybody just calls him Jah."

"Let me see what I can find out."

"Thanks, Warren, I would appreciate that. Hey, a friend dropped by, so I'm being a little rude right now. Can I give you a call a little later?"

"Yeah, Bent, that's what's up. Hopefully when I come to see you, that friend will be gone."

"I'll make sure, Warren. You stay out of trouble."

"I'll try, but I can't make any promises. Take it slow, boo."

"Bye."

I hung up and walked back to the sofa near Daniel. "Sorry about that."

He flashed that gorgeous smile. "Hey, Bentley, I didn't mean to eavesdrop, but did I hear you say 'Seth' and 'PGC' in the same sentence?"

I eyed Daniel with suspicion and nodded. Damn, that was not the smartest move to have that conversation in front of this guy I didn't know.

"I thought so," Daniel said. "Is that who you were booking for when I came to see you?"

I warned Daniel that I didn't know him very well and even if I did, I wouldn't discuss my client roster with him unless I was sending him out on a go-see or a booking.

"I understand," he said, "but when you told me about the job, I thought immediately that it had to do with Seth Sinclair and his band of merry men."

I tried to keep a cool face, showing no surprise. "So you know Seth?"

"Yeah, and I don't mind telling you —"

I felt nervous for a split second as a disturbed expression flashed across Daniel's face.

"— meeting him turned out to be one of the worst moments of my life," Daniel said. "That guy gives the devil suggestions."

"That bad?"

"That bad."

Daniel said he'd met Seth five years ago at a party where he was booked to just go and be a party guest. Since he was one of the younger guys there, he said he was picked to keep the king company that evening.

"Next thing I know," Daniel said, "I'm being showered with expensive gifts and more money that I ever thought I'd make at such a young age."

I asked if Seth moved him to California.

Daniel shifted on the couch. "No, he kept me here, but I made several trips to the West Coast before it started getting crazy."

I drew my brows together and asked with an urgent tone, "What do you mean, crazy?"

"First of all, Seth Sinclair and his cohorts

think they can buy any man or boi they choose. And when they tire of them, which is quick, they pass them around just like an old pair of pants they've outgrown. It took me almost two years to get away from him and those horny old men."

I closed my eyes, praying that Jah would get the hell out of there. I thought about getting on a plane and going out there myself to bring him home to the safety and sanity of Miami.

"Daniel, are you telling me the truth? And why didn't you tell me when I told you about the job?"

He shrugged. "It wasn't my business. I knew if it was Seth, then he was paying you a lot of money to find bois for him."

"I was finding models for his representative," I said, defending myself. I had a sudden feeling that I'd shared too much information with Daniel. What if he was actually sent here to fish for information from *me?*

Daniel asked who Seth had picked at the party. "Let me guess. Someone young, good-looking with a nice ass and pretty big package. If this guy is a friend or one of your top models you should warn him before he gets caught up in that crazy shit." Daniel buried his face in his hands for a moment. "Sometimes I wake up in a cold sweat thinking about some of the stuff that man had me do."

My head was spinning with bad scenarios involving Jah and Seth. Now I was really worried about Jah, and curious at the same time, but I didn't want to pry too much. I got the gist of what Seth Sinclair was up to. Daniel just confirmed my thoughts. I asked Daniel how he got away.

"I had to meet with several attorneys and sign lots of papers saying I would never talk about this crap."

I gave him a puzzled look. "Then why are you telling me?"

"Because I know you probably signed some papers as well," Daniel said, "and trust me when I tell you that crossing Seth Sinclair is not a wise move. That's why I was up in Chicago. I was there tending to a friend of mine who didn't listen to Seth's warning, because when these people say 'watch your back' they mean it."

Oh, shit. I immediately thought of Wilson and his dead friend. This couldn't be a simple coincidence. "What happened?"

Daniel shook his head and stood up. "Look, Bentley, I've said too much already. I just came over here to see if we could finish what we started in your office, but I'm suddenly out of the mood."

I stood. "I'm sorry, Daniel, but I'll have to give you a rain check on hitting the sheets. After talking to you, I need to check on my friend."

He looked at me with the sad expression of a missed opportunity. "Yeah, you do that. I'll be around and you're going to like what I got to offer."

I smiled, remembering the visual of his huge dick in my office.

"I took a year off from sex after dealing with Seth and company," Daniel said. "I wanted to make sure those people didn't leave me any gifts I wouldn't want, if you get my drift. So you were going to be my foray back into having a normal sex life."

"I guess I should be honored."

"Yeah, you should be."

Daniel leaned over, gave me a peck on the forehead, and vanished out the door.

THIRTY-THREE

Alexandria opened the door of her apartment in a chic art deco building not far from the office. It was painted a soft shade of orange, like cantaloupe, that relaxed me as I stepped inside. Her cozy furniture was faux suede, so as soon as I sat on the couch, I sunk down and got comfortable.

She had the flat screen on while the coffee table offered a spread of nachos, pineapple slices, mixed nuts, and popcorn.

"I feel like we're about to watch a football game," I said playfully, popping a nacho into my mouth.

"You're gonna help me score a touchdown," Alex said, looking so different than she did at the office. Her hair was pulled back in a ponytail but fell in soft wisps around her cosmetic-free face. She wore no jewelry. And baggy pink sweats had replaced her femme fatale, form-fitting skirts and blouses. No spiked heels tonight; she wore fluffy white shearling slippers.

"We're about to switch on the baby-daddy shopping channel," she said, aiming the remote at the DVD player under the flat screen. It was attached to the wall facing us.

I chomped some pecans and cashews, feeling a little nervous about this. "Alex, tell me what you're looking for again."

"Intelligent, handsome, healthy, tall, and allergy-free." She said it like she was ordering ingredients in an omelet.

An introduction played from the sperm bank, explaining that she would have a choice between men who wanted complete anonymity and men who wanted to play a role in the child's life.

A gorgeous blond showed up on the screen first. "Hi, my name is Greg. I'm a full-time surfer, so I have great coordination and balance. I have very low body fat and long, lean muscles. I'm six-three and weigh one-sixty —"

I looked at Alex, who was mesmerized. But she said, "Sounds a little skinny."

I looked at her harder, wondering if she was going to consider what was obvious to me. "And?"

"Shhh, he hasn't mentioned his education yet," she said.

"— and I was on the dean's list at UCLA,

but I decided not to go to law school," he said. "My family's pretty all-American. My mom stayed home while my dad ran a chain of restaurants. So I love to cook —"

"He makes the cut," she said, clicking to the next guy.

"Pause!" I ordered. "Alex, you'd cross the color line to find some sperm?"

She looked at me like I'd just asked her if she'd eat at dinnertime.

"Of course I would," she said. "What's the big deal?"

I yanked up a nacho chip covered in gooey cheese and a jalapeño slice. "I guess it's not a big deal, since you're biracial yourself."

She smiled, aiming the remote, but she paused when I said, "That baby would come out superlight. French vanilla. A drop of coffee in the cream."

She pushed the button. "Hush, Bentley Dean. I'm 'bout to find the darkest brotha on here and put him on the list, too. It doesn't matter to me."

"Well go 'head with your bad self," I teased. "I like lookin' at these dudes, too. I'm still trippin', though, that we're shopping for a sperm donor through a DVD."

She smiled. "Welcome to the new millennium. You should see the Web sites. You can pick the sperm donor's hair color, eye color, race, religion, ethnicity, height, and weight. Then you click and up pops that type of sperm, and they tell you which sperm bank has it."

It seemed like the good old-fashioned way was easier than all that. "So, Alex, you're an equal opportunity sperm seeker?"

"The sperm bank told me not a lot of black guys donate," she said. "In fact, they said some sperm banks have no black sperm!"

"Why?"

She shrugged. "They didn't say. These guys get paid. One donor said he made sixteen grand over four years."

"Why aren't more brothers signing up to donate? They could get paid and help black women and couples get pregnant."

Alex scooped up a handful of mixed nuts and popped a few in her mouth. "Maybe they're getting pregnant the natural way, without all the formalities. Personally, I think this is safer. All the donors are screened for HIV and other STDs. But when you do it naturally, you have to have unsafe sex. Yuck!"

She clicked on the next guy. "Hi, my name is Edward —"

"No!" Alex and I exclaimed in unison.

We laughed.

"Guess we agree on that one," she said. "Next!"

"I'm Anthony," said an olive-skinned man with dark wavy hair and warm brown eyes.

"Italian?" she asked.

"Beautiful comes from any country," I said. "Definitely Italian or Latin, but no accent."

"I have an MBA from Stanford and a BA from Yale. I play soccer, I'm on a debate team, and I'm a marathon runner. I own a software company and I love to hike in the mountains."

Alex stared. "I wish this were a dating service." She sighed. "His fine ass would be mine!"

"You'd have to fight me for that dude," I said playfully.

"Sorry, Bentley, the FDA said gay men can't be sperm donors, due to the HIV risk."

"For real?"

She nodded.

"This is a trip," I said. "What's next?"

"You help me pick my baby daddy. I get artificially inseminated. And you become a godfather."

This was still feeling a little wild for me, so I reached for more nachos and looked up at yet another man offering to help Alex make a baby.

THIRTY-FOUR

Over a week had passed and still no word from Jah. I'd left so many messages on his cell phone that now it was full and not accepting any more messages. I was worried, so I called Daniel to see if I could get some more information out of him. He told me he had already told me too much and was worried about his safety. When I asked him what he meant by that, he told me that it would be best to just stop worrying about Jah because when he got a little older, he would be released to pasture by Seth and his cohorts.

That would have reassured me, except for the fact that Daniel's tone of voice made me doubt that what he was saying was true. Was Daniel trying to tell me that he escaped, but too many others didn't? Seth probably picked boys like he was casting them as extras in a film of his sick, sordid life.

I went to the office early, trying to stay

busy and not worry as much, but it didn't work. Almost every hour, I would call Jah again or look on some of the celebrity blogs as if they would provide answers. I decided that a long workout might help, but as I was leaving my office, Alex walked in, looking grim.

"We've got a big problem," she said, standing there with her arms crossed. She had that look like her brain was going in a million directions, trying to solve a problem.

"Alex, what's wrong?"

She shook her head. "I just got a call from Seth Sinclair's office saying that they could meet with me tomorrow, but I have a conflict."

"What kind?"

She explained that she had a meeting that had been set up for a while with people from Serena Williams's company. The tennis star was doing a line of active sportswear and wanted to use a black agency to find female models for the catalogue's online Web site. Alex said the job was a sure thing if she showed up.

"What do you suggest we do?" I asked.

"I was thinking," Alex said, "maybe you could go to California and meet with Seth."

My thoughts raced over the pros and cons of her idea. "Do you think he'll be there? I can't imagine he would attend an introduction meeting," I said. But what if Seth did attend the meeting? Could I corner him and find out what was going on with Jah? Would he even remember me?

Alex threw up her hands. "I don't know, but unless you want to handle the meeting with Serena's people, this sounds like the best plan."

The expense of a last-minute ticket made me pause. I asked Alex about it, and she said Seth's people were willing to purchase my ticket.

"I bet they fly you out there first class," she said. "You don't have anything tomorrow, do you?"

My schedule had nothing that I couldn't reschedule. We decided to call and tell Seth's people that I'd be there in Alexandria's place. This was just too big an opportunity for us to turn down, for several reasons. Alex and I agreed that tomorrow we could both score big contracts for the firm. Contracts that would keep us in business for a couple more months and maybe even make some money.

As Alexandria and I talked, I made a plan to go to the gym, then head home and pack to stay in Cali a few days, because Alex said she could handle the agency while I was gone. "Alex, do we have enough young ladies for the Serena deal?"

"Yeah," she said, "because I knew there was a chance we'd be up for the deal. So I've been recruiting hard. We'll be fine."

She said she had been planning to stay with her girlfriend and offered to have her contact recommend a hotel close to the production company's office. I said I'd take care of it myself.

"Alex, I'll holler at you before I leave."

"Thanks, Bentley. Glad we could work it out. Hey, did you ever hear from Jah?"

I shook my head. "Not yet, but maybe with this trip I'll be able to see him." Maybe I wouldn't confront Seth. Maybe instead, I would try to find Jah at his place in West Hollywood.

"I hope everything is okay with him," she said. "He's still a young kid."

"Tell me about it."

As I put my last pair of sweatpants and underwear in my suitcase, my cell phone rang.

"Hello?"

"Bentley, this is Ramon. What's shaking?"

"Hey, Ramon, good to hear from you. What's good with you?" I looked around my bedroom, wondering what I was forgetting.

Ramon said, "I was just thinking about you and thought I'd give you a call."

"That's cool. How's school and basketball?"

"It's all good. What you got up for tonight?"

"I'm just packing." I spotted my phone charger on the dresser and tossed it into my suitcase. "I have a flight out to Cali first thing in the morning. Why?"

Ramon sounded disappointed. "Aw, nothing. I was thinking about dropping by, but sounds like you busy. When you coming back?"

I headed into the bathroom, refilling the little bottles of shampoo and cocoa butter in my toiletry travel bag. I told Ramon I'd be gone a couple of days, and that I wished he'd have called earlier so that we could have hooked up. He said cool, maybe we could hang out when I got back.

"I'd like that, Ramon."

"Have you heard from my home boi, De-Marco?"

I put a new toothbrush in my bag. "No, I haven't. Should I?"

Ramon made a disgusted sound. "I don't know. He hasn't mentioned anything, but that nigga always got some stuff going. If he calls you, just be careful."

I was smart enough to not be played by some young gangsta like DeMarco and wouldn't take any of his calls. But was this the real reason Ramon was calling or was he trying to get in where he fit in himself? Did this youngster have a crush on me and didn't know how to go about telling me? I told him I appreciated him giving me the heads-up.

"No problem. Have a safe trip, boss."

I checked out my reflection in the mirror. Good thing I'd gotten a haircut that still looked fresh. "I will. Hey, maybe I can come check you out at one of your games when I get back."

Ramon sounded geeked. "That would be cool! I'll send you a schedule through e-mail. I think the address was on your card."

"Yeah, it is, and do that. Take care, Ramon."

"I will."

THIRTY-FIVE

When Seth Sinclair walked into the conference room he looked a little bit startled. I figured it was because he remembered me. I stood up as he walked down to the end of the table. He was wearing white pants with a pink shirt and white sweater. It was a very high-class country club look that I saw a lot of in Miami.

Seth looked and sounded annoyed as he said, "I thought I was meeting with a female. You don't look like an Alexandria."

"She's my business partner and couldn't make the meeting, so I'm filling in for her. It's good seeing you again, Mr. Sinclair," I said as I extended my hand toward him.

"Do I know you?" he asked without offering his hand.

"Yes, we met before," I said, a little offended that this asshole didn't remember meeting me.

"I don't remember you, but that's not

unusual," he said with an arrogant tone. "I meet a lot of people. I can only give you fifteen minutes. I have a golf game." He sat down.

Fifteen minutes would not be long enough for me to find information about Jah. For a moment, I didn't know if I should start with telling him about our company or Jah.

"Did you hear me?" he snapped. "I don't have a lot of time."

I kept it cool and professional. "Yes, Mr. Sinclair, we would love the opportunity to do business with you on your next film. We have a roster of people, both male and female, that you might be interested in as extras and under five."

He shook his perfectly groomed head. "We don't shoot a lot of films in Miami. There aren't enough tax breaks." Seth wasn't looking at me, but out of the floor-to-ceiling glass window overlooking a busy street. This guy was so full of himself.

"We can make it happen anywhere in the country you need us to," I said.

"Fine. Just leave your card with my assistant, Alice," he said as he stood up and headed toward the door, again without a handshake or any acknowledgment.

With his back facing me, I stood up and raised my voice. "Mr. Sinclair, where is Jah?

I need to talk to him to make sure he's doing okay."

Seth turned around and looked at me incredulously. "Who?"

"Jah, the young man you moved out here. He's a good friend of mine and I'm a little worried about him."

He looked at me as if I were insane. "I don't know who you're talking about. Why would I move some young man out here? I'm a married man."

I stared hard into his eyes. "You really don't remember me, do you?"

"No, why would I lie about something like that?" He stared back at me just as hard.

"I met you at the party in Miami. I supply models through your assistant, Sterling. We met right before the party. That's where you met Jah." I didn't know why this dude was trippin'; surely he remembered me. I knew he was doing this to say I wasn't important enough for him to remember me. I worked for him and should act accordingly.

Seth walked close to me. He stared me straight in the eyes and pointed his finger so close to my nose that I could almost feel it.

His voice was deep and angry. "What kind of bullshit game are you playing with me? Do you know who the fuck I am?"

382

I didn't flinch. "I'm very much aware of who you are, Mr. Sinclair. I'm just trying to find my friend. He's a good kid and he's very impressionable. A man like yourself could really have a lot of influence over him."

He looked at me with shock that I had the gall to talk to him like this. "Look here, I don't know what you're talking about! Are you trying to extort money or business from me? I will call the FBI on you so fast, you won't know what hit you."

I shook my head. "Mr. Sinclair, I'm just trying to find my friend. Can you give me the address of where he's staying?"

He squinted at me. "Get the fuck out of my face. I don't know you or what you're talking about." He shouted, "Leave my office! Now!"

"Just tell me where Jah is!"

He balled his fists. "Do I need to call security?"

"No, sir, I don't think that's necessary because I mean you no harm. I just want to make sure Jah is all right. When I do that, I'll be out of your way."

He almost did a double take as I spoke. I bet nobody had the balls to stand up to him like this.

"I'm not Jah's parent or guardian and if

he wants to stay here with you, then there's no way I can make him come back to Miami."

He looked at me like I was in deep shit. "You have no idea who you're fucking with, but you'll find out soon enough if you ever come to my office or anywhere near me talking shit. You got thirty seconds to get out of my office or else you might find yourself flying out that window."

I felt like I was on autopilot. Trembling inside, but not really afraid. Just fueled by my protective need to find Jah and make sure he was safe. "I'm not afraid of you, Seth. Just tell me where I can find Jah."

He glared at me, his eyes saying a million unspeakable things. "We're done. Leave the premises." Seth Sinclair walked out and slammed the door.

Outside in the parking lot, I stood by my rental car and texted Warren, asking if he'd found out anything about Jah's where-abouts. Warren usually texted me right back, so I stood in the hazy California sunshine, waiting a few minutes for a response. Nothing came. So I drove back to my hotel.

I felt proud that I'd stood up to Seth. Not that I'd gotten any information out of him, but at least I tried. Then it hit me that I'd completely blown any chance of Picture

Perfect supplying people for his films. What would I tell Alex?

Thirty-Six

Just when I thought my day couldn't get any crazier, it did. I ordered room service and was thinking about my meeting with Satan Sinclair and how I was going to get him to tell me where Jah was. Warren finally texted me back. But it obviously wasn't meant for me:

Hey, Baby — you ready for some of this dick? Are you going to put on the purple panties I like?

I started to ignore it but instead I texted back, "What?"

A few seconds later, he sent me another text that was clearly intended for someone else:

You know the panties you like to wear, dude. Hey, my boi Bentley is still asking questions about his boi. I told him I couldn't find out anything yet but he keeps asking. Good thing he don't know about the Wentworth asshole. He could make big problems for Seth.

Rather than text back, I quickly saved the message in my phone. What was Warren talking about? Who was Wentworth? And his reference about Seth made it sound like Warren was "in" on protecting Seth. Plus, his reference to me and my questions about Jah made it sound like he wasn't on my side. Was Warren double-crossing me? I stood there, stunned, wondering if this man that I loved and trusted was actually working against me.

The hotel phone rang. Nobody knew where I was staying, except for Alex and Seth's people, so I answered.

"Mr. Dean, would you like fries or chips with your club sandwich?" the friendly female room service attendant asked.

"Chips are fine," I said.

"Good choice. We do homemade chips and I think you'll like them better than the fries."

When I hung up, another text came in from Warren. I guess he'd gotten his numbers and names straight, but hadn't realized that he'd texted me earlier.

Hey, Bent . . . how did your meeting go? I'm still trying to find out some information on your boi but everybody is being tight-lipped. How long are you in Cali? I want to see you before you leave.

I simply texted back, "K!"

About twenty minutes later, my room service order arrived. I signed the check and let the attendant out the door. Starving, I sat on the sofa and just as I picked up one of the quarters of my sandwich, my cell rang. It was sitting right next to me and when I looked down at the screen, my first thought was, *It couldn't be.* The name on my phone was KIM BOSTON. Could this day get any more strange? I put down the sandwich and picked up the cell phone.

"Hello?"

"Bentley, is this you?" a tearful Kim asked.

"Kim, what's wrong? Yes, this is Bentley. What's going on?"

She sounded frantic. "You need to come to Detroit right away. Something terrible has happened."

This made no sense. Why in the world would Kim be the one to call me with bad news? About who? I shot up to my feet.

"What, Kim? What's wrong?"

"It's your father," she said quickly. "I think

he's had a heart attack. I don't know if he's still alive."

I paced the hotel room. This made no sense. Why would Kim know something had happened to my father?

"My father? What happened?"

She sobbed. "I called 911 and they just showed up. They put this machine on him. Then they put him in an ambulance."

I struggled to connect the dots. Kim, my father, ambulance, hotel room? "Where are you, Kim? Is he going to be all right?"

"I'm still at the hotel. We were in bed when it happened." She sobbed. "I think you need to call your mother and sister and tell them to get to Mercy Hospital as soon as possible."

Did Kim say hotel and bed? Heart attack? What was happening? My own chest squeezed tighter and my head spun. She was crying, out of control.

"Kim!" I exclaimed. "Kim, talk to me. What are you doing with my father?" The idea of them being together in bed in a hotel room for the reasons that most grown folks do, well, my brain just refused to go there. Even when I remembered Alex's playful dish about Kim's new wealthy boyfriend. "Kim?"

She sighed loudly. "Bentley, we have to

talk. I didn't want to tell you over the phone."

"You have to tell me something because this is the craziest shit I've ever heard."

She spoke softly. "We didn't want to hurt you."

"Oh, I've been hurt! My father stopped talking to me because I told the truth," I exclaimed, losing my patience with her lack of explanations. "What! Tell me, Kim!"

"Your dad and I, well, we both missed you so much, we sort of bonded over missing Bentley Dean the third."

"Bonded?"

The image of fine-ass Kim with my father — that shit was crazy.

I walked quickly toward the bathroom, sure that my empty stomach would retch up something.

"Bentley," Kim said with a pleading tone. "Don't be upset. Your father loves you so much. He misses you like you wouldn't believe. I somehow thought I could bring you both back together."

Yes, today registered as the craziest day of my life. Kim thought she could inspire my father's reconciliation by fucking him in a hotel room?

"Kim, this is the most whack —"

"Bentley, are you still in Miami?"

"No! I'm in California."

"Then you need to get on a plane and get here. Call your mother."

She said it like all this was so matter-of-fact. I caught my reflection in the mirror; my skin was pale and my eyes were wide with shock. I started tossing my things back into the suitcase.

"Kim, you and my father?"

"I don't want to get into that right now, Bentley. We can talk once you get here. I don't think we should go into this over the phone."

"We already did," I said. "I have to get off this phone to get in contact with my mother and sister. I also need to see when I can get a flight out of here."

"Would you like me to send your father's private jet?"

I stared at the phone. So she had that kind of clout in Father's life?

"No, I'll make my own arrangements," I said, wondering now what kind of relationship Kim had with my father.

"Okay, I'll see you when you get here and if there are any changes, I'll call you."

"Thanks, Kim."

I hung up and started pacing the hotel room, wondering what I should do next. Did I call my mother or should I let my

391

sister break the news to her? Was my father still alive and would I ever have the chance to tell him how much I loved him? I felt tears coming, but told myself to man up. This was no time for tears.

I called the hotel concierge and asked for help with getting a flight to Detroit and a car service to take me back to LAX. She was very helpful when I told her the situation and promised to call me in ten minutes with arrangements.

I paced again, scratching my head like my hair was protecting my thoughts on what I should do next. I picked up my phone and hit the speed dial with my mother's number. The phone rang several times and suddenly my mother's voice came on sounding so cheerful, but telling me that she was not around for chatting right now and to leave a message. I didn't. Instead, I called my sister's number.

Her nanny answered. I quickly announced who I was and told her I needed to speak to my sister immediately. A few minutes later, Anna was on the other end of the phone.

"Bentley, what a pleasant surprise," Anna said.

"Sis, have you talked to Mother today?"

"About an hour ago."

"Where is she? I tried reaching her on her

cell but I got her voice mail." I zipped my suitcase, holding my car keys, ready to leave.

"She's at the casino with that young stud of hers. What's going on, Bentley? I hear stress in your voice."

I exhaled. "Something is wrong with Father. I think he had a heart attack."

The line was silent. Then Anna shrieked, "What? Tell me you're kidding, Bentley. Don't play with me. Where did you hear a thing like that?"

It felt so strange to say, "Kim called me and told me a few minutes ago. Something about a hotel and them being in bed."

"Oh, God, then it must be true," Anna cried.

"What in hell is going on between Kim and my father, Anna?"

She was quiet. I could hear my angry, scared heartbeat pounding in my ears until she said, "We can talk when you get here, Bentley. You are coming home, aren't you?"

I was sick of people not giving me answers today! "I'm trying to get on the next flight." I raised my voice. "Tell me about what is going on between Father and Kim!"

"Get on a flight and get here, Bentley. I need to find Mother and get to the hospital. Have a safe flight, brother dear. Bye."

When I hung up from Anna it appeared
the room had joined my head in spinning.

THIRTY-SEVEN

I got out of a cab and rushed through the electronic glass doors of the emergency room of Mercy Hospital near downtown Detroit. It was almost the end of February and the city was bitter cold. When I entered the warm hospital, I went straight to the information desk and asked for my father.

"Oh, Mr. Dean, I was alerted to look out for you. Let me notify security," the receptionist said.

Security? This couldn't be good, I told myself. Why would I need to be escorted by security? Was my father already dead? Or was this something my mother ordered in an attempt to be grand? A few moments later, a tall black man in a dark blue rent-a-cop suit told me to follow him. He had a somber look on his face and I knew this wasn't good.

As we rode up the escalators, I saw many patients in wheelchairs with plastic IV bags at the top of the chair and I realized this was the first time I'd ever been in a hospital. I followed the guard down a long hallway and then through two double doors. Once behind the doors, we passed a series of waiting rooms until we got to the end of the corridor and the security guard opened the door. I followed him in and immediately saw my mother and sister staring out the window in a mournful embrace.

"Mother, how is Father?" I asked and she turned around. She was crying, with tears streaming down her face. Just the sight of her caused me to start whimpering like a puppy, blinking back my own tears.

"Bentley, I'm so glad you made it safely," Anna said as she kissed me on the cheek and rubbed my shoulders. My mother was still crying and I hadn't gotten a word out of her about my father's condition.

"Where is my father, Anna? Is he still alive?"

Anna looked at me with a somber face and said, "Just barely." She and I had always looked alike, except she had long black hair that she usually wore pin straight. Today it was twisted up in a barrette. With a blue velvet warm-up suit, she wore no makeup and her eyes were red-rimmed and puffy.

"Where is he?"

"In the operating room, and he's already been in there for three hours."

"Did he have a heart attack?"

"Yes, and the doctors said it was a massive one. They found blockage in six arteries. They say it is amazing he's still alive and if Kim hadn't called the ambulance when she did, we surely would have lost him."

Kim. I still didn't understand why my father was with my ex. I guess there was no better time than now to find out.

"What was Kim doing with Father, Anna?"

"I tell you why your father is with Kim, Bentley. He thinks because I have a young boyfriend he would get a youngster as well. He's just an old fool being used by Kim."

I turned to Anna and asked, "What is Mother talking about?"

Anna's face turned red. "Bentley, I didn't want to be the one to tell you, but Father has been going out with Kim for about six months. They've been quite the couple and all of Detroit has been talking about it. I'm really quite surprised you didn't hear about it in Miami. You should have seen the two of them in Washington during the inauguration. They were all over each other."

I just stared at her, wondering if I was

hearing this right. "Tell me you're kidding. Where is she now?"

Anna looked at me like she was so sorry that I had to deal with all this at once. "They put her in the general waiting room. This is a private area, and even though Mother and Father are no longer married, the head of the hospital knew our parents when they were together and thought it was best that he keep Mother and Kim in separate areas."

"So how long is the surgery? What does the doctor say?"

Anna said, "It can last up to ten hours and we haven't had any updates. This is a serious surgery, but Father has the best doctors in Michigan."

I looked at my mother, who was standing there trembling with her arms crossed.

"Mother, can I get you something to drink or eat? You don't look well."

She glared at me. "I'm *not* well, Bentley. My husband is in there fighting for his life and I may never get the chance to tell him I love him or make him laugh with my silly questions. I've spent over half of my life with that man. Now I'll never get the chance to walk into the Links Ball on his arm or play golf at the country club."

Anna put her arms around our mother

and said with a soothing voice, "Mother, tell me you're not really worried about that. Let's use our energy to pray that Daddy will be all right." She was right. My father was fighting for his life and Mother was worried about some social club. I had to admit that sometimes my mother could be so petty. But I could tell from her tears and the way that she was shaking that she was concerned about my father. And she had admitted she still loved him. That was a good thing.

Five hours later there was still no word on how my father's operation was going. I guessed this was a case of no news was good news. My mother, sister, and I sat in silence in the nicely furnished waiting room, exchanging magazines and newspapers.

"Mother, have you eaten today?" Anna asked.

"I'm not hungry," she replied.

"You need to eat something, Mother."

"Yeah, Mother, Anna is right. Do you think they'll deliver something up here?"

"We might have to go down to the cafeteria," Anna said as she looked at her watch. I looked at mine. It was a little after six.

"I'll go down and get something for us," I said. "What would you like, Mother?"

"Bentley, I told you I'm not hungry."

"Just get her a sandwich and a soda, Bentley," Anna said. It felt strange that us kids were the ones talking to our mother like we were the parents, taking care of her.

"If you two are going to force me to eat, then I don't want any sandwich." Mother had a way of talking like a drill sergeant. "Get me some tuna salad on some lettuce and maybe a tomato slice. I have my club function coming up in May and I'm not going to let your father be the cause of me gaining weight. And I don't want a soda. Get me some black coffee, Bentley."

"Okay, Mother. Anna, what would you like?"

Anna hugged herself. "Just a sandwich, Bentley, and a bottle of water."

As I left, I said, "Okay, I'll be back, but if the doctor calls with any news, text me, please."

"Will do."

I got on the elevator and punched B. Just as the elevator door was beginning to close, I heard someone yell, "Wait a minute!" It was a familiar voice and I pushed the door open button. In walked Kim Boston. She seemed surprised to see me and I was equally shocked to see her. She not only looked older, but she was dressed like a matronly socialite with a fur coat and gaudy jewelry.

"Bentley Dean the third. How are you?" She kissed me on the cheek and it smelled like she was wearing a perfume my mother wore when we were children. I remembered it being my father's favorite.

"I'm okay, Kim. I guess I shouldn't be surprised to see you here. Anna told me you were in another waiting room."

Kim shook her head. Her eyes were bloodshot and glassy. "At least your sister has been able to retain her class. I wish I could say the same thing about your mother. Have you heard anything from the doctors? This wait is making me more nervous than I was when B. D. first had the heart attack."

That took me back to the image of Kim in bed with my father. I know I just looked at her with a completely puzzled expression. That just seemed so *wrong.* I forced myself to talk. "No, we haven't heard anything. Thanks a lot for getting my father to the hospital. If he survives this, then I guess you saved his life."

"You don't have to thank me. I mean, what else was I going to do? I love your daddy."

I stared at her, waiting for those words to

sink into my brain. "When did that happen?"

"What?"

"When did you fall in love with my father?"

"About six months ago. I saw him at a golf tournament and he invited me to dinner. We started talking about you and I think we connected over the fact that we both missed you so much. We've been together ever since. He really is the best thing to ever happen to me, Bentley."

The elevator reached the bottom floor and I held the door as Kim walked out into the hospital cafeteria. Once we reached the buffet-style serving line, Kim asked me if I would like to join her for dinner so that we could catch up on things.

"I need to get the food back to my mother and sister."

"Bentley, please try and talk some sense into your mother."

"About what?"

She placed her right hand on my arm. I looked down at it, feeling strange that she had shared her body with me and now was sharing her body with Father. "Letting me be the first one to see B. D. once he's out of recovery. I'm sure when he opens his eyes, I'll be the first person he'll want to see. I mean, I was the last person he saw before collapsing."

I screwed up my face. "Spare me the details, Kim. And I think my father will want to see my mother and the rest of his family first."

Kim put her hand out. She was sporting a huge diamond that was almost blinding. "I'll be family soon, Bentley."

"What does that mean?"

She beamed a huge smile. "Your daddy and I are getting married. We're engaged."

That would mean my ex-fiancée would become my stepmother. Snap! "Are you serious? Kim, tell me you're kidding."

"What? Just because you didn't want me, doesn't mean all the Dean men have lost their senses."

"Are you doing this to get back at me, Kim?"

"No, Bentley, I honestly care for your father. He's a great man and now I know where you get a lot of your good qualities." I looked at Kim and realized she was trying to be nice during this very difficult time. Still, it was hard to think about her with my father. Was I just being selfish or deep down did I wish my father and mother would get back together again?

"Kim, I'll talk with you later. I need to get

some food for my mother and sister." Shaking my head, I looked at the selection of sandwiches the cafeteria had.

Thirty-Eight

When I got back to the waiting room with food for my mother and sister, they were with a middle-aged white man with a white coat. He was talking to my mother, who was crying. I wondered if something terrible had happened.

"Anna, is everything okay?" I asked.

"Bentley, this is Dr. Welsh. He was the lead doctor on Daddy's bypass operation. Dr. Welsh, this is my baby brother, Bentley Dean the third."

I shook his hand. "Nice to meet you, Dr. Welsh. Please tell me my father is going to be okay."

He had serious brown eyes and deep wrinkles on his forehead. "It was a tough surgery. There were more blockages than we anticipated. Right now your father is in the recovery room, but he has a tough road ahead of him. I was just explaining to your mother and sister that we will keep him heavily sedated the next couple of days and just hope everything turns out for the better."

"When can we see him?" I asked.

The doctor said, "We need to give him a couple of hours and I think we should just do one visitor at a time. He won't be able to talk to you or even see you, but he might be able to hear you. It will be days before he'll be able to respond to his family."

Anna touched his arm. "Thanks, Dr. Welsh, I think my mother should be the first person to see him."

The doctor nodded. "Let's try not to wear him out. I know you want to see him, but he's in a very delicate state right now."

"I understand, Dr. Welsh," I said. "I agree with my sister that my mother should see my father first and then if you think it's okay, we'll visit with him."

The doctor looked as if he were going to ask a question. "That sounds like a plan. Now if it's okay, I'm going to go talk to Ms. Boston. I understand she is your father's lady friend and I think she is very concerned about Mr. Dean's health as well."

"I will talk with Kim when it's time," my mother said. She was stony and iron-voiced. She clearly still loved our father, no matter how angry and tough of a façade she presented. Maybe there was a chance that this crisis could bring them back together. Maybe my wishes were going to be granted.

"Mother, are you sure? Anna and I can talk with Kim."

"Yes, Mother," Anna said.

"Don't be silly. I can talk with Kim. Are you two afraid I might slap the poor girl? I, Lucinda Dean, know how to treat people. I taught you two."

"You're right, Mother. I just don't want you to stress yourself," I said.

"I don't even know what stress is, darling. Now let's move on to the next thing."

Anna and I looked at each other with questioning looks as my mother marched out of the room.

THIRTY-NINE

Almost forty-eight hours had passed before it was my turn to see my father. But before I went in, I borrowed my sister's car, went to the neighborhood where my father owned rental homes, and picked up a little gift for him.

I was a little nervous before I went in because Mother talked about how bad he looked and how he was heavily sedated and still hadn't opened his eyes. Mother, Anna, and Kim had all spent a little time with him, and the doctors urged us not to stay longer than fifteen minutes because he would need all of his strength for a complete recovery.

I walked slowly into the hospital room and saw an Asian nurse messing with the tubes connected to my father. His eyes were closed and his face was ashen. Bentley Dean, Jr., certainly didn't look like the vibrant man who told me how disappointed he was with me and my choices. I still couldn't believe such a smart man couldn't understand that I hadn't made a choice about being gay. If I'd had a choice it would have been to be the son he wanted. I never wanted to disappoint my father, but I wasn't going to be miserable, either.

I nodded at the nurse, took a seat, and just stared for a moment at my father. His head was positioned so his eyes, though closed, were looking toward the off-white ceiling.

"Has he woken up yet?" I asked the nurse.

"Not yet. I would give him another day or so and then maybe we can expect some movement from him."

"Do you think he can hear me?"

The nurse adjusted some tubes and turned some knobs on the machines around the bed. "Maybe. I think it's okay to talk to him and maybe massage his arms and hands."

"Okay."

"I'll be back in about ten minutes, so enjoy your time with your father."

"Thank you."

When the nurse left, I put my hand on top of my father's hands, which felt rough and warm.

"How you gon' scare us like this, old man?" My throat felt raw despite my playful tone. "You know we'd be a mess without you. I don't know if you're happy that I'm here or if you're still mad at me, but nothing, and I mean nothing, was going to keep me away. Maybe now might be the only time that I can talk to you and not have you say, 'I'm the father.' This time you're going to have to listen to me."

I paused for a moment, then I reached into my leather jacket for the gift. I pulled out the little white-and-blue cardboard box that held a small White Castle cheeseburger. I knew he would not be able to eat it, but I thought if he could smell it, maybe it would bring back to my father the memories that it brought back to me anytime I saw a White Castle drive-in or when I smelled one of the mini-burgers. Whenever that happened, I always thought of my father and the great times we'd have on our Saturday excursions to the South Side of Detroit.

"I know you can't eat this, and the nurse would most likely kick me out of the hospital, but I brought you a little gift." I looked at his motionless face.

"I went back to the old neighborhood where you bought your first rental property. You remember how you used to take me with you and how sometimes you'd let your tenants pay me the money? How proud you were of me? When your tenants would ask me what I was going to be when I grew up, how I would always say that I was going to be just like my father."

I stood up over my father and put the cheeseburger close to his nose. I didn't know if he could smell it, but it was worth a try.

"Father, you've got to get well," I said over a hot lump in my throat. "We still really need you. I need you. And even though we've been out of each other's lives for some years now, I don't think it's too late for us to catch up. Father, I never meant to disappoint you. I was just trying to do what you taught me and that was to always tell the truth, even when it hurts, and to always be proud of the Dean name. I've tried to do that."

His face blurred through my tears.

"It's the real reason why I couldn't lie to Mother, Kim, and you. If you were going to love me then you had to know who you were loving. Does that make sense? I need you to recover because I want you to understand that I really have become the man you wanted me to become. I'm still concerned about those less fortunate than me. I'm doing something that I love, and I treat and respect all people equally no matter what their stations in life are."

I heard the door crack. I turned and saw the nurse coming back in. I shot her a look and she recognized that I needed a little more time, so she closed the door. I put the cheeseburger in its box and into my jacket pocket.

"Now I know you may think my being gay was something that I chose just to get on your nerves, but, Father, you really have to know better. My greatest joy has been being your son and I've missed you terribly. I need my father back, even if you don't like everything about me. We're going to have to learn to respect each other's differences so that love can return. So will you get well so we can have that chance?"

I knew my father couldn't answer me, but suddenly I felt his hand squeeze mine. I looked at his face and even though both of his eyes were still closed, I saw long tears streaming from his eyes. And a few seconds later, tears warmed my own face and I knew God was going to give my father and me a second chance.

FORTY

When Anna and I pulled into the garage of her house, I made an announcement.

"Father is going to be fine and our family is going to be just like it was when we were young."

"What makes you say that?" Anna asked from the driver's seat.

"It's just a feeling I have, Anna."

"So what?" She turned off the engine and looked at me skeptically. "You got some kind of time capsule, Bentley? Times changed. We've changed."

I sat, enjoying the silence. I'd decided to stay with Anna instead of at the family house because I didn't know if my mother's young boyfriend was shacking up with her. I was in no mood to deal with that.

My sister and her husband had more than enough room. They had bought one of the huge mansions that white Buick executives had abandoned during the Detroit riots in the sixties. It was large enough where I could have my privacy and had a two-bedroom apartment right behind the garage. Normally I would have stayed there, but Anna's nanny was currently occupying it.

"I know times have changed, but I think when Father gets well, I'm going to make him understand me. I need my father, Anna, and I think he needs me."

She opened the car door. "I'm sure you're right, Bentley, but both of you are still stubborn Dean men. Just like grandfather. How are you going to change that?"

"We both are going to have to bend. Almost losing him forced me to realize how much I need my father."

She looked at me like my optimism was ridiculously unrealistic. "What are you going to do about Kim? I mean, that has to be uncomfortable for the both of you."

"This isn't about Kim. It's about me and Father."

She shook her head. "But she is a part of his life now. I don't know how we're going to decide where Daddy is going to recover. I thought about bringing him here so Mother and Kim wouldn't split him down the middle."

"Does Mother want him to come to the house?"

Anna got out of the car and I followed her, but we ended up standing in the garage, talking over the car. "Yes, those are her plans. When I asked her about Kim, she told me not to worry about Kim. That she would take care of that."

"What do you think she has up her sleeve?"

"Heaven only knows, my brother."

My father was coming home from the hospital. Mother had won the battle and he was coming back to the family home. Mother had hired a private nurse and finally agreed to let Kim come and visit.

I was still at Anna's house having a cup of coffee when I realized it had been over a week since I'd checked my messages or computer. I wondered what was going on with Jah and if he was all right.

I listened to my messages. There were a couple of calls from Warren, Ramon, Alexandria, and Wilson. But no calls from Jah. When I checked my computer, I found several e-mail messages from people, but nothing from Jah. I decided to call Alexandria first, so I hit the number three autodial on my phone.

"Hey there, partner. Are you all right?" Alex asked after a couple of rings.

"I'm doing okay. Sorry I haven't been in touch. Do we still have a business?"

She chuckled. "Business is fine. How is your father?"

I felt so relieved to tell her, "He's not a hundred percent yet but he's finally been released from the hospital. And can you believe, he's coming to my mother's house?"

Alex made a play shriek sound. "What? How did that happen?"

"Mother insisted and I think he's too weak to fight," I said with a laugh.

"How are you two getting along?"

"You mean me and my father?"

"Yeah."

I sipped my coffee. "I think we're going to be fine. I think the death scare and the operation have changed him quite a bit. But we'll see."

Alex was typing with noisy clicks on her keyboard as she asked, "When are you coming back to Miami?"

"Possibly in a week, but I can come back sooner if you need me." I imagined her juggling my work and her own and feeling overwhelmed.

"I think I can hold the fort down. We got the Serena Williams deal, but that doesn't start until April."

"That's great."

Seth's people obviously hadn't gotten back with her, because she sounded completely natural when she asked, "How did your meeting in L.A. go?"

"Not well, but I don't want to talk about it over the phone. I'll update you when I get back."

Alexandria said, "Okay. I've got some amazing news for you when you get back."

I set my coffee cup down hard in protest. "Oh, you can't do that to me. I need some exciting news. Please tell me."

"Okay," she said excitedly, "I really wanted to see your face. But I'm so happy, I'm about to bust." She squealed, "I'm pregnant!"

I smiled. "What? That's great. Which one did you choose?"

"The basketball-playing, Harvard MBA guy, so you know my baby will be athletic and smart."

I remembered his picture and imagined a mix between him and Alex. "I'm so happy for you. When did you find out?"

Alex had a tone like she was confessing. "Actually I've known for a while but I didn't tell anyone because I heard a lot of ladies miscarry when they first try it."

"So it happened on the first time?"

Alex laughed. "Yeah, I didn't need to buy

all that sperm!"

"Well, Alex, I'm really happy for you. I hope this means I'm going to be a godfather or something like it."

"A godfather for sure. I'm really going to need your help, Bentley. But not right now. You need to stay as long as you need to, to help take care of your father."

Looking around Anna's kitchen reminded me that I was still in Detroit. "Yeah, I'm going to see if he needs any help with any of his businesses."

I could tell Anna was smiling at the other end of the line. "Bentley, it's great hearing your voice and I'm happy your father is on the mend."

"Yeah, me, too, and thanks for looking out for me. I promise to make it up when I get back to Miami."

I was still smiling when we hung up, until I immediately called Warren. I didn't get an answer, so I left a message and sent him a text. I went back to my computer and decided to check my Facebook page because Jah used it all the time and maybe he'd left me a message there.

When I pulled up the pages there were no new messages on Facebook. But I did see something on the running log that caught my attention. It was a posting from Wilson stating that he would be attending a memorial service for his good friend, Jarvis Wentworth.

Wentworth was an unusual name and I didn't recall Wilson ever telling me his friend's last name. I thought back to the text that Warren had mistakenly sent me and wondered, could there be a connection? Could Warren be involved in this somehow? And who had the text been intended for?

I placed a call to Wilson but got his voice mail. I left him a message asking him to give me a call when he got a chance. I called Warren again and still couldn't get in touch with him. I sent another text message telling him I was in the city and if he had time, I wanted to take him to lunch. I didn't want to ask him about the text over the phone because I wouldn't be able to tell if he was telling the truth or not.

I walked into my parents' bedroom suite and my father was sitting up and looking at the television. He actually smiled when he saw me walk into the room. I went over and kissed him on the forehead and whispered that I was glad he was home.

"I'm not going to be here long, son. That woman isn't going to drive me crazy."

I smiled. "I guess you're talking about my

mother. What has she done now?" I asked as I pulled a mustard yellow chair closer to the bed. I gazed around the large room, noticing all the changes my mother made after her divorce. She had replaced the oak bedroom furniture with new modern leather furniture and very bright colors like light purple and yellow. I knew my father wasn't going to like this.

"She hired some white lady to give me baths. Can you believe that?"

"You mean the nurse?"

Father just shook his head in dismay.

"What are you watching?"

"CNN, that's the only thing worth watching."

I glanced at the TV. "Okay. How have they been treating our new president?"

"Okay, I guess, but I think the Republicans are waiting on him to make his first big blunder. I sure hope this stimulus package works."

I watched his mouth as he spoke. "Your speech has really improved, Father. The doctor told us it might take a couple of weeks."

"I'm always ahead of the game, Bentley. You know that about me."

I nodded. "Yeah, I do. But I have to tell you, it was pretty hard to see you like that."

My father looked at me with a face full of confidence. "Check with me in a couple of months and I'm going to be brand-new, son."

Part of me couldn't believe I was sitting here in my father's house, talking with him. "I'm just glad you're here. I hope you'll listen to your doctors so you won't suffer any setbacks."

For about an hour, my father and I remained mute with the only sound being the television. Just as I was getting ready to go downstairs and fix myself a sandwich, I heard my father's voice.

He said, "Bentley, I can't tell you how happy I am to have you back in the fold, son."

"I'm happy to be back, Father," I said as I blinked back tears.

I walked through the back door of my sister's house into the kitchen and the aroma of something good. I'd forgotten what a fine cook my sister was.

"Dang, that smells delicious. What are you making?"

"Just searing some chicken breasts with mushrooms and onions. How is Father?"

I smiled. "Looks like he's getting better every day."

"I'm going to go over and visit with him after I finish this."

I warned her, "Call Mother first. She's a tough gatekeeper."

"I wonder what she's up to?" Anna asked over the sizzle of food.

"What do you mean?" I asked, leaning closer to inhale the delicious scent as she pushed the chicken around the pan with a spatula. "Do you think she wants to get back together with him?"

"Ha!" she said. "The way they were fighting at the end of their marriage, I doubt it." Anna turned and looked at me. "So, we haven't really talked about Father and Kim."

"And I don't want to talk about it. I'm going up to my room. What time is dinner?" I asked as I put my feet on the first step leading to the second floor.

"In about thirty minutes it should be all done. Oh, yeah, I got the Heather Headley gospel CD for you. I think you'll love it. I put it on the bed."

"Thanks, sis."

When I got to my room, my cell phone rang. It was Wilson.

"Hey, Bentley, I got your message on my phone and on Facebook. What's going on?"

"How was the memorial service?"

"It was very moving," he said. "A lot of

people showed up."

"What did Jarvis do for a living?"

"He was a hairstylist. He used to be one of the most popular ones in Chicago until he started going to Los Angeles every chance he got. He was trying to break in on that celebrity clientele."

"Do they have any leads on who did this to him?"

Wilson sounded sad. "Not to my knowledge. And to be honest, I don't think the police are even looking. They don't give a damn about a black man. Especially if it's a black gay man."

I shook my head. "I hear you. So did he have any success in getting to celebrities?" I asked, wondering if it was possible Jarvis knew Seth.

"Yeah, but he used to always say he couldn't talk about it because once a star found out you talked about working with them, they would drop you like a hot rock."

I sat on the bed, hoping that Wilson would give me some clues. "You think his secret boyfriend could have been a celebrity?"

Wilson sounded like he wondered why I was asking so many questions. "I guess so, but why do you ask?"

I played it cool. "Just a hunch I'm following up on. I'd like to see the people who did this caught."

"Wow, Bentley, thank you. If you could find out anything, I know Jarvis's family and I would be very happy."

"I don't know if I'm right but I'm going to do what I can. I'll keep you posted."

"Thanks, Bentley. Take care."

"I will, Wilson. You take care of yourself."

"For sho."

I threw my cell phone on the bed and picked up the Heather Headley CD and inspected it for a minute. I went in the bathroom and washed my face and brushed my teeth. When I came back into the bedroom, my phone was flashing. I picked it up: Warren.

"Where have you been hiding?" I demanded.

"I haven't been hiding," he said, with his usual coolness. "I'm just out in Los Angeles handling some business. You still in the Motor City? How's your father doing?"

"Much better." I hated feeling suspicious of Warren, but I didn't think he was being straight with me. I guess "straight" was a funny word considering the nature of our relationship. One of the reasons I put up with some of Warren's crap was because I felt he would always give me all the story.

"That's good. Are you two going to make up?"

"I think so."

Warren chuckled. "Great. Maybe he'll give you his team if he wants to take it easy. Don't forget me, because you'll need a good general manager."

I wasn't in the mood to entertain his narcissistic nature. "I doubt if that happens," I said dryly, "but I'll keep that in mind. So I guess I won't get a chance to see you. I think I'm heading back to Miami in a couple of days."

"I can always come down there to check on my boi," Warren said.

"Yeah, I know." I wanted to ask Warren what he knew about Wentworth but I was still worried about not being able to tell if he was being truthful. But how else was I going to find out if Seth's gang had anything to do with Jarvis's murder? On one hand it didn't make a lot of sense for someone so rich and powerful to want a Chicago hairdresser dead, but then I knew that people like Seth would do almost anything to protect their secrets. When you got right down to it, guys like Seth had more issues than *Essence* magazine.

"Okay, Bent, I gotta run."

"Hey, Warren, can I ask you something?"

"Sure, boo."

"Who is Wentworth?"

Warren didn't answer. A deafening silence hung between us.

"Warren, are you still there?"

"I don't know a Wentworth. Hey, I gotta run."

Click.

FORTY-ONE

My sister's house was quiet and I had the place to myself. Anna, her husband, and the kids were spending some time with my father. I'd been over there earlier and now I was getting ready to enjoy some microwave popcorn, pizza, and the Oscars.

When I sat down in Anna's plush, all-cream family room, the awards had already started. Even though I didn't watch the Oscars every year, I was intrigued because this one looked different. Before the first major award for best supporting actress was announced, five former winners came out on stage and talked about this year's nominees. I thought that was very nice and especially enjoyed it since one of the former winners was Whoopi Goldberg. She'd been one of my favorite actors ever since I first saw her in *The Color Purple.*

I hadn't seen any of the movies the nominees had appeared in. But I knew that neither of the two African American actresses would win. The two most likely split the black vote in the Academy. When Penelope Cruz was announced the winner, I started to turn off the television to do some work. But I decided to stick around and see how Sean Penn fared for his role in *Milk.* That was another movie I hadn't seen, but I'd heard that both Penn and the movie were great.

Just as I reached down for my glass of wine, something on the television set off a slow burn through my body. It was Seth Sinclair in the audience. And the camera was slowly zooming in on him with his wife looking at him with adoring eyes.

"Joining us tonight," the host said, "is Seth Sinclair and his lovely wife. Seth is one of the most respected men in Hollywood. And maybe one day, our second African American president." The audience clapped as Seth smiled proudly and waved to the crowd and camera.

I felt sick to my stomach. It had nothing to do with the combination of the pizza and popcorn I'd been eating. But it had everything to do with my rage.

Then I thought about something my father once told me. When he got ready to purchase his football team, a wealthy white real estate developer tried to steal the franchise from him. Bo Sexton and Father had once been friends, often playing golf together and even vacationing as a foursome with their wives. But the relationship soon soured.

Because, Father believed, Bo got jealous when Father's wealth suddenly became much greater than Bo's. Turned out, Bo had invested in a bad real estate development with the hopes of cashing in on luxury condos that were scheduled for construction along the Detroit River. Around the same time, when Bo found out Father was getting ready to increase his assets by acquiring the team, Bo tried to outbid him.

But when the day of the deal and bidding came around, Bo silently bowed out. My father was strutting around his office like a peacock. I asked him why or how he got Bo to drop out. He simply took a puff of what he called his victory cigar and said, "Bentley Tre, our secrets always outweigh our strengths. So be careful with whom you share your secrets, and even more mindful of who finds them out."

Seth Sinclair had secrets. Many secrets. Maybe even one that could knock him off his perch. And maybe one of those secrets had fallen into my lap.

Jah. I was almost certain that my young friend was in danger. And I blamed myself as the reason he was in this mess. Had I not invited him to the party, he never would have met Seth. Damn, if I hadn't taken the job, their paths never would have crossed.

I had to do something about Jah and Seth. And if my hunch was correct, it could save Jah.

With my cell phone in one hand, I read Sterling's number as I dialed it on the land-line on the coffee table. I imagined he was at the Oscars, so I was prepared to leave a message. I would use the one word that would guarantee a return call.

After two rings, Sterling answered.

"Sterling, this is Bentley Dean. I need to speak with Seth."

"I don't think Seth wants any more conversations with you, Bentley Dean. I strongly recommend that you lose my number and forget you ever met me or Seth."

I spoke confidently. "But you see, Sterling, there's no way I can do that. Remember, it was you two who came into my life. I will decide when this relationship ends."

His rage shot through the phone, which I held away from my ear. "Motherfucker, do you know who you're talking to? Is this a threat? My boss doesn't take kindly to threats from anyone. Do you know what that means?"

I stayed cool. "Sterling, to be quite frank with you, I consider what you just said as a threat. And my father taught me not to view threats favorably. So are you going to set up the meeting, or must I do it?"

I watched the camera zoom on to Seth on television one more time as his right-hand man shouted into my phone.

"Are you smoking crack or something, asshole? Do you think my boss gives a shit about some modeling agency guy? Or better yet, a gay-ass pimp?"

Stunned, I looked at the phone, as if it would tell me that yes, this bastard had just called me a pimp. My insides blazed from a slow boiling simmer to a red-hot barbeque pit. And I had taken enough from this gofer.

My voice threatened to crack with anger as I said, "I'm done playing with you two. I have a message you can relay to the great Seth Sinclair with his fake Hollywood life —"

"You know, Bentley, Seth and I deal with haters like you every day —"

"It ain't hatin' if it's true," I said.

"If what is true?"

"Allow me to finish, asshole. Tell your

431

boss, if my friend Jah is not safely back in Miami in forty-eight hours, I'm going to the police."

Sterling said, "Go to the police. Nothing will happen. There's no way you can prove anything."

I said confidently, "Tell Seth to try me and I will go to the police and the press with the one word that can destroy him." The truth was I had no evidence except for my gut feelings and anecdotal stories from Daniel and Wilson, plus that strange text from Warren.

"Word. What are you talking about?" Sterling shouted. "What word?"

I paused for dramatic effect. This was, after all, Oscar night. Then I did a Hitchcock whisper into the phone: "Wentworth."

And the world between me, Sterling, and Seth suddenly became silent.

FORTY-TWO

My last day in my hometown almost felt like spring, even though it was the end of February. I had the driver stop by my mother's house so that I could say good-bye to her and my father.

"How are you, Mr. Dean?" asked Doris, my father's nurse, as she opened the double front doors. A gust of lemon furniture polish greeted me. I was always so impressed with the sight of our double staircase and two-story foyer with the giant chandelier. It just looked so regal.

"I'm fine, Doris. Where's my mother?" I stepped into the huge foyer.

"She had some errands to run. I expect her back in an hour."

I glanced up the staircase. "How's my father doing?"

"Better than yesterday," Doris said as she closed the doors. "And I'm sure he'll be even better when he sees you."

"I don't know about that, Doris," I said with a slight smile.

"Oh, I'm sure of that," she said. "You should hear how he talks about you while I'm taking him through his therapy. He's so proud of you! Told me how you'd started a business in Miami without any of his help."

"He did?" The red panes in the stained-glass window on the doors behind her caught my eye. I remembered how I had thought about blood bonds the day Father had banished me from his house. What a difference five years could make!

"Yes, he did brag about you," Doris said. "Right now, he's sitting on the sofa in the master suite. Go on up there."

I walked up the stairs and entered the bedroom, where Father was sitting on the leather sofa. He wore blue striped pajamas and a brown robe. He was reading a newspaper, but when I walked in, he immediately put it down.

"How are you feeling today, Father?" I bent to hug him. He returned a weak hug, but I did feel strong hands patting my back.

"I'm doing better. Feeling more like my old self. Here, take a seat," he said as he put his hand on the spot next to him.

"Father, I don't have much time. My flight leaves in a couple of hours and I have baggage to check."

He looked disappointed. "I'm glad you stopped by. I have something I want to talk to you about."

"Sure, Father. What's going on?" Were we finally going to talk about Kim? I didn't know if I was ready for this conversation but whatever my father wanted I would do.

"I need your help."

"Doing what?"

"With one of my businesses. I don't know when my doctor will let me go back to working full-time. And to be honest with you, I kind of like this life of taking things easy. But I'm anxious to get back to my own place and resume my life."

Did that mean a love reconnection was impossible for my parents? "So has Mother gotten on your last nerves?"

"I don't pay her no mind."

"I know."

"Besides, I miss Kim and I don't think she feels comfortable here."

"I can understand that. I mean, the first time she came to the house was with me."

"That was a long time ago, son."

"Is that your way of telling me that we're done with this Kim conversation?"

"For now, but I know we'll discuss it at some point. She is not going anywhere."

"Cool."

My father got serious and spoke in a tone as if he were wearing a business suit. "Now, Bentley, I want you to know that what I'm going to ask you to do doesn't mean I accept or understand your lifestyle. I don't ever think I will. But you're my son. And if your mother and I raised you right, you'll be okay."

This was the conversation I had been hoping to have for five years. I spoke firmly. "I don't expect you to accept my lifestyle, Father, but it's important that you at least love and respect me."

Father's gaze softened as he looked at me. "You know I love you. But I've always told you, Bentley, you have to earn respect. That's not what I want to talk about. Hopefully there will be days on the golf course where we can get to that point."

I nodded. "That's cool. What do you need me to do, Father?"

He got businesslike again. "I need you to come and oversee my football team."

If someone had told me just a month ago this would happen, I would have never believed them. I let the words bounce around in my head for a few seconds, to make sure that yes, my father had just said that.

"I hired a new general manager right before the heart attack," he said. "But the draft is coming up and I need somebody with my best interest to make sure we make the right picks. And to make sure my money is being well spent."

I looked back at him with a serious expression over the disbelief that made my jaw threaten to drop open.

"Bentley, I know how much you like football and how one day you hoped I'd turn the team over to you."

"Father," I said with excitement and respect. "Wow, that's cool. Are you sure you want to do this?"

He nodded. "Now don't get me wrong, Bentley. I'm not ready to give up the team yet. But one day I will and it won't hurt for you to get a little experience by going through a draft. The guy I hired used to play professional football and I think he'll be good for the club."

A thousand thoughts shot through my mind. "I need to talk this over with my business partner, but I'm sure we can work something out. Will you need me to be here? Or can I do some work from Miami?"

Father almost smiled. "That's the good thing and why I think this will be so perfect. The combine and the draft will be in Fort

Lauderdale, so you'll be able to do a lot of work from there. Which, by the way, your mother has been on me to buy you a bigger place. So I guess you can start looking."

I shook my head. "That won't be necessary, Father. I'm really happy where I live now."

"Nonsense, Bentley. You're going to be a team owner and you need to live in a place befitting one. Besides, you're Bentley Dean the third. We know lots of people in Florida. I'll have my real estate guy locate some places. What's that place down there? Star Island?"

"That's one of the places," I said, "but can we talk about that later? I don't want to miss my flight."

Father looked at me as if he would miss me. "Okay, get out of here, but let me know something as soon as you can. I want to send my general manager down south to meet with you."

"I will." I hugged him again. "I love you, Father. And I'm really happy you're back on the mend."

"Yeah, I know, son. Thanks for coming up and spending some time with me. It's meant a lot. I think we'll be okay."

"I *know* we'll be okay." I stood.

"Have a safe flight."

"I will."

I gazed at my father, glad that he looked stronger. The color had returned to his face. And the whites of his eyes were as bright as the snow that had greeted my return to Detroit.

A hot wave of melancholy seeped through me. All of a sudden, I wasn't in such a hurry to return to sunny Miami. Tears burned my eyes, so I turned and headed toward the door.

"Bentley."

I turned to face him. "Yes, Father?"

"Thanks for the cheeseburger."

I smiled. "Anytime, Father."

FORTY-THREE

As I sat in the waiting area of the Northwest Airlines boarding area, I thought about the last couple of weeks, my father, and my life. At the same time, I found myself studying couples, both straight and gay, as they came into the area. Would I ever engage in public affection with another man?

I glanced at my watch. I had about thirty minutes before my flight would board, so I walked over to the newsstands. I was immediately struck by how most of the magazine covers featured our new first lady, Michelle Obama. Soon even Oprah would be sharing the cover with Michelle on the April issue of *O* magazine.

The only people rivaling the first family on magazine covers, sadly, were singers Chris Brown and Rihanna. Here we had another black man who would most likely do jail time for being unable to control his temper, and a beautiful young girl who was willing to accept that in the name of love. It made me think back to a time when I was seeing Kim and Warren at the same time and I couldn't get Kim to leave. I was so mad that I started an unnecessary fight. But I never thought of hitting her. My father had told me at an early age that that was never an option.

As a television over the magazine stand streamed with a news ticker, I noticed an item about the California Supreme Court looking into the validity of Proposition 8. I envisioned myself standing before a minister or a judge to marry a man. Who would be at my side? Would times, and my father, change enough so that he might be there? The doctor had told us if he survived the surgery, it could add another twelve to fifteen years to his life. Now that would be a change that in my wildest dreams I could believe in. But hey, my father hadn't thought he'd live to see a black man elected president.

I purchased a couple of magazines and returned to the waiting area.

Damn. I hadn't arranged a car service to pick me up from the Miami airport. I pulled out my phone and called Mitch's cell number. He picked up after the first ring, sounding happy to hear from me.

"Bentley! You still up in the snow zone?"

I laughed. "I'm at the airport."

"How's your dad?"

"Much better. Thanks for asking, Mitch."

"Do you know how lucky you are to have him back in your life?"

"I do."

"Yes, sir, you're very lucky, Bentley. I was thinking about that today when I was having breakfast. I had always wished the same for me and my daddy." Mitch's voice had swung into a melancholy tone and I felt sorry for him.

"Your father knows you loved him, Mitch. I know that."

"Yeah, you're right. When will you be back in town?"

"In a couple of hours. That's why I'm calling. I was wondering if you could pick me up at the airport. I didn't think to arrange transportation." I looked up at the monitor and saw my flight number flashing. NOW BOARDING was blinking brightly.

"Sure, I can do that. What airline and what flight?"

I pulled out my boarding pass. "Northwest flight 571. It arrives at three twenty-five."

Mitch said, "Let me jot this down. Okay, I got it. I'll meet you outside baggage claim. I'll be in my sports car."

"Thanks, Mitch. Maybe I can buy you a drink after I land?"

"I never turn down a drink for a friend!" He laughed. "So you got a deal. Have a safe flight."

"I will. See you in a couple of hours."

"Bye, Bentley."

I shut my phone and headed toward the boarding door. As I reached the door, I opened it to shut off the power. It rang. WARREN flashed across the tiny screen.

"What's good, Warren?"

Warren screamed, "Bentley, what in the fuck have you done? You're gonna get us all killed!"

"What are you talking about?" My heart raced as I followed the stream of passengers onto the plane.

Warren shouted, "What did you do to Seth?"

"What?"

"Nigga, you heard what the fuck I said! You're fucking with the wrong people, Bentley." I had never heard Warren so furious. His voice was higher-pitched and nervous. "You gonna let that young punk be responsible for ruining or ending both of our lives?"

"Are you talking about Jah?" I had reached the inside of the plane and already the flight attendant was giving me that "you know you gonna have to turn that off" look.

"You know damn well I'm talking about him! But let me tell you something, Bentley Dean. You're not takin' my black ass down with you. Stupid fuckin' move, Bentley. I thought you were smarter than that."

"Warren, chill. I'm getting ready to take off. I'll call you when I get home."

"Naw, nigga, I'll call you. But take my advice and watch your back."

Click.

My flight arrived at Miami International Airport thirty minutes late. As soon as I got off the plane, and turned my phone back on, it vibrated. Was it Mitch, wondering where I was? No, Mitch most likely knew that the flight was late.

I looked at the phone, which showed three missed calls from Warren. Several new texts included one from Mitch telling me to come outside of the baggage claim door. The next one was from Warren.

Dude, I really do care about you, but you're fuckin' with the big bois and this shit is serious. I'm going to lay low for a minute and suggest you do the same.

Disturbed, I deleted the message, then questioned if that was wise. I went to the baggage claim area and waited for my bags. I always hated this part. MIA had to be the worst when it came to baggage. I started to call Mitch and let him know it might be another thirty minutes before I was outside.

But oddly, the bags started to come down the turnstyle and mine were some of the first ones out. I grabbed them and headed for the door.

Outside, it seemed like Miami had been blessed with a cleansing rain. The damp air smelled sweet with early spring. I looked for Mitch or his car, but didn't see him. I walked across the street to where I saw rental car buses but no sign of Mitch. I walked to the other island for pickups and thought maybe Mitch was driving around the airport looking for me.

I stood there looking, then called Mitch. His voice mail clicked on, so I said, "Hey, Mitch, I'm here. Looking for you."

I waited a few minutes. Still no Mitch. *Maybe I should just catch a taxi,* I told myself. As I turned to walk toward the stand, I heard a familiar voice.

"Hey, B, it looks like you need a ride."

I turned. There, standing on the driver's side of the car, was Jah. He was like a mirage. I wanted to run and hug and kiss his face, but I couldn't move. It felt like I was standing in wet cement shoes.

"Jah!" I shouted as my voice broke.

"In the flesh." He smiled and his eyes sparkled with the happiness that I was feeling. Jah's hair was a mess and he wore disheveled workout clothes, but he looked good.

"What are you doing here?"

"I called Mitch, looking for you, and he told me he was heading out to pick you up. I told him I would do it."

For a moment, I held my breath to keep from crying. I grinned in triumph. Finally, my feet decided to move me toward Jah and the car. We met at the back of the car and hugged each other tightly for seconds that turned into minutes. When I finally released him, he said, "Boi, do I have a lot to tell you."

"I'm all ears." Then I realized Jah still had the car. I gave him a quizzical look.

"I got to keep the car. Don't you think I deserve it?"

"Jah, you deserve it and so much more."

FORTY-FOUR

Later that evening Jah moved slowly into the kitchen as if he were wading through fog. His eyes were groggy and confused. I was cooking, and seeing him there momentarily startled me. As I patted down the turkey burgers I was grilling I stared at him for a moment longer than usual. I still couldn't believe he was back here in my condo. There had been times when I wondered if I'd ever see him again. As the silence stretched out for a few more moments I finally said something.

"How did you sleep?"

"Okay. What time is it? How long was I asleep?"

"A little after seven and only for a couple of hours."

"I must have been tired and I haven't been sleeping well."

"I hope you're hungry."

"Yeah, I could eat a little something."

"Good."

"What are you cooking? It smells good."

"Turkey burgers and fries."

"Good."

Jah was wearing a white V-neck T-shirt and some black-and-white pajama bottoms. He looked like the young man that he was and not the beaten man that Seth and company tried to turn him into.

"Do you want something to drink?" I asked as I poured a can of Coke over a clink of ice cubes.

"I want some water but don't worry, Bentley, I can get it myself. I don't need a life of people waiting on me." I wondered if this was my opening to talk about the life that Jah had just escaped, but I waited a few minutes to see if he was going to bring it up.

I took the turkey patties off the grill and placed them on a white plate covered with a paper towel. I could hear Jah opening the refrigerator and pulling open the crisper where I kept cold water.

When I looked at Jah he refused to meet my eyes and I suddenly noticed his tear-stained face.

"Jah, are you okay?" I moved close to him and put my arms around him.

"How could people treat other people like

cattle, Bentley? What did I do to deserve Seth? Haven't I been through enough? Why wouldn't God give me my happy ending, or does he just hate me?"

"God doesn't hate you, Jah, and your time is coming. Trust me."

"I don't know. I just want somebody to love me," Jah said. Tears were streaming down his face and I guided him with my hand to the bar stools.

"Come on, sit down, Jah, and you know I love you."

Jah sat at the bar and said, "I know you do, Bentley, and I'm sorry for not listening to you, but you know what I mean. Somebody I can spend my life with. A romantic life."

"You just have to be patient and you're going to have to deal with what happened to you the last couple of months."

"Deal with it how? Right before they let me go, Seth and Sterling warned me that they would track me down and hurt me if I told anyone."

"Don't even mention those sick mutherfuckers, Jah. Don't waste your breath. Their day is coming and it will be a huge payback," I said, not really certain that anything would happen to a powerful man like Seth Sinclair, but that's what I thought Jah

449

needed to hear.

"I'm just glad he let me go. I mean, I was basically a prisoner in a high-rise condo. Not able to come and go as I pleased because of the huge bodyguards blocking every exit. Why would Seth think I was the kind of guy who would sleep with all his friends because he told me to? One of the first things I told him was how I had been saving myself for the first man I fell in love with."

I placed my hand on Jah's knees and they were shaking. I looked at his usually warm face and saw no signs of forgiveness. That was a good thing.

"Look, Jah, you're handsome and fresh. But that's all those guys saw. They didn't see what I see and everybody with any sense who meets you sees. You are even more beautiful here," I said as I beat on my chest.

"For real?"

"For real, for real," I said, trying to elicit that trademark smile from Jah that I was used to. Just when it looked like I was going to get it I felt my phone vibrate in my pants. I pulled out my phone and said that it was Alex. I told Jah I needed to take the call and left the bar and walked toward the terrace.

"What's going on?"

"Gosh, I'm glad you answer this phone. I got some bad news," Alex said.

"What?"

"Do we have a client by the name of Gabriel? I think he might have worked that party you booked some time ago."

"Yeah, I know Gabriel. What about him? What has he done now?" I asked, thinking about the last time I'd seen Gabriel and his bitchy ass on Lincoln Road. I braced myself for what Alex was about to tell me. If he'd done something to embarrass the agency I would make sure he never worked in Miami again.

"I just got a call from Miami University Hospital. They found one of our cards in his wallet. It seems as though he was beaten badly. He's heavily sedated and they don't think he's going to make it. Your card was the only thing besides his driver's license."

"Are you serious?" I was now on the terrace wondering if the evening wind or what Alex was telling me was causing the chill on my naked arms.

"Dead serious. Do you know if he has any family? If he survives tonight the hospital said they might try to operate to save him, but they need to get in contact with next of kin or his employer. Right now they think that's us."

451

"I don't remember him mentioning his family, but I can go down to the hospital and check on him," I said. Before Alex could answer I got another call coming in. It was Warren. I told Alex I'd call her back shortly.

"Warren, what was your message about?" I asked.

"Where are you, dude?" There was a coldness in his voice I'd never heard before.

"I'm home. Where are you?"

"In your city and I need to see you. I want to make sure you don't do something crazy to my bois in California."

"What are you doing here, Warren, and why didn't you tell me you were coming here?"

"I had a little business to take care of." Again I heard that coldness combined with that over-the-top masculinity Warren always put out on display. Suddenly I felt a mix of rage and loathing churning inside of me. It finally dawned on me that the man I was in love with might be a cold-blooded murderer or a henchman for Seth and his crew.

With each phone call I was becoming a major part of a rapidly unfolding catastrophe.

"What kind of business you got here, Warren? Did you have some business earlier in the year in Chicago? Do you want a movie career that bad?" My voice grew louder and shriller and I saw Jah walking toward the terrace. I put my hand up, instructing him not to come out. I didn't want him involved in this shit.

"What are you talking about, Bentley? Stop trippin'," Warren said. Now his voice was strangely pitched and I knew I was right about his involvement in Wilson's friend's death and most likely in Gabriel's beating.

"I'm not tripping and if I were you I'd get a good lawyer, Warren."

"You won't say anything, Bentley. They will lock me up for a long time and you don't want that to happen to the man you love. Come on, Bentley, I'll do whatever you want me to do. I'll stop dating females and devote myself to showing you what a good lover I can be. I will beat that ass down three times a day. I might even let you try to do me."

I looked out at the ocean; the waves looked like they were fighting against each other and every now and then I could have sworn I'd seen a shark. Maybe they were coming inland again, but this time I would be prepared.

My voice broke and I shouted into the phone, "Warren, the only thing I want you to do for me is never call me again!"

I then clicked off the phone and let the ocean of tears flood from my eyes.

It took about an hour for me to pull myself together. I was still very angry, but a glass of wine made me mellow. I told Jah what I thought was happening and the two of us held each other as we prayed for Gabriel's full recovery. I called the hospital and they said he was still in intensive care and couldn't have visitors unless they were next of kin. I got his doctor's name and promised to call back later. Only when I thought about Gabriel did a little of my anger drain away.

I hit the speed dial on my phone and seconds later I heard Mitch's voice on the line. I asked if his boat was available and when he said yes I told him what had happened and that I might need to disappear for a week or two. I knew Seth and Warren would be angrier than a dope boi's pit bulls, but soon their focus would be on a defense that would keep them from being property of the state.

"Just tell me what you need me to do, Bentley. You can keep the boat for as long as you need. If you need a place to stay I have some friends who have a private island near the Bahamas. No one could find you there."

"I will call you when I'm done. Thanks, Mitch. You're a good friend."

"And you're a brave man, my friend. I'm so proud to know you."

When I got off the phone I told Jah I needed him to take me somewhere.

"Where do you want to go, Bentley?"

"I need you to take me to the police station."

Jah looked quizzically at me and then asked, "Bentley, are you sure you want to get involved with this? Seth can be ruthless. I don't know what I would do if something happened to you."

"Nothing is going to happen to me, Jah, but I can't let this slide. I have to take a stand and I need you to help me."

"How can I help?"

"If the police want to question you about Seth and his crew you've got to tell them everything, even the stuff you don't think is important. You and I can stop all the madness from happening to anyone else."

"Whatever you say, Bentley."

"That's my boi," I said as I gave Jah a big hug, squeezing him harder than I'd ever hugged any man other than my father.

■ ■ ■ ■

When Jah and I walked out of the Miami police station I don't think I ever felt prouder of two men. A mild drizzle fell, but it was clean and not like the heavy dirty rain from when we had arrived at the station three hours earlier.

"So, do you think they believe us?" Jah asked.

"We did what we could, Jah. We told the truth."

"So, what do we do next?"

"I'm going for some time for myself. Would you like to join me?"

"That would be nice, but I need to get back to school and get my life back on track. I've got a lot to do if I'm going to be a lawyer and help kids like myself."

"That's good, Jah. I know you can do it."

"For real?"

"For real, for real," I said, laughing at Jah's innocence. At least he hadn't lost that totally.

"I'll start out tomorrow like it's the first day of my life," Jah said, his voice vibrating with happiness.

"And so will I."

As we reached Jah's car I looked up and

noticed the morning sunrise, and before we got in I looked over at Jah and admired his smile, lingering there for a few moments. Then I asked him a question.

"What's that smile about, Jah?"

"I was thinking about all I have to look forward to."

"Your future is as bright as that sun," I said, noticing the sun once again.

"Thanks to you. Do you know how much your friendship and love mean to me?"

"I think I do."

"I'll show you with my new life."

"I think I'll start me a new life," I said, smiling to myself and relaxing my body into the smooth leather of the passenger's seat. Droplets of rain pattered on the windshield and I felt a yearning to stick my head out and enjoy the morning rain.

"Oh, yeah, and what you gonna do with this new life, sir?"

I looked directly into Jah's eyes bright with excitement and then foolishly suddenly let down the window and stuck my head out and let the rain caress my face and shouted in a voice that sounded like I was singing, "I'm going to learn how to dance in the rain!"

ABOUT THE AUTHOR

E. Lynn Harris is the author of ten previous novels and the memoir *What Becomes of the Brokenhearted.* His recent novels, *Mama Dearest, Basketball Jones,* and *Just Too Good to be True* hit the bestseller lists in the *New York Times,* the *Wall Street Journal, The Washington Post,* and other publications. Harris divided his time between Atlanta, Georgia, and Fayetteville, Arkansas, before his death in 2009.